THE
LOST
LEGENDS

Tales of Myth
and Magic

Archgate Press

ACKNOWLEDGMENTS

There are dozens of people I could thank; I hope you all know who you are, because I'm only going to mention a few.

At first, this book was destined to be a mere collection of stories, but when Renea McKenzie joined the project it became a well-edited collection of stories. Being well-edited is what makes a collection worth reading, and my own meager efforts weren't going to be enough to lift this anthology out of obscurity. Thanks to Renea's tireless work, professional experience, and lofty standards, I can proudly call *The Lost Legends* an outstanding collection.

Furthermore, *The Lost Legends* wouldn't exist at all if not for the efforts of Ryan Swindoll. Not only did he contribute some very fine writing, he also handled all of the lovely artwork and layout design. His visual instincts breathed life into the project and transformed this anthology into something unique, bold, and a lot of fun.

I am also indebted to Rachel Neumeier, whose encouragement gave me confidence as I began a project I had no idea how to finish.

Finally, I could not accomplish anything without the love of my incredible wife. Christine, I don't deserve you.

For the friends and family
who encourage us while we write.

TABLE OF CONTENTS

FOREWORD

The Lost Legends started as a dream to give talented fantasy authors a chance to slip the surly bonds of industry expectations and finally tell their favorite stories. Naturally, we demanded impressive writing and fresh, unforgettable ideas. (Who wants to read a collection of failed trunk stories and half-efforts?) But within these boundaries, the authors who contributed to this anthology were free to go where their pens led them.

I promised that nothing would be rejected merely for being too long or too short, for being too traditional or too ambitious, or—horror of horrors—for being too *different*. (Yes, even science fiction and fantasy authors get rejected for the crime of being too weird.) With no one to stop us, we put our passions on the page until we'd built the book you've got in your hands.

You might be surprised to discover how many rules authors are expected to follow. Industry trends, flash-in-the-pan hashtags, and imperious reviewers are always building a cage around storytellers, and, sadly, it's not unusual for successful authors to publish their "passion projects" only after reaching retirement age.

But times have changed. Today's readers have shown an incredible willingness to purchase books published anywhere, by anyone, and many writers are still being caught off-guard by the realization that they are in control. It's like we've been sitting in a car and waiting for it to start, only to figure out we've been holding the keys all along.

With writers now firmly in the driver's seat, the world of storytelling has changed. And while *The Lost Legends* is a collection of wonderful stories, bursting with magic, monsters, and mayhem of all sorts, it's also a celebration of the new world that today's writers and readers are building together.

Read on.
–Adam D. Jones

IDNA'S JOURNALS

Adam D. Jones

When the old woman finally died, the leather-bound journals were taken from her dim house and hastily arranged on a pyre.

The curious town folk gathered to watch, dotting the grassy hilltop on all sides. Further back, their wooden houses surrounded the hill and stood as silent sentinels, holding lanterns by their outstretched eaves. Above them, even the stars peeked through the dusk to join the audience, but the scene before them was disappointing.

Her journals looked ordinary. Everyone in Crow Hill had seen Idna and knew about her writing; there was nothing ordinary about any of it. She was always sitting under a tree or in the shade of someone's house or barn, and from her perch she would watch passersby with a cackling grin while she wrote endlessly—madly, some would say—filling blank pages with wild strokes. They expected her journals to appear sinister, or even arcane, but the books sitting on the pyre appeared completely normal. Their plain leather covers, coated with dust, quietly awaited their fate.

When torches became the only light, all eyes turned to Hild. She stood tall over the pile of tomes and cast her gaze downward, as if defying the dusty books, telling them she was not afraid of them. Two men on the hilltop held torches low, letting the bright fire almost touch the books, and looked to Hild for permission.

Glancing up, Hild noticed the surrounding onlookers were no longer staring at the books. Their wide eyes watched her now, waiting. *It's like the day they first saw me.*

She remembered five years ago when she rode into Crow Hill on what was still the only horse in town. The settlers left their homes and formed a crowd to greet her, parting as she plodded down the lone street. They were silent at first, but after taking in her fine horse and her silk clothes, they began asking questions. She explained that she had been a record keeper in the Capital, but after an early retirement she was looking for a new home, a place on the quiet frontier where she could relax. Hild expected more questions, but before she could even dismount from her saddle, they asked her to take over the recently vacated job of town overseer. From the moment she swung down from her horse and her boots made their first imprints on Crow Hill, nothing happened in the settlement without the approving nod of Hild's sharp chin.

Hild returned her thoughts to the journals. The people of Crow Hill had often asked her to do *something* about the strange woman who, if the rumors were true, could see through walls, speak to crows, and, if she slept beneath your window, could even listen to your dreams. Some whispered they had seen Idna standing at the edge of town on dark nights, face to face with shadowy figures.

"There's one like Idna in every town," Hild would always say, "a hundred of them in the Capitol."

But Hild's tolerance of Idna's ways didn't stop her from being curious; more than once, Hild had fought back the instinct to wrestle a journal away from the old woman's wrinkled hands. Even now, as Hild stood over the pyre, her mind raged to finally know why these books were so important, why Idna wrote in them all day, every day, never stopping even when she'd filled every page and had to scribble on the backs.

And the answers might be in those pages, she thought. *Just a hand's width from the torches.*

Hild considered the dry, yellow pages Idna had left behind. It would only take her a few days to pore through them all, if Hild read all day and night. The surrounding men and women held each other close and watched the journals with fear, and Hild wondered if it was possible to ask them to wait, to burn these books another time.

No. Hild shook the idea from her head. *They came here for a conclusion. To feel safe. I'll let them have their peace of mind.*

Her chin dipped in a decisive nod; the men saw it and lowered their torches.

Eager flames reached out and blazed through the old, dry paper. Red cracks spread through pages that curled and blackened in their own heat while fire rose high from the pyre, spiking quickly and driving the men back. The leather covers melted into smoldering lumps that fell into the collapsing ash. A log broke in half and tumbled, kicking up dirt and debris that leapt toward Hild.

The smoke surprised everyone. A dark cloud burst from the pyre, reaching out with impossibly thick tendrils that fled the hilltop and raced through the crowd. Plumes rolled down the hill on every side to grope through the onlookers who shut their eyes to the stinging smoke. They covered their mouths and cowered while rolling clouds shrouded them like a funeral veil. The smoke rambled past, rushing beyond the settlers, then beyond their homes, and finally disappearing across the dusty plains. The citizens of Crow Hill were left standing in startled silence, surrounded by a few wisps of smoke and staring at a fire that had somehow already burned down to its final embers.

Everyone turned their backs to the pyre and made their way down the hill, treading carefully in the quiet night. Hild, her boots covered in soot from standing so close, took a long, skeptical look at the pile of ash and then made her way down, her eyes low, keeping to herself until she stumbled into someone.

"Eli." She had bumped into one of the farmers. "Forgive me. We seem to have lost our light."

They stopped walking. The farmer stared at her, directly into her eyes, but his face grew distant, like he was looking at something just beyond the hills. "Hild. Our minister…" His eyes narrowed into slits. "Came here, what, five years ago?"

Hild nodded. "That's right…"

His face awoke with sudden clarity. "Because you wanted a simpler life!" He was grinning now. "Not because someone finally took a close look at those records you kept in the Capital, eh?"

Hild gasped. Nearby faces turned her way, and she straightened up to bear their scrutiny.

He can't know that! No one in this forgotten hole of a town could—that was the reason Hild had spent the last five years of her life counting thankless cattle and smiling at unattractive children.

She was prepared to deflect him when a memory forced its way into her thoughts. A stray puff of smoke blew past while unfamiliar images played in her mind.

"Your barn..." Hild shut her eyes. She could see Eli setting bails of hay on fire, and she realized with a shudder that this memory was not her own. "It burned down last year...and you... asked for donations..."

Eli's eyes widened.

The two stared at one another while their neighbors shuffled past. Hild and Eli finally parted, sharing one last, distrustful look.

And the people of Crow Hill walked home along scattered paths as the remaining smoke wisped between them, whispering secrets that pushed them apart.

THE LUCK STONE

Kristen Bickerstaff

A oife hated these stupid boots.

She cracked an eyelid open and dragged one ponderous shoe up into the air. She held the boot up until her leg trembled from the weight, then let it drop to the ground with a loud *thunk*. The iron sole clanged against the loose white rocks scattered around the quarry mainway, shocking Bran into jumping off of his perch on the boulder next to her. He shot her a baleful look, his dark eyebrows cranked down low.

"I don't see why I had to wear these," she complained. Even with the layer of leather between her and the iron, the soles of her feet itched abominably.

"They're mule-kickers," Fynn said from under the brim of his outlandishly large southern hat. She couldn't even see his sharp features underneath the brim, tipped down as it was to shield his face as he napped. "It's so you blend in. Well, as much as *you* can blend in. Not many with elvish blood this way, and you know how superstitious the folks in Grimnal can be. Can't have potential clients turning us down on sight alone."

Aoife ignored the comment about her appearance, though she did tuck a stray white lock of hair back under her kerchief. The tight braided coil of hair trapped under there itched too, and her own foolishly large hat trapped the sweat trickling down her scalp, making her feel grimy. She thought longingly of the last time she'd had a bath, before their ill-fated river job a month ago.

Blend in. She rolled her eyes. By the look of the menagerie of people hawking their wares on the quarry's mainway, blending in was laughable. Between the hedgewitch cloaked in smoking incense (and not much else) and the merc whose stone-colored skin spoke of at least a drop of troll blood, she was not the oddest one here.

The hat did hide her dully-pointed ears, she had to admit, though there was no hiding her distinctive green-gold eyes. Or the thick strokes of her brand, white lines stark against the brown skin of her cheek, elegant in their cruelty. Aoife traced its familiar outline, a circle broken by a jagged slash. Even Grimnalians who'd never so much as smelled the bluebell-scented air of the Vyoathe Forest would know what it was. Only one sort was branded on the face in the so-called Civil States. *Murderer.*

"I bet these stupid rock-tossers care more about that than my boots," she said, mostly to herself. She raised her other foot and let it *thunk* to the ground once more to distract herself from thoughts of the past.

"Will you stop it?" Bran growled, his already-ruddy face flushing more. "Drivin' me mad."

"I hardly think I'm the cause of your madness," Aoife said. "You were cracked when we found you."

Fynn chuckled, the noise muffled by the silly hat. Bran said nothing, glaring at her boots as if waiting to swat one down the next time she raised it.

A gust of wind kicked up, and Aoife tilted her hat down to shield her face. The dust splattered her chest and neck instead, the smell of hot gravel assaulting her nostrils. Quarries. She hated quarries too, almost as much as these itchy iron soles. But, they'd finally run out of coin, and the rough-and-tumble sort near the southern quarries *always* had need of a knife. Or a boot.

Wrinkling her nose, Aoife picked at her ragged tunic to shake the dust out. She thought longingly of the bathhouse at the guild, with its three pools and its steam room always ready for any merc who needed it. As if sensing her thoughts, Fynn reached up and patted her hand.

"You'll be back in your leathers soon," he said, his deep voice holding a note of sympathy under his usual wryness. "We just need enough coin to get us back to Greengleann."

"I told you we shouldn't have taken that river job. As soon as we get to Greengleann, I'm buying a curse for that *vaksha* captain."

"You can buy as many curses as you want once we get

back home," Fynn promised.

Home. The word still stuck in Aoife's chest, even after ten years of living in the high city of men. Greengleann's cold, black granite walls, stuffed full with people, could never inspire the same longing in her as the towering oaks of Vyoathe, shrouded in shadow and emerald, lost to her now.

Another gust of wind blew down the mainway, sending them all into coughing fits and shrouding the boulders and vendors in a white cloud. The hedgewitch's wailing chants wove through the dust. A shiver crawled up Aoife's spine.

"Hate quarry jobs," Bran mumbled once the dust had settled.

"That's a little ironic, given that's where we found you, rock-tosser," Aoife said with a wink.

Fynn still bore the scar across his chest from the brawl Bran had saved him from, some five years back, the last time Fynn and Aoife found themselves in Grimnal province. A crew of miners had gotten tired of Fynn's unnaturally good luck at cards and decided to take their winnings back by force. Before Aoife could run over to assist, Bran barreled straight through the brawl, tossing miners right and left and cold-cocking the one with the knife. Quite the job application, Aoife always thought.

"S'why I hate 'em." Bran crossed his arms, squinting at another group of mercs, probably from the Grimnalian guild, laughing loudly as one of them juggled knives to pass the time. "Been three days roasting out here, an' no jobs."

A bell rang, its sonorous voice rolling from the quarry and down the mainway, enhanced by some charm no doubt.

"Finally," Aoife sighed.

She jumped off the boulder and walked to their banner—a thin pennant with the black bounty-hunting sigil sewn on a green field. Brushing off her tunic, Aoife subtly checked that all her hidden knives were in place. Bran took up a spot next to her elbow, looming a full head over her and casting some blessed shade. Fynn stayed on the ground, but he did tilt his hat back, his dark eyes scanning the mainway eagerly.

The quarry workers spilled out of the dusty pit and flowed down the mainway, the first few not so much as casting a glance at the vendors who lined the sides. Slowly, a quarry worker here and there peeled off from their fellows: a young man with hope gleaming in his eyes lingered in front of the hedgewitch, two rock-tossers built for brawling taunted the troll-man in a strength contest, and a hard-faced woman covered in dust approached the knife-thrower. But none paused at Aoife's banner. She scanned the crowd, trying not to make eye contact with any one person and seem overeager.

A squat man almost as wide as he was tall shoved a few of his comrades to the side, wading through the human river to her side of the mainway. The way his eyes raked over her body squashed any dim hope she had.

"Trouble," she muttered.

"Don't judge a book by its cover," Fynn said, remaining on the ground. "If he offers up coin for a job, we'll take it. I'm tired of baking out here."

Bran grunted, though whether that was a grunt in agreement with Aoife or with Fynn, she wasn't sure.

"Oy! You selling?" the squat rock-tosser asked as soon as he was in earshot. He trundled up to their banner, stopping just a foot short of Aoife. She could smell his breath from here, rank with chew-leaf and the Lady knew what else. His dust-covered leathers were stained with mottled dark patches, and his dishwater-colored beard bore the trademark yellow stains of a chewer.

"Do you have something you need us to find?" Aoife asked, fighting not to wrinkle her nose in disgust.

The man grabbed himself, grinning with all five of his remaining teeth. "Oh, I got somethin' you can find. What's the price?"

Apparently some Grimnalians weren't above tangling with an elf-blood, or a murderer. Aoife rolled her eyes and pointed to the banner. "We're bounty hunters, not whore-mongers. Check two tents down the road."

"But I like the look of *you*," the man said with a leer. One grubby hand shot out and grabbed at her tunic, smearing the white fabric with brown stains. "Let's see what you've got to offer."

Something blurred in her peripheral vision. Bran roared, charging the man, at the same time that Fynn popped into existence over the rock-tosser's shoulder, short sword drawn, the speed enchantment tattooed on his neck glowing white against his dark brown skin. The man howled, ducking under Bran's swing, splattering carmine drops across the white gravel from the wickedly curved knife sticking through his hand. He fell to all fours, still shrieking, then rolled over, grasping his wounded hand as if offering it to the sky.

"I win as usual, boys," Aoife said with a smirk. "Although if one of you could get my knife back, I'd be obliged."

Bran bent down, lightly tapping the man's forehead with his giant fist. The man's cries cut off abruptly as his eyes rolled back into his skull. With a small, satisfied smile, Bran ripped the knife out of the rock-tosser's hand. He wiped it off on the man's dirty jerkin, then flipped it back to Aoife, who snatched it from the air and made it disappear.

"Nice work," a deep voice rumbled to the right of them. It belonged to another quarryman, though this one's jerkin was clean under the dust, his beard neatly trimmed. "If you're done poundin' on Harrit, I got a job for you."

Fynn's face shifted from cold anger to amiable charm

so fast, it was like he'd donned a mask. He took the man solicitously by the elbow, like some courtier in a high house, and pulled him away from Harrit's unlucky body.

"Of course," he said. "What can we do for you, sir?"

The man scoffed. "I'm no 'sir.' Just Petro. And I want you to find whoever killed my brother."

"I'm sorry for your loss, Petro," Fynn replied smoothly. He tipped his head to the side, inviting Aoife and Bran to step closer. "I assure you that we're the best for the task. We've never had a hunt end without bringing back the prey. When was your brother taken?"

"These three nights past, in the city. He was there visitin' his sweetheart; she took work at the high house, tryin' to earn coin for the two of them to marry. Instead, he got a knife across his throat."

"Robbery?" Aoife asked. She tried to keep the dismay off her face at the mention of "the city." Petro had to mean Kamzal, a good two-day's ride away. If they had horses. Which they didn't.

"That's the thing." Petro frowned, scratching his beard. "His purse was still on 'im. Mel, his sweetheart, found 'im when he didn't show up to see her on the usual day. Wasn't more than a couple streets away from the high house, nice part of town. Seems they killed 'im for no reason at all, 'cept his luck stone was missing."

"Luck stone?" Fynn leaned in closer, his eyes sparkling with curiosity. He was always one for gems. "What kind of stone was it?"

Petro shrugged his large shoulders. "Just some rock Jek found in the quarry a few years back. It's a pretty rock, don't mistake me. Blue as the summer sky, with lots of mica scattered through. Shone like a star in the candle light. But, just a rock. You find some odd ones, every now and again. Lot of luck it did 'im in the end."

Something in the back of Aoife's mind chimed at the description, but, for the life of her, she couldn't pull it out of her distant memories. She shook it off and paid closer attention to the task at hand.

Fynn's face fell, but he pushed on. "Did your brother hold any grudges? Did he play at cards while he was in the city? Owe money?"

Funny how Fynn always jumps to someone getting in trouble over cards. Petro shook his head.

"Nothing like that. Jek was a quiet sort. Didn't even drink much, truth be told. Our father did enough of that for us both." Petro spat on the ground, narrowly missing Aoife's boot. She clenched her jaw but said nothing. *Once a rock-tosser...* "He did stop by the pub near the high house now and again, usually with Mel. I went there with 'em, a time or two. The Fat Grouse."

"Anything else you can think of?" Aoife asked. A name of a pub and a missing rock were hardly the best clues, but they had started jobs with less.

"That's it. I just want to know who did 'im. He was my only blood left, and he was a good sort." He jammed a hand in his limp, dusty belt purse, coming out with twelve coppers and a half-silver. "This is all I've got for now. Pay comes again in six days. Take this now, go to Kamzal and see what you can find, and come back by pay day. If you've found the rudding bastard and bring proof, you'll get double. If you've got nothing, well, at least you have this and I know I tried."

Aoife traded a disappointed look with Bran. That money was barely enough to buy them a stay at a flea-infested boarding house for a night. It certainly wasn't enough to get them to Greengleann. But this was their first job offer in three days...

"Deal," Fynn said. His hand blurred, then reappeared at his side, jingling the coins. The tattoo on his neck bloomed with light once more, and Petro gaped at his empty palm. "We'll leave tonight and see you by next seven-day. With the head of your brother's murderer in our bags."

Aoife turned her laugh at Fynn's theatrics into a cough. Petro nodded, seeming satisfied.

"You can find me at the pub in town when you come back. I thank you."

With that, he trundled off, rejoining the flow of quarrymen headed back home.

"He talks almost as little as you, Bran," she said as soon as Petro was out of earshot. "If words were coin, you'd both be rich as dragons."

Bran grunted, then looked at Fynn. "Why'd you take it?"

Fynn shrugged. "It's coin. If nothing else, we get to Kamzal with it and find a better paying job to pad our pockets. This Jek sounds like a simple man. I'm sure his murder was a simple thing. Should be no problem for us." He winked and brushed off his clothes. "Now, let's see if we can find a cart into the city that we can ride with. I'll be happy to leave this rock heap behind us."

Aoife sneered in the direction of Harrit's prone body. "At least I can agree with that."

Another roar of outrage let Aoife know that Fynn had succeeded in making their coin multiply at the card table once more. She smirked into her ale and polished it off, letting the tankard clunk back on the scarred wooden bar. Well, at least they'd had some victory tonight. No one in the pub had much to say about Jek beyond the fact that he was a quiet fellow thoroughly in love with his Mel. They were at a dead end, with no leads beyond the almost-bride, now almost-widow, whom they would meet with tomorrow.

The air was hot and close in The Fat Grouse; that ever-present mineral scent floated about in an invisible fog. She exhaled through her nose, trying to clear it, but it was no use.

The back of her neck itched, and she glanced out of the corner of her eyes to the left. Sure enough, a woman seated next to her man, both the fine-looking sort that fit right into The Fat Grouse's clientele, was staring right at her. The man's vest, straining over his large paunch, was embroidered with what looked to be silver thread around the collar, and the woman had a shining chain hanging about her neck, with a pendant that she clutched tight to her heart.

As their eyes met, the woman's fingers tightened even more around the pendant while her other hand made a flurried motion at her side, a warding sign. Aoife reached up to check that her headscarf was still wrapped firmly over her ears and hair, as her hat sat on the bar beside her. Her fingers brushed smooth hair instead of fabric, before resting on the dull point of her ear.

"Lady's skirts," she mumbled, tugging the scarf quickly back over her offending features.

It was too late. The woman whispered something urgent in her man's ear, and whatever she said must have been rousing, for his ale-reddened face turned purple. The woman let go of her pendant to clutch the man's sleeve, and the triangle sacred to devout Grimnalians swung forward. The sort of devout Grimnalians who burned demons like Aoife in bonfires.

Time to go.

Casting her eyes around the bar, Aoife caught Bran's attention from his position leaning against the wall by the card table. She flicked her eyes at the door and he nodded. They'd arranged to stay the night in the barn of a grubby inn close to the outer walls; Bran and Fynn wouldn't be hard to find. Tossing a copper on the bar, Aoife muttered the words of a small "don't-see-me" charm and grabbed her hat. The charm wouldn't stop anyone looking directly at her from seeing her, but it encouraged people to look past her and, once she was out of sight, ignore her presence entirely.

Stuffing the hat on her head, she moved casually toward the back of the inn, as if she were simply visiting the privies. The heavy footfalls behind her, caught by her sensitive hearing, let her know that the ruse wouldn't be enough to shake the interest of the devouts. She picked up the pace a little, and instead of going out the door in front of her to the innyard, she ducked into the kitchen. She heard her pursuer swear, then speed up, but he was too late. Aoife was out the window and scrambling up the inn's walls to the roof by the time the man crashed into the kitchen, startling the cook and her two assistants, who met his demands for where she went with confusion, having not seen Aoife pass at all.

On the peak of the roof, Aoife sat down, as comfortable on her perch as she was on the ground. She'd give it a few minutes to make sure the devouts hadn't decided to follow her outside, then she'd leave. Besides, the night air, finally cooling from the day's blistering heat, was welcome after the stuffy inn, and she liked the higher view of Kamzal's wealthy district. Lantern lights glowed like yellow stars against the gray stone of the buildings, glinting off the rare, expensive panes of glass and casting dancing shadows on the cobblestones.

Being up this high reminded her of racing her brother up the branches of the Vyoathe oaks, higher and higher until the tree limbs she climbed became little more than twigs. After the race, which she always won, they'd sit atop the trees for hours, swaying in the breeze, watching the world go by in companionable silence until their aunt's angry screeches called them down. Sighing, Aoife rubbed the center of her chest with the heel of her hand and shoved the memory down deep with the rest of her childhood. The oaks and Bres were gone, and she had a job to do.

She scanned the rooftops until she found the walls of the high house, just a few streets away. Kamzal's mayor had a fine residence indeed, made of the smooth gray stone so prized here in the south and sporting intricate carvings around the glass-paned windows. Most of the windows were dark, sensible at such a late hour. Aoife was just about to turn away when a spark of light, quickly extinguished, flared in one of the upper rooms on the third floor.

Curious. If the high house was laid out like those in Greengleann, the first floor contained entertaining rooms and the staff quarters, the second, the quarters of the mayor and his family, and the third, lesser-used rooms like the study and guest quarters. There shouldn't be any lights on the third floor at this time of night.

She'd never been one to ignore a mystery, she thought, fingering her brand as she studied the house. No matter what the consequences. The light flickered again, this time in the next window over, before winking out once more.

"A little reconnaissance to cap the night off," she whispered to herself. "What's the harm in taking a look?"

The buildings in this district were stacked almost on top of each other, making for an easy path from rooftop to rooftop until she reached the plaza where the high house reigned alone. From there, she scampered up the walls, hoping her "don't-see-me" held as she wedged her fingers into the miniscule handholds between the smooth gray stones. She waited atop the wall for a heart-pounding moment, ready to leap back down if a cry of alarm rang out, but none came. Once down, it was easy to wend her way through the carefully cultivated garden she dropped into—all hardy shrubs and flowered vines thanks to the south's harsh climate—back up the walls of the house, and down into the chimney closest to where she'd last seen the spark of light.

She crept slowly down, bracing herself against the

sooty walls and sending her thanks to the Lady that the mayor's staff had declined to light any fires this night. Just above the opening, she hovered, waiting. Her sensitive ears picked up no sound, however, so she dropped down, a plume of ashes rising around her. She thought longingly once more of the copper tub in the guild's quarters in Greengleann, but the lightest of footsteps snapped her back to the present.

Aoife froze, debating whether she should climb back up the chimney and hide, but the footsteps grew no closer, and she realized they were coming from the next room over. Breathing a sigh of relief, she ducked out of the chimney, brushed herself off, and looked around. She had dropped into a cozy library, chock full of leatherbound volumes and cushy chairs. A desk covered in scrolls and an inkpot sat near the window. All in all, a fairly ordinary library, though a glance at the book titles and the preponderance of triangles blazoned on the spines let her know that she definitely should not be caught by the mayor on her little nighttime excursion.

A quiet scraping noise from the next room announced that her quarry was still occupied. Should she go out the window and peek in through the outside? Climb back up to the roof and look for another entry? In the end, like always, she settled for simplicity. She opened the door of the library just enough to slip through, then ducked into the next room before whoever was sneaking around in there fled. Anyone taking that much care to be quiet was certainly not supposed to be here.

This room had no window to let in light; Aoife waited for her eyes to adjust. She wished again that she'd inherited the night vision of her mother's people, but she was stuck with her unknown human father's eyesight and left blinking like an owl. A sharp intake of breath, then a snap of fingers, and a small flame of light flickered in the middle of the room, attached to no candle she could see.

She'd seen that magic before…

The flame gave her only the briefest of moments to take all the details in. A man cloaked in black, broad-shouldered but lean as a willow branch, stood before her, right hand just pulling out of the jewelry box he was obviously pilfering, left outstretched to maintain the light. The fingers of his right hand were curled around a huge blue stone trailing a silver chain and glittering in the warm light. *Shone like a star in the candle light,* Petro's voice muttered in her mind.

But the resemblance of the gleaming jewel to Jek's not-so-lucky stone was the last thing on her mind as the light illuminated the high cheekbones, dully pointed ears, and features she could have sketched with her eyes closed. Her breath caught as her eyes met a green-gold gaze that matched her own, right down to the pale eyebrows above, arched in surprise.

"*Ishen?*" she whispered harshly, almost choking on the endearment.

"*Isha,*" said the man, his lips quirking up in that familiar ironic smile. "Fancy meeting you here."

"How…why…Lady of the Moon, I thought you must be dead!" Her voice cracked on the last word, and she didn't need her brother's hushing to tell her that she needed to speak quieter. The air squeezed out of her chest as she traced Bres's features, familiar yet foreign after all these years. She noted the new scar above his eyebrow and the sharpness of his jaw, shed of the last remnants of adolescent softness. Relief and joy flew through her body until she thought she would burst from it, relaxing muscles she hadn't even known were tensed.

Then she remembered the last time they had parted. Her fingers crept up to the brand through no thought of her own. "When you didn't come…when I couldn't find you…"

Bres closed the distance between them in two long

strides, the flame bobbing at his shoulder, until he stood just in front of her. He reached up to trace the cruel lines of scar tissue etched on her face.

"Oh, Aoife, what did those fools do to you?"

Aoife covered his fingers with her own, as if she could keep him close to her with such a light hold. She cast her eyes down to the floor. "No more than I deserved. It was my knife, my choice." *My damnation.* She shook her head. "What are you doing here, Bres?"

That smile again. "I could ask the same of you. I thought you safe in the forest all this time, not traipsing about Grimnal in boots I could hear a mile away."

Aoife grimaced as she stared down at the offending footwear, then glanced back up at her brother, drinking in the sight of her only true family, here and alive and whole. A piece of her lost home, finally within reach. She let Bres take her hand and walked with him toward the door, with no thought to where they were going or what she would do. She followed automatically, as she always had.

But even as she moved, a small, dark voice in the back of her head drowned out her happy hopes of reunion. She looked to the stone, still dangling from his fingers.

"Why are you stealing that stone?" she asked, her footsteps dragging to a halt.

"Always the curious cat, *isha* dear," Bres chided. "It's a long story. I'll tell you all about it later." A muscle in his jaw twitched, as if it cost his face effort to keep the smile pasted on there. She stayed put.

"How long have you been here?" she countered, thinking of Jek, murdered only a few nights before within reach of the woman who loved him, with only his worthless luck stone taken. To take a life was the highest crime of her people, casting them forever from their patron goddess's light, forbidding them the trees of their birth. Surely, her brother had not stooped so low, and not for something as trivial as a *stone*. Not after what she had done to save him from this fate once before.

"Come, let's leave this place for somewhere we can talk more freely. I've got a hideout outside the walls," Bres said, tugging her hand once more. His expression was still pleasant, almost teasing. But annoyance flashed in his eyes, just as it used to when they were children and he had to wait for her short legs to catch up to his long strides as they moved through the forest. "You don't want to get caught by the mayor. He burned the last elf he found in this city."

Aoife shook herself, as if she could rid herself of doubt as easily as a dog could shake out water in his coat. What Bres said made sense, and they really shouldn't tarry here any longer when at any moment a member of the household might awake. She snuck up next to him, earning another brief smile. They moved silently together back through the hallway and up the chimney.

Aoife sighed in relief as her boots hit the dust beside the high house. But that feeling flew away like a bird as a cry of alarm echoed through the courtyard. They had climbed down the side of the house instead of the back for expediency's sake and were now in clear sight of the two guards who manned the iron entry gates.

"*Vaks*!" Bres cursed under his breath and then took off. Aoife stumbled behind, tripping over her heavy boots.

They dashed across the garden, reaching the wall easily. But Aoife heard the ominous crank of a crossbow, and her heart nearly leapt out of her chest. She scrambled up the wall after Bres. The fear and adrenaline rushing through her veins prompted stupid fumbles though, and she nearly fell from the wall twice. Fynn and Bran would have laughed to see her like this. She didn't feel like the competent professional she was, but the scared girl-child who had run through the dark forest chasing her brother's shadow.

Thwack. Aoife yelped in surprise as a crossbow quarrel bounced against the stone right above her hand. Bres, already at the top of the wall, glanced down briefly. A chill ran through her at his emotionless expression. Then, without a word, he vaulted over the wall, out of sight.

She couldn't lose him. Aoife let that thought speed her limbs as she made a last harried push over the wall. There was no time to climb safely down. Bres was halfway across the plaza, his black cloak billowing behind him. Sucking in a breath, Aoife leapt off the wall, her arms pinwheeling as she fell. The ground slapped her feet through the heavy iron soles of her boots, pain racing up her ankles and shins. She groaned, nearly falling over, but forced her ill-used legs back into a run to catch up with her brother.

The boots were too heavy. She'd never catch up with Bres this way. Just as her brother reached the edge of the plaza and turned back, she bent down to tug them off.

"Wait for me," she hissed. "I'll be right there."

Bres cocked his head to the side. Even from this distance, Aoife could see that strange, blank expression spread over his face again. His eyes filled with cold calculation, and her heart dropped into her stomach. She'd seen that look once before, standing in a moonlit grove, her knife dripping with blood. Staring at the body that had fallen on top of her brother, hands still wrapped around Bres's neck.

"Bres, wait!" she called out once more, not bothering to be quiet.

One boot was off, and she almost had the laces undone from the other as Bres's hand fluttered at his side. A blurred, dark shape dove in front of her, letting out a small *oof* as something hit it, then crashed to the cobblestones beside her.

The moonlight gilded the new arrival's face, dark skin pulled taut with pain over familiar sharp features.

"Fynn?" she cried out.

He smiled shakily, but it quickly turned into a grimace

as he tried to sit up. Aoife scanned his body and spotted the small hilt of a throwing dagger protruding from Fynn's stomach.

"You *vaksha* idiot!" she said, smacking Fynn on the shoulder.

The shouting from inside the walls grew louder as more guards undoubtedly joined the first two. The iron gates creaked open. She looked to the alley where Bres had stood, but he was gone.

"Sweet...Aoife, you're the only woman I know...who would hit a man...for saving her life," Fynn said, panting with pain.

"That dagger wasn't meant for me!"

Even as she denied it, her eyes flicked back to the hilt. Bres had always been an expert with knives. If he threw a blade, he aimed to kill. The low placement of the knife in Fynn's side didn't make sense to her. *Bres would never hurt me,* she told herself.

Fynn made a doubtful noise that turned into a groan as his body shuddered involuntarily. "I hate to...rush you, but I think...your friend...poisoned this blade."

Bran lumbered out of a nearby alley just as the iron gates opened enough for a tide of red-and-black uniformed guards to spill out. He lifted Fynn up on his massive shoulder as if the other man weighed no more than a sack of potatoes, and then the three of them escaped into the night, Aoife hobbling along on one boot.

The benefit of staying in the slums of Kamzal was that no one asked questions when someone barged in dragging a moaning, knife-stuck man as city patrols marched by. The stablehand took one look at them and decided he'd rather wash his ignorance down with a cup of ale at the inn's bar. Only the horses were there to complain about the noise as Bran lifted Fynn up into the small loft and looked at Aoife for direction. She was the most experienced healer of the bunch.

"Beg the innkeep for some hot water and some cloths," she said. She was surprised how calm her voice was even as the panic rising inside threatened to choke her. She drew in a deep breath, taking comfort in the smell of warm straw and horses. "Everything else we should have in our packs."

Bran nodded and left. Aoife flew up the ladder and ripped open her pack.

"Who…was that?" Fynn choked out. His skin was now tinged with gray, and his eyes had become bright and unfocused.

Aoife ignored the question, desperately digging around in her overstuffed pack. Her mind refused to think of what had happened in the courtyard. Instead, she focused completely on saving Fynn's life. Finally, her fingers grazed leather, and she triumphantly yanked out her medical kit. Hastily unrolling the wrap with shaking fingers, she pulled out a small glass vial filled with a green, mucky substance.

Fynn made a face. "Is that bitterroot?"

"Drink it," Aoife ordered, uncorking the vial and tipping it to his lips.

"I'm not sure…if I'd rather take my chances…with the poison," Fynn said, though his breathy voice and small shudders gave lie to his joke. She lightly slapped his face, and he obediently parted his lips and drank, his mouth twisting as the expensive antidote to most common poisons slid down his throat.

While they waited for Bran, Aoife cut away Fynn's dusty tunic. The knife hilt stood out starkly just beneath the left side of his ribcage. Too far down for any real damage. Her mind churned as she stared at the offending hilt.

"So, are you going to…introduce me to your

knife-wielding friend? I'm impressed with the skill...although I can't say I approve of his target at the moment," Fynn said, his voice already smoothing out, the pained hitches in his breath growing fewer and farther between.

Lucky for Aoife, she was spared an explanation when Bran reappeared with a steaming crock of water and a bundle of grayish rags that she supposed were as close to clean cloths as the innkeep had. He handed them up to her and then moved to stand guard by the door.

"How about you tell me why you were in that plaza in the first place?" Aoife said, wrapping her fingers around the knife's bone hilt. "It'll give you something to distract yourself while I do all the work."

Fynn's chuckle turned into a loud moan as she drew the blade out. Luckily, it was short enough that it had only caused surface damage. Bres always preferred small blades for greater accuracy, content to let his poisons do the killing for him. Aoife dipped a rag into the hot water and began cleaning the wound, holding Fynn down with one hand as he jerked up with each touch of the cloth. When she was satisfied, she plucked a needle and thread out of her kit and went to work on closing the narrow slash.

"We left The Fat Grouse just after you. I'd been a little too successful in getting our coin to multiply, and there were some bad sports." Aoife rolled her eyes. Fynn was a good enough player that he didn't *need* to cheat, but that never stopped him once he was on a roll. "We decided to walk by the high house before heading back here when we saw you disappear down the chimney. So we waited to hear whatever inexplicable reason you had for breaking and entering into the mayor's domain." He cocked an eyebrow at her meaningfully.

Aoife pulled her next stitch a little too tight, prompting a wince from her friend. She loosened the thread a little as she pondered how much to tell Fynn. He'd been her closest companion since she'd first shown up to the merc guild in Greengleann in little better than rags from her year searching for her brother in every town between the Vyoathe Forest and the capital. But she hesitated to betray Bres, even to Fynn. Even as that small, dark voice grew louder in the back of her mind.

"I saw a light in the window," she finally said.

"And?" Fynn didn't bother asking why she'd gone to investigate.

"There was a thief in the upper levels. I surprised him, and we both escaped as the alarm was raised." It wasn't *quite* a lie. The alarm had been raised as they were escaping, just not when they were still in the high house. She tied off her last knot and unrolled the clean bandages she always kept tucked away in her pack.

"But you knew him," Fynn said, his dark eyebrows drawing down. "You called out his name and said 'wait.'"

"It doesn't matter," Aoife snapped, ignoring Fynn's stare. She finished padding the wound and briskly motioned for Fynn to sit up so she could wind the bandages around his torso. And if she used the opportunity to slide behind him and out of view so he couldn't see her face, well, so much the better.

Silence fell between them, only the quiet nickering of horses filling the air. Aoife tied her last knot and patted Fynn on the shoulder to let him know she was done. He shifted slowly until he sat propped against the sloping wall of the loft.

"Aoife," he said, his face devoid of his usual winking humor. "You know I'm not one to pry. We all have our secrets, past sins that we'd rather leave to the years behind us. But whoever that man was to you, he's no friend of yours now. The knife is proof of that much."

"If you hadn't charged in there in some ill-advised attempt to save me, there would *be* no knife," she said, her eyes unwillingly glancing down to the blood-covered blade.

Fynn shook his head. He paused, as if searching for the right words.

"Aoife...the knife was already in the air when I started running across the plaza. If I hadn't used my charm, I would have been too late." He patted the tattoo on his neck as if it was some faithful steed. His eyes were dark with pity that she'd rather not see.

She'd heard enough. She stood up, nearly bumping her head on the roof, and turned her back to Fynn and his words. Sliding down the ladder, she ignored Bran's grave look and burst past him out of the stable, still with only one boot on. Neither of her companions followed her. They knew better than to approach her when she was in a temper—after the first few times *she* had thrown a knife at them.

In the predawn shadows, the innyard took on an eerie air, its broken fence and wilting garden more ominous than they looked in the harsh light of day. One shadow stood darker than the rest, pressed against the broken-down tool shed. She took a moment to unlace and remove her boot, gratefully pulling her sore foot from the stinging iron, then stepped lightly amongst the cabbage heads and drooping herbs to cross the garden.

The shadow separated itself from the shed, becoming a familiar broad-shouldered silhouette cloaked in black.

"*Isha*," Bres said. It was too dark to see the expression on his face. "I knew you'd spot me. Come, let's leave this hole. You'll like where I'm staying much better, away from these dirty humans and their dust-choked city."

Aoife bit her lip and moved no closer to him. "My pack is in the barn."

"With your humans?" Bres said. She didn't need light to hear the sneer in his voice.

"We're half-human," she reminded him. He spit to the side, giving her all the answer she needed. "And they're my friends. I've been traveling with them for years now."

Since you left me, she left unsaid. Her fingers itched to touch her brand again, but she kept them folded into fists at her sides.

"That doesn't matter now," he said, stepping closer. He rested one finger under her chin and tilted her face up to look at him. "The Lady herself must have brought us together again. Surely, you won't stay with them when you could come with me instead? Once my job is finished here, we'll be flush in coin. I'll take you anywhere in the Civil States you want. Or we'll cross the sea if you'd rather, and start a new life on the Peninsula."

"The Lady turned her face from me the day I took a life," Aoife whispered, her eyes flicking to the setting moon, cold and distant in the sky. She bit her lip, wrestling with the old scars of abandonment and self-incrimination before adding, "This has been all I've known since that day. I've had no one else."

Bres folded her into his arms, holding her tight. "You've given up much for me, *isha*. Don't think I've ever forgotten. If I had known you were out of the forest, I would have died before I stopped searching for you."

Wrapped in the warm safety of his arms, Aoife blinked furiously to hold back tears that had sprung up at the words she'd longed to hear for over a decade. That dark voice broke in through her thoughts just as Bres drew back, shouting its vile poison in her mind. It spoke of the knife, the stone, and the blankness in her brother's eyes. *Not now*. She shoved it down and took a step back, stuffing her trembling fingers in her pockets.

"I need a day," she said.

Bres's hand fluttered by his side, and she tensed even as she told herself she had no reason to. But all that he pulled out was a small folded piece of parchment. She took it from his outstretched fingers before disappearing it into her sleeve.

"I thought you might say as much. Meet me there,

tomorrow at moonrise. I'll have finished my job, and we can be off together. Say whatever goodbyes you need to your pets and come away with me." He kissed her brow, his lips cold and smooth. "Thank the Lady for bringing you to me."

He melted into the shadows once more, leaving Aoife standing barefoot in the garden as the sun began its ascent in the sky.

oife crept into a rocky vale at the foot of the mountain range that sprung up just outside Kamzal's walls. The gray stones were painted with shadows as clouds scuttled above, shrouding the moon's white light with their gauzy fingers. She was late, but she didn't think Bres would care. Her preparations had taken longer than she'd thought they would. She scanned the craggy rise in front of her but saw no shadows but her own.

"*Isha*," Bres said from behind her.

She whirled around, heart pounding in her chest. Discreetly, she wiped her clammy palms on her favorite leather trousers. She wore no hat tonight, no headscarf. Bres still wore his large black cloak, and it floated in the breeze flowing between the rocks.

"I knew you'd come," he said, that ironic smile twisting his lips. He came forward, arms wide to embrace her.

She stepped back, surprising a frown out of him.

"I only came to say goodbye," she said.

"What?" That muscle in Bres's cheek jumped. "You can't leave now. I need you by my side."

"I think you need the only witness of your crime well away from the scene of it," she whispered, her voice shaking as she spoke.

Bres advanced on her. She danced back another step, careful to stay out of his reach. He cocked his head, looking for all the world like the concerned older brother she desperately wanted him to be. The shadows atop the rocks to her right rippled.

"Aoife, what nonsense is this?"

She took a deep breath, straightening her shoulders and looking Bres square in the eye. "Did you kill a man near the high house six nights past? For the stone he carried in his pocket?"

The smile died on Bres's lips. He waved a hand in the air as if to scatter her words away.

"*Isha* dear, there are forces at play you don't understand. These Grimnalians don't even understand these stones they carry in their pockets and around their necks. They think them only pretty baubles." His fingers fluttered, and a stone appeared in the palm of his outstretched hand, its silver flecks sparkling even in the darkness. "These stones are *dangerous* and worth my weight in silver to my employer. Don't you recognize them from our lessons? They're *spéir* stones."

Aoife sucked in a breath, her suspicions confirmed from the first time Petro had mentioned the luck stone. *Spéir* stones were highly potent magical objects, able to hold an infinite number of enchantments that would break any ordinary material. A warlock could slowly store enough destructive spells to take out an army in one, then use it with no effort in one blow. They occurred rarely in nature, appearing here and there throughout the centuries and then disappearing like a myth. There must be a small vein here in one of the quarries, and if any powerful magic users realized it before the vein disappeared, they'd descend upon Grimnal in hordes to tear it apart.

"My employer's spies had been instructed to relay any rumors of shiny blue stones that seemed to bring luck with them. Eventually, we heard whispers that the mayor's wife in this backwater was spotted wearing a pendant that matched the description. He sent me here to discover for myself. I've an enchantment on me that burns whenever I draw close to a high-powered magical object."

Bres rolled his shirt sleeve back, and Aoife gasped. His arm was covered in elaborate tattoos, all sharp edges and ugly patterns, some dangerously close to overlapping as they covered almost every inch of his smooth brown skin. He tapped one particularly thorny tattoo, but Aoife's eyes were drawn to the large chain circling above it.

"That's a binding curse," she whispered. "Oh, Bres, what did you do to make a warlock bind you so?" Binding curses were rare, requiring a blood sacrifice from the user and very specific parameters. They were usually only placed on highly dangerous familiars who couldn't be trusted to wander the realms unchained. The punishment for disobeying an order from whoever held the binding curse was death.

Bres shrugged and dropped his sleeve, the tattoos hidden once more. "It doesn't matter. He's promised to lift the curse if I can bring back a stone. So, when that dumb rock-tosser walked by me as I scouted the high house, my arm burned, and I grabbed my chance. He fussed too loudly, so I shut him up."

At her brother's callous dismissal, Aoife thought of Mel's pale, tear-streaked face as they'd questioned her this morning. She'd spoken mournfully of how Jek always took extra time to find her favorite flowers when they were in season. How they'd dreamed of a small house in the town to call their own. How she heard his voice calling for her in the night. Aoife squeezed her eyes shut and rubbed her hands against her face as if she could wipe the sorrow away.

Bres stepped closer, placing his hands on her shoulders. "See, my sweet sister? It's all a misunderstanding. Come with me, see me earn my freedom, and then my promise stands. Anywhere you want, I'll take you."

"How will you take me anywhere if your warlock kills

both of us to keep the source of the stones secret?" she asked.

Bres shrugged, his face inscrutable in the shadows the moon cast on him. "I'll figure a way out of trouble, once the binding curse is lifted. I always do."

"*Always*?" she hissed, shaking his hands off her shoulders. She touched her brand, feeling the thick ridges beneath her fingertips. "Adair would have killed you that night if I hadn't saved you! And then you disappeared, nowhere to be found as they chained me with iron and pressed a hot brand to my face!" Her voice dropped low as she added, "I cried your name as they did it. Over and over again, I screamed for you to save me, as my skin bubbled and my hands burned from the chains. But you didn't come."

"I never asked you to kill him!" Bres shot back.

"What else was I to do?" The words spilled out of Aoife's mouth like hot lava, burning her lips as they went. Tears streamed down her face as she traveled back through the years to that terrible night. "There was no one around to call for help except for Fianna, naked and screeching as her husband choked the life out of you. I tried to pull him off, but he wouldn't stop. Your face turned blue. I saw it in his eyes that he wouldn't stop, not this time, not after all the times before. I did what I had to do."

"As did I," Bres said coldly. "I couldn't come back to that damn forest after that. I had to get away, and I had to do what I had to survive. You don't understand that."

"*I* don't understand that? You knew they would toss me out! You knew no one who had taken a life could stay beneath the Lady's oaks. All that bluster about thinking I was safe in the trees…did you really think I was dumb enough to believe that?" She blew out a breath, shaking her head. "No. Your lies have cost enough lives, mine included. I can't let you leave with those stones. Any warlock who is rotten enough to lay binding curses on people isn't someone who should have such a precious thing. Only destruction will follow."

"That's not your decision to make, *isha* dear. We're family. The only family we have left, as those fools in the forest made perfectly clear. Come away with me, and it will all be fine. We'll be together, family. As we should."

"Family doesn't abandon each other in hardship. They don't let each other face the darkness alone," she said, still hoping for reason from him. "Or watch those they love walk a path to damnation. Bres, please. Give me the stones and turn yourself in. It's the only hope you have to preserve your life. We'll find a way to break the binding. I promise."

"I always knew you for a fool." With those harsh words, Bres stepped away, all pretense dropped, his face gone cold. He tutted like an old nanny as he fingered the hilt of one of the many knives sheathed in his belt. "A shame you have no one to back up your righteous mission. You have a choice. Either come with me or die alone among the rocks. It makes no difference to me. But you know I can't let you go."

At the blunt threat coming from what should be trusted lips, Aoife was struck mute. Her eyes were stuck on Bres as if by staring at him she could change his cold heart.

The moment of frozen shock cost her. Bres's hand fluttered at his side. She barely had time to recognize the lethal shape of the knife flying toward her before a clang of metal broke her reverie. Diving to the side, she crashed to the rocky ground, landing awkwardly on her wrist. The pain swept the breath from her. Gasping for air, she waited for a final blow from Bres.

As her heart kept beating and no knives sprouted from her body, reason came back to her. She rolled over then got to her knees, cradling her injured wrist against her chest. Two knives lay nearby, Bres's poison-dipped blade and a larger one with a carved wooden hilt.

Fynn stood with his knife to Bres's neck, panting. The enchantment on his neck was already dimming. He'd used it too quickly in succession when he wasn't at full strength. The distance from the rocks behind Bres where he and Bran had waited must have been too great for him in this state. He wouldn't get another burst of unnatural speed tonight.

Bran crossed the vale from his own hiding place, moving as if he were made of rock himself and swinging the large mace in his hand idly as he neared her brother's other side. Bres's eyes darted from left to right, nostrils flared and face reddening with rage.

"You filthy little snake," he sneered at Aoife as she stood up, her wrist throbbing with each movement. "You dare betray me?"

"She told you," Fynn said. "Family doesn't let each other face the darkness alone. Good thing you wear that stupid cloak so you're easy to identify."

Bran prodded Bres's side with the handle of his mace and extended one meaty hand. "Stones," he said simply, twitching his fingers.

Bres spat into his hand. Bran studied the fat, slimy gobbet for a moment, as if it held a message for him, then casually backhanded the other man. Bres's head snapped back with the impact, and he stumbled.

Aoife opened her mouth to cry out a warning, knowing her brother's penchant for trickery in a fight. But by that time, Bres had already swept Fynn's feet out from under him and kicked him in the side, right where his knife had landed the previous night. Fynn howled and tried his best to scrabble away as Bran grabbed for the black-cloaked thief and caught nothing but air. Aoife barely had time to move before she felt her brother's arm wrapped around her neck and the cold kiss of steel against her skin.

"Now that we're on more even footing," he said, as casually as if they were discussing the events of the day over a mug of ale, "let's take my pretty sister's advice and be reasonable. You two will drop your weapons and leave immediately, or I start cutting pieces off of her. And then it will be your turn."

Bran helped Fynn to his feet, supporting him with an arm across his back. She knew them both well enough to recognize the panic welling in their eyes. Fynn traced the lines of his tattoo, murmuring the activation under his breath, but they remained dull and black.

"You would truly do this?" she asked, so low that only Bres could hear. "Have I always meant so little to you, *ishen*?"

He scoffed and pressed the knife harder against her skin, sparking a bright line of pain, followed by wetness as blood dripped down her neck.

"If there's one thing that damn forest taught me, it's that you can't let anyone mean more to you than yourself. You were useful to me for a time, but that time is long past. Say your goodbyes, *isha* dear."

Lady, if you ever bore me love, guide my hand, Aoife prayed. *Help me make things right.*

Aoife's brand burned like a fire as Bres drew his hand back. His knife glittered in the moonlight that poured down through the sudden break in the clouds. Fynn and Bran both cried out as one. They seemed to move in slow motion, too far to do anything but catch her corpse. She did not share their alarm. The awe the moonlight inspired in her warred with the grief twisting in her heart. The Lady, it seemed, was offering her a second chance. To make amends.

She spun quickly, pressing her body against Bres's larger one and wrapping one arm around his back. She held him close, her bad hand trapped between their bodies.

Footsteps and shouting assaulted her ears, but they came from miles away. Bres's eyes widened, his lips parting with surprise. Blinking stinging tears from her eyes, she twisted the knife she'd driven into his heart a little deeper, just to be sure. His nerveless fingers opened, his own weapon clattering to the rocks, still smeared with some of her blood.

"I love you," she whispered to him. "Still. And always. But I'll sin no more for you."

His lips twitched, but whatever precious last words he had been about to speak spilled out with his last breath. His dead weight sagged against her, almost bringing her down. Reluctantly, she let him slide down to rest on the ground.

There were no clouds in the sky. Moonlight drowned the vale as Fynn and Bran hobbled toward her. Aoife tipped her face to the sky and drank in the blessing.

The Lady herself must have brought us together. Perhaps she had.

It was easy in the light to find the stones. They weighed as much as an iron block in her hand. She rubbed a spot of blood off the pendant.

"What'll you do with 'em?" Bran asked.

"The pendant I'll dedicate at the Lady's temple in Greengleann. Their vault is tighter than most dukes'. Hopefully when Bres doesn't appear, the warlock will think the original tip was a dud. Jek found the stone a few years ago. The vein is probably gone by now."

"And the other?"

"To Petro, of course," she answered. "I think he could use a little luck."

THE PROBLEM
WITH ELVES

Ryan Swindoll

Grandmother once said, "Never toss out a rotten egg. I never did." She had one slipper in the grave when she told me that, and had I been a mite older, I would have asked her to clarify her meaning.

It was in the last hours of autumn before the deadly frost that I found myself distracted in Grandmother's labyrinth of forehead creases. They cut and crisscut inscrutably. Standing at her bedside, all but fourteen years upon this globe, I looked for a way out of that wrinkling maze. Her comment about the eggs did not offer me an exit. Grandmother was my last living relative. Why was she carrying on about eggs? It vexed me. I did my time in a scullery as a child, and I can assure you, saving the rotten eggs was the broad road to unemployment.

In need of clarity, my focus drifted downward and found a vista atop that walnut between her eyes. I quietly surveyed my childhood in those harrowing trenches. That dented knoll was my doing. Grandmother had raised me alone; her principal means of tutelage was flexing that all-powerful, all-knowing Knot.

I was a curious child, and sickly, too—an unfortunate pairing. One of my earliest predilections was that of magic and its usefulness as a means to stave off boredom. Once I ate three cloves of garlic at midnight in a vainglorious attempt to float the cat up the chimney. It caught halfway, disappointingly, and did not survive the fateful fire Grandmother stoked the next morning. Even so, the Knot kept me from more perilous ends. When I climbed the roof with a satchel of spoiled cabbage and sampled it, arms outstretched, intent to crack the mystery of magical flight, the Knot put a stop to it. Grandmother did not say a word; she let the Knot do the winnowing work.

I take comfort in knowing that I did not face my perennial struggle with curiosity alone. Indeed, I had as company a great many ridges in Grandmother's brow. The Arch of Suspicion. The Accordion of Surprise. The Scowl of Reckoning—yes, the Scowl of Reckoning alone was a champion worthy of knighthood. When I determined as a lad to become the greatest mage the world had ever seen, I never imagined doing so outside the safety of Grandmother's scowl.

At her deathbed, still puzzling about the eggs, I had few options available to comfort her. I told her I loved her. I recited part of my catechism—Grandmother always liked that. Then inspiration came to me in those blessed wrinkles: an opportunity to mend the lines my mischief had drawn; to send my grandmother without seam unto the pale gold palisades of Heaven.

I fumbled in my pocket and retrieved my magic bean.

I had pilfered the bean from the forest on the north end of town. The faint odor of brimstone hung about the clearing. We lived near elves—at least everyone suspected so—and the bean confirmed this. Elves never let them out of their sight, which made my find miraculous. I'd heard about magic beans from the children whispering in the market: white as chalk, slender, cylindrical: the secret ingredient to elvish magic. No human to my knowledge had ever held a magic bean except for those witless fools in the fables, and I knew those tales served only to frighten children from their natural curiosity in magic. I snatched the bean and escaped the forest. Heroically, I resolved to save it until a moment of true necessity where its power could be used for the good. This was that moment.

The bean, small and smooth, proved easy enough to hide from the Knot. Feigning a cough, I slipped it in my mouth. Only a child would believe themselves capable of channeling the latent powers of a magic bean. I knew not whether to chew or swallow whole; such was my folly. In the end, its mildewed secretion made the decision for me. I gagged it down and waited for the magic to hit my digestion.

Grandmother reclined with her eyes at half mast, Knot

none the wiser.

I winced as a bloat of magic ballooned in my gut. Magical foods like cauliflower and cheese typically required a half-hour minimum to kick in, but the bean had worked in under a minute. I acted fast and burped—just enough magic gas to touch the Knot and smooth the ripples that rounded it. My invisible powers worked upon the creases. Grandmother's face lifted. Her lips parted as she experienced a complete and weightless calm. To be honest, she looked fourteen years younger. I had not reversed her age nor delayed her death, only briefly interrupted the bond between her body and the earth, an elementary trick of magic. But the effect was exactly as I had hoped. The consternation between her eyes vanished. She seemed finally at peace. Free.

We both took a deep breath—though mine was cut short by a sharp pressure in my stomach where the magic continued to bloat. I gasped in pain. Grandmother roused, tilting her head to study my countenance. Always looking out for me, dear Grandmother, even on her deathbed. I clenched a cheerful smile, enough to distract her from the cold panic collecting upon my skin. Never having swallowed a magic bean before, I could only guess whether I had crested the peak of its magical potency.

I had not.

A bubble of magic gas growled through my gut. Grandmother blinked in alarm as her weightless arms began to float up from the sheets. Then my two feet lost contact with the ground. Everything in the chamber, from the rocking chair to the bedpan, undertook a sudden and urgent apotheosis. The thatchwork roof rent apart in a torrent of vertical lift and the fluorescence of God broke upon us, shining down as we rose.

The magic was clearly out of control. I grabbed Grandmother's wrist, and I thrashed the air to make our escape. Flecks of twinkling sweat flung about the dissolving room. My legs kicked desperately—yet, as in a dream, I remained very much in place.

Finally, I could no longer contain it. I broke wind, shamefully loud and in Grandmother's hearing. Grandmother sobered out of death. The wet odor of rotten eggs singed our noses, and I wondered how quickly she would recant her line about saving them. Her wrinkled brow reincarnated the Arch, the Accordion, and the Scowl in succession. At last, the Knot pierced me with its beholding stare—too late to save us, too late to shield us from what was to follow.

Suspended between Heaven and Earth, I glanced upward into the swirling vortex of rocking chairs, quilts, and ceiling tar. It lifted us up, up to a bright center, out of this world.

Then the intestinal pain broke me, and I blacked out.

My eyes popped open to a brilliant lemon ceiling where edge and beam could not be seen. Reflex pivoted me into a sitting position. My gut felt stretched; it folded with residual pain. Shining yellow walls met my gaze in all directions, confounding me. The walls looked inwardly illumined, as if the builders had skinned the bright sun and papered the walls with the peelings.

In front of me, a mystical door opened. Gliding in like a gentle breeze came a young woman, tall, with flowing white hair and luxurious gold robes. Her kindly face struck me as familiar, like a long lost sister. I puzzled on her identity as the lady shuffled to a nearby table and poured me a glass of sparkling water. Was this the Holy Lady herself? Given the circumstances of my last moments on Earth, I found this reception to Heaven well exceeded my expectations.

Presenting the glass, the woman said in a soothing

Gaelic voice, "I find a glass of water settles well before the presentation."

That voice, that accent made me gasp. "Grandmother?"

The lady smiled with radiant affection, yet with no smile lines. Her forehead shone clean as porcelain. She seemed lighter than air, half her former age and twice her former height. Dumbstruck, I accepted the glass from her youthful hands. The water bubbled like millions of tiny minnows leaping to make a joyful escape. Sucking in my resolve, I drained the glass. The leaping water required a strange effort to swallow, but it tasted effervescent. A hint of lemon that matched the walls.

I politely masked my burp.

"Come, child." Grandmother gestured magisterially to the open portal. "The presentation begins on the hour."

"Wait," I requested, feeling my shame. "We're dead, Grandmother, aren't we? I'm so sorry, I shouldnt've—"

"Curious boy!" she inflected. "Always running ahead. Don't worry about that now. The presentation will make all things clear."

I found my legs and slipped uneasily off a white, cushioned lounge seat. The antechamber was otherwise sparsely furnished, prefiguring an entrance into a more dazzling space. The air felt fizzled dry; the floor tinny and hollow. I caught the scent of something foul, though I supposed it to be my own breath still serving the halo of that magic bean.

Grandmother led me into a broad and circular room with a domed ceiling. Mirrors lined the rim of the room, making the interior feel infinite. I watched our reflections find their way to a platform in the illustrious center where stood a polished round table and three golden chairs. In one of the gold chairs sat an olive-skinned monk, silent, ageless, and the room's only occupant besides us. Tufts of white hair orbited his bald head like a procession of clouds. And, like Grandmother, his skin shone immaculate.

"This is Alzo," said Grandmother in courtesy as we joined the monk at the table.

Alzo bowed.

I peered at the man expectantly. "Grandfather?"

Grandmother and Alzo shared a look of amusement. I'd never met Grandfather, but the idea that she'd married a monk fit easily with my picture of her moral inflexibility. The monk seemed to consider the proposition, but he rendered a muffled reply, "No-no. No-no. Please, my name is Alzo."

Grandmother waved. "Alzo and I are old friends, back before you were born. He's here to learn how to give the presentation, so I've asked him to sit in. Pay him no mind." She folded her hands neatly on the table. "Now. The presentation. I'm sure you have many questions, and you are welcome to ask them when the presentation has ended."

The bright mirrors dimmed tawny, then fell to dark rust. Grandmother motioned me to turn around. The rim of the room blinked with inward light, and the mirrors began to reflect activity from another time and place. Scrying magic. I saw a great multitude of moving faces in hazy environments I found difficult to place. My ears hummed with speech and sound, overlapping and indistinct. Each mirror fixated on its own perspective; the greater meaning remained a blur.

My eyes latched on a black cat in the focus of one scene. "That's Arthur," I cried, "inside the magic mirror!" The cat licked his paws on the sitting room mat, very much alive and not burned. I noticed then the familiar trappings of Grandmother's cottage: the old oil pastoral, the stain on the hearth. "But how is he—"

"Dear boy, this is the echo of your past," Grandmother mused.

I watched, mesmerized. Each scene took shape in my understanding. I found mirrors here and there depicting the hanging straw above my bed where, annually, I battled the whooping cough. Those prickling patterns I'd recognize anywhere. The Straw Knights. Characters I'd invented to go on adventures for me.

On different mirrors, I saw Norban and me playing jacks in the alley out of the summer heat: trading barbs, boasting of wagers and winnings. I watched myself cheat Norban mercilessly. With a pinch of dried fish, I could slow the ball's descent and snatch more jacks than was humanly possible. I felt less jubilant about my mischief now.

I looked elsewhere. Many figures I didn't recognize, forgotten by time. I wondered if any were my parents who'd abandoned me at birth.

In another mirror I sat as a young child at Grandmother's rickety table, refusing to eat the soup, thin and sour. I caught myself pouring the bowl into a window pot the moment Grandmother turned her back.

My cheeks burned and I pinched my lower lip between my teeth, for Grandmother saw the whole thing now.

In yet another mirror, older, I ate the soup. Later, when I burped and inexplicably moved the rocking chair, the curious link between indigestion and magic became known. The discovery entranced me. My reflection in other mirrors was raiding garbage piles and practicing childish tricks. An ignoble beginning. There was Constable Wembley shouting me down as a lad when I magically tipped a manure cart on his shoes.

I stifled a laugh at the memory. Grandmother and Alzo turned to stare at me across the dark table. My throat closed.

The mirror behind Grandmother showed urine falling on the back wall of the public house.

"Can I ask," I coughed to draw their attention away. "This is not my entire past, is it?"

"Every part," she assured me in the dark.

I sunk in my chair. The Knot would have bulged many

times larger if it had grappled with all of my transgressions. Avoiding the mirrors now, I cast a sidelong glance at Alzo who sat in a wakeful meditation. I do not recall him ever blinking. My entire past, watched without a word of explanation, uncovered and exposed upon the eyes of Grandmother and this perfect stranger. An unbearable fate.

"Why must we watch this?" I pleaded and winced.

At once, the mirrors ceased. Sunny illumination refilled the room, and I shielded my eyes. Bright yellow accosted me like that time I had a hangover, a memory I was glad we did not relive. My focus returned to Grandmother, beautiful, noble, posture ramrod straight. She stared at me as if expecting an answer to what we had seen.

I did as I had growing up: I studied her brow to interpret what she was thinking and what I should say. Her brow remained wiped clean, a blank slate. Frankly, it made it impossible to wriggle a line in my defense, to atone for the damage my life had caused.

"I'm rotten," I strained, addressing my abject confession to both Grandmother and the monk. "My past—you see it. I'm not proud of it. I don't see the purpose in reliving it."

"Ah, the purpose," Grandmother intoned. She swept back a loose strand of hair so that it all tucked symmetrically. "Nobody gets into Heaven without first watching the presentation with their Grandmother." She and Alzo opened their palms splendorously. "Heaven is clean. It is perfect. It abounds in possibilities. But there is one thing Heaven cannot abide."

"Magic," Alzo resounded like a gong.

My heart hammered with the reverberations.

"Magic is a putrid thing," mulled Grandmother. "It corrupts the natural bonds things have for one another. Its mischief spreads falsehoods, stokes the embers of pride, and kills cats. It leaves the most unpleasant odor in its wake."

"Grandmother," I begged in a whisper, "I'm really sorry about Arthur. I really thought he'd climbed down."

"Are you willing," she solemnly continued, "to surrender your magic? To end this spectacle of forgery? It is a generous exchange I offer you. Your magic for a new life."

I looked at my cowering face repeating in the infinite mirrors. Since I was a boy, I'd devoted my life to plumbing the secrets of magic, an ambition no mortal dared master. And all I'd done in my short years on Earth was use it for ill gains and frivolous fun. I was heartbroken. Was there nothing I could do to make up for the waste?

"Grandmother, please," I tried once more, "is magic really all bad?"

The room dropped into darkness, and the mirrors showed Grandmother and I in our fateful final ascent, lingering above the Earth. Grandmother and her Knot betrayed a look of shriveled terror.

"Enough," I said, wiping my eyes. "I will relent of all my magic. Only please forgive me, Grandmother. I'm sorry for everything I put you through."

The lady appeared self-satisfied. "Then the presentation is over." Her ageless face looked at Alzo, and the monk patted the table with his right palm.

"The beans, lad."

I searched his expression for some clue. "The magic bean? You mean, the one I found in the forest? I used it by your bed, Grandmother. That why—it's gone."

Alzo's white eyebrows furrowed. "The others. Heaven will not have you until you return them."

"But I don't have any more," I explained in earnest.

Grandmother rose to her feet, towering over me. This was a new and frightful experience of Grandmother who otherwise had been known for being quite short and easily lost in crowds. Her brow bore not a ripple, yet her gaze felt more severe than even the tightest of her old scowls. My ears burned in her radiant heat, and, for the second time, I caught a whiff of something foul.

"Come now, child," she coaxed. "Six more beans remain unaccounted. Heaven does not abide a liar. But—" She signaled Alzo to stand. "If you speak true, you can prove it with your purity."

Grandmother and Alzo evacuated the platform and I followed, lagging. No sooner had I stepped off the center platform but the round table fell away and the floor opened its maw over the whistling tops of white clouds.

"Leap, child!" Grandmother commanded over the wind. "Leap over this chasm. If you speak true, Heaven will float you blameless to the other side. But be advised. If you've any impurity, any lingering rot, Hell will snatch you down by the shackles of your lie."

I forced myself to exhale. The air left me breathless, and I stumbled to my knees. Had I even one more bean—or a generous helping of beef stew—I could have delivered myself from this awful trial. But Grandmother had stripped me of both my magic and my pride such that I nearly threw myself into the gaping hole to be done with it.

Only one question tethered me back. "Grandmother," I asked, "you told me you never tossed out a rotten egg. Why?"

The lady frowned—at least, I think she did. The telltale wrinkle was missing from her face. She squinted into her recollection, and after a terrible silence, Grandmother dismissed my question with a surly answer. "It was a metaphor, child—about you. I always saved you from your rottenness, whenever I could. Obviously, I tossed out the real eggs."

"That can't be," I gasped in a peril of thought. "The pantry was full of them."

Grandmother tilted her jaw.

"You knew I practiced magic," I accused her. "You cautioned me—scowled at me, sure. But I dare say you encouraged it. The soup was dreadful, but it was magically potent. It took a long time before I acquired the taste."

I grew more certain of the test before me, and it was not the one my captors were presenting.

"You're elves!"

Alzo and Grandmother snapped a fierce look at each other before shedding their magic illusions. Their ears thinned, their clothes frilled, and the scent of brimstone leaked from their golden bodies.

"He could smell us, Alzo!" the sallow elf masquerading as Grandmother cursed. "I told you we needed to cast proper disguises!"

"Marta, you ninny," the bearded elf clipped back, "we would've had time to mask it had you not insisted on rehearsing this Heaven nonsense. He's a hack magician, not an altar boy."

"He's a threat," Marta fumed at me. A blazing wreath encircled her head; the flames licked over the pit. "And there are two ways to deal with threats. Fix them—or nix them."

I took several involuntary steps backwards.

"Where are the beans?" Alzo angered.

The elves of the fables were illusive and mischievous, but always principled. I knew they had not gone to the trouble of abducting me only to kill me for speaking up for myself. "I took one—just one! If more are missing, perhaps I can help you find them."

Marta stamped her elven hoof. "That's exactly what we're trying to avoid here! Eating a magic bean would've killed any mortal, but you—you survived. There's only one explanation."

"Practice," I declared.

Marta screeched. "Your mother was an elf! If you, a bastard elf, introduce magic to the humans, they'll spoil the planet!"

"They'll raze the forests." Alzo took a step toward me.

"They'll slay the mythical beasts." Marta joined his advance.

"They'll banish the elves and Other Worldly creatures." On the far wall, elves in white suits stepped out from the mirrors. Behind me, a shout: commotion about an escapee. I was running out of time.

I sympathized with my hands in plain view. "And that would all be terribly bad. But what if I keep magic a secret—find a way to use it for the good?"

"You're a mistake," Marta seethed, fingers undulating. "A mistake not worth fixing."

I had my dumb fists and nothing else. But before I could deliver my first and would-be only blow, two bony fingers pinched my ear and pulled me back. A wrinkled thumb forced open my fist and planted a clicking collection of six white morsels. My gaze shot upward and locked eyes with Grandmother's Knot, bulging with all the worry of love. "Time to fly," she scowled.

"The missing beans!" Marta and Alzo lunged into action.

I clapped my hand over my mouth. This time I chewed.

A surge of sulfuric gas overtook my breath, knocking my assailants back. I warped the magic against the encircling mirrors, shattering them, exposing observation rooms where more elves either fled or attempted attack. A blast of magic through my digestion flung them all against the walls. I wrapped my scrawny arm around Grandmother, and we leapt together through the opening in the floor. We plummeted toward Earth. Spinning around, I caught one last glimpse of that elven Other World before wisps of cloud obscured my vision, that shining golden disk we narrowly escaped.

As dawn rose over the frosty mountains, Grandmother and I fell upon the shattered remains of the family cottage. I gripped my gut in an agony of pain, barely conscious of how fast we flew. I did everything in my power to deliver Grandmother safely to her broken bed, gently as a feather lights upon snow. I even managed to flutter a tattered quilt over her.

She wheezed softly with exertion. "I was saving them—for you, Merlin."

I endeavored to show Grandmother what I concealed in my palm. The sixth bean I did not swallow, saved for a special purpose. With one bean, I could engineer a cleaner form of elven magic and create a kingdom where human folk lived in peace and harmony, despite the elves. It was the least I could do to honor Grandmother. Faced with a rotten egg like me, she did the unthinkable and made a soup out of it.

But alas, I could hardly move. I was overbrimming with magic gas. Every twitch proved searing. I could only utter a catechism of moans, and between my gasps for air there came a punctuation of heavenly wind.

Grandmother's knot relaxed as she began to laugh, hard and hearty, and she laughed until she died.

LILA

Rachel Neumeier

"Lila" previously appeared in an anthology of Rachel Neumeier's work titled *Beyond the Dreams We Know: A Collection.*

They unfolded from pebbles, first. From limestone pebbles in driveways and planters; from the quartz inclusions in river rocks, from sharp-edged bits of flint along the edge of the old quarry where the rock had long ago been broken and left lying.

They came out of the water, too. From the foam where the little waterfalls of the river dashed down the mountain, from the still pools where the deeper water lingered in shadowed eddies, from the cold green quarry lake where children swam during long summer afternoons. They were the colors of the stone and water: foam white or cloud grey or translucent green. The white ones were streaked with rust along their breasts and the undersides of their wings; the green ones dappled with shadowed grey and blue.

Sometimes they left behind fragments of shells, not quite like ordinary eggshells: delicate layers of pale stone on the outside, glistening and nacreous on the inside. Mad collected half a dozen broken shells, but the remnants were fragile, and overnight the pearlescent layer sublimed like ice kept too long frozen, leaving behind only curved layers of ordinary limestone or chert.

The dragons were far too small to frighten anyone. They were the size of sparrows, mostly, or occasionally as large as starlings: wingspans as long as a woman's hand, whippy tails twice as long again. The children of Springdale tried to catch them in nets, but once their wings were dry they were quick as hummingbirds. Only a few of the more persistent and energetic boys caught one that way, and discovered to their disappointment that the dragons would not live through the night if kept in a jar or aquarium, no matter whether you punched holes in the lid of the jar or what you tried to feed them. Then the dead dragons would dissolve into the air like the nacreous layers of their shells, and you would be left with only a few uninteresting bits that might be bone or chips of limestone, or at best one or two curiously shaped little teeth. The scientists collected a few or paid the boys to do it, and so did the reporters, but with no better result. If there was a way to keep a dragon alive once you caught it, no one had discovered it yet.

One morning near the beginning, Lila caught one as it emerged from a limestone pebble. She brought it in through the pet door, as proud of herself as if she'd caught a mole or a mouse. The dragon was one of the little streaky white ones, pretty and delicate as a porcelain ornament, but now with its neck limp and wings trailing. Mad took it away from Lila and held it curled in the palm of her hand while the little dog danced on her hind legs and yipped to have it back.

Mad was sorry the little dragon was dead, but Lila was so pleased with herself that she didn't have the heart to say so. "You're a brave, bold hunter," Mad told the little dog. "But please consider sticking to moles in the future, yes?" And she put the dragon out of the way on a counter so she could check Lila's face and neck and legs for injuries. Lila knew all about moles and mice and hadn't been bitten since puppyhood, but dragons were as new for her as for everyone else and she might not have realized how long and agile they were. Like snakes, really. That was a disturbing thought—

"They're not poisonous," Boyd Raske said from the kitchen door, propped open now to let in the breeze. "Or at least the one that bit Tommy Kincaid wasn't."

Mad nodded to him, not at all surprised that he had dropped by, or that he'd recognized her sudden fear. Boyd Raske noticed a lot; a little too much, sometimes. And he kept track of everyone in Springdale. Particularly anybody who might be grieving or angry or thinking about getting into trouble. He'd had been making a point of wandering by Mad's house every day or so since Christmas. Since her mother's funeral, in fact. She supposed that one day he would stop coming by. When that happened, she figured, she would know she was…over it. Or at least, over it *enough*.

But she said only, "Good to know, Deputy. Tommy got bitten, did he?"

"I know. It *would* be Tommy. If that boy didn't have more lives than a cat, he'd be dead as a doornail." Boyd stepped into the kitchen and stroked Lila under the chin with the tip of one finger, smiling when the little dog wiggled in Mad's arms and licked his hand.

When she'd first met him, Mad had assumed Boyd simply spoke naturally in clichés, as politicians spoke in soundbites or preachers in sonorous exhortations. Later, she had decided he was probably doing it on purpose to amuse himself, or maybe to amuse her.

She'd been the one to start it: she'd met the new deputy at the gallery, when he'd been looking for paintings to dress up the Bateman's little house, which he was renting. Something about his expression—lack of expression—as he studied one of her paintings had led her to comment that mostly she painted clichés because clichés sold better than originality. He'd been looking at one of her portraits of Lila, and he'd nodded solemnly and answered, "Clichés are comforting. If they're the right clichés." Then he'd bought a different painting, the one of the maple branch where the leaves at the top of the painting were all the colors of autumn fire, but the ones that dipped into the shadowed pool were ambiguous, as green and translucent as the water, so that it was impossible to tell where the tree ended and the water began, impossible to tell whether the leaves were real leaves or somehow themselves shaped out of green shade and water.

Of all her paintings in the gallery at the time, that one had been Mad's favorite. She had never asked Deputy Raske what he saw in it, or where in his little house he'd hung it. And though he knew she'd painted it, he'd never said a word about it to her.

Now Mad said solemnly, "Tommy's taken so many years off his mother's life, I expect she's practically turning in her grave."

"Mrs. Kincaid is a resilient woman, fortunately. Did Lila get bitten?"

"Apparently not." Mad ran her hand once more across the little dog's feathered ears and set her on the floor. Lila immediately hurled herself at Boyd, who caught her handily when she leaped at his chest. He tucked her under his arm, petting her firmly. She looked even smaller and more elegant in his big hands, all fluff, the kind of little dog who ought to be curled on a velvet cushion with a pink rhinestone collar and painted toenails. Not that anyone who knew Lila expected her to sit inside on a velvet cushion when she could be out in the yard, digging for moles or hunting mice through the overgrown lilacs. Or catching newly hatched dragons.

Boyd crossed the room to peer thoughtfully at the dead dragon on the windowsill. "Shame," he murmured. "Pretty little things. I don't suppose you want to paint this one?"

Mad shrugged. "No. Not now." She felt uneasy and faintly annoyed, and uneasy with her own annoyance, which she knew Boyd—Deputy Raske—had done nothing to deserve.

"Figured probably not. I'll take it away, then." Boyd folded the poor crumpled thing up in his handkerchief, glancing at Mad for permission. "Unless you want to take it into town yourself? Might do you good to get out of this haunted house for an afternoon."

Mad rolled her eyes. "What are you, Tommy's age? It might be crumbling around the edges, but haunted?"

Boyd said mildly, "For you, it is." But he avoided an argument by talking to Lila instead. "Tough lady," he told the little dog. "Good job keeping the garden safe." Then he added to Mad, "Not as tough as she thinks she is, though. You might want to keep her in. Or on a leash. Poisonous or not, the little dragons do have teeth, and you've got a good many more up here than anywhere in town."

Mad shrugged. She was still annoyed, but only a little. She was fairly certain that Boyd could no more stop himself offering helpful, protective advice than he could stop breathing.

Her house, perched among and atop the limestone bluffs above Springdale, was nearer the quarry than the town and nearer the river than either: just the kind of country best suited to produce dragons, apparently. Mad had been one of the first people—maybe *the* first—to see a dragon crack open a pebble and unfold its damp wings. Not the first to report what she'd seen, though. Leave that to boys like Tommy Kincaid, or to men of unimpeachable reputation like Deputy Boyd Raske.

Mad's discretion had been only so much use. One of the reporters and two of the scientists had been very persistent; the reporter wanting to ask Mad all about her mother; the scientists wanting to walk over every inch of Mad's property, collecting samples of the rocks and earth and water. The scientists had been tolerable, actually. But it had taken Boyd to get rid of the reporter, once the woman realized who Mad was. Who her mother had been.

That was probably why Boyd had driven up from town today. Just to make sure the reporter had not come back.

"We're fine," Mad told him. "Thanks for taking care of that, though." She nodded toward the handkerchief hiding the dead little dragon. "I know they like to look at them before they start dissolving."

Boyd shrugged. "I'm going that way anyway." He turned toward the door, then turned back. "I expect I'll swing by tomorrow. Need anything?"

"No," Mad said immediately. And then, more firmly as he hesitated, "No, Deputy. I said, we're fine."

"Of course you did." Boyd stroked Lila once more, set her on the couch, touched a finger to his hat in casual salute, and was gone.

For three more weeks, the dragons were everywhere in Springdale: perching along the eaves of people's houses, chasing the bees that buzzed around the crabapple blossoms in the town square, spiraling up in alarm when the church bells rang for Sunday services.

Then, about as soon as everyone got used to them, they were gone. The first ones had emerged from pebbles and river-froth near the beginning of April. On the second of May, they gathered in flocks like blackbirds in the fall. On the fifth, they all spiraled suddenly up into a cloudless sky: the size of sparrows and then the size of bumblebees and then the size of gnats and then gone.

For a few days, everyone in Springdale expected them to return, or at least descend somewhere else, maybe miles away—maybe hundreds of miles away, like monarch butterflies or ruby-throated hummingbirds. But if they came back to the ground anywhere, it must have been somewhere without people, because no one reported it.

By the end of the next week, all the reporters were gone, even the one interested in Mad's family history, and the fickle attention of the American public had been recaptured by celebrity scandals and the sudden revelation of the new president's love child. The people of Springdale turned back to important concerns, such as the dreadful performance of the high school football team and the unseasonable weather, which was very dry and warm for so early in the year.

At the beginning of June, when everyone had practically forgotten the dragons, they started emerging again.

But this time they didn't emerge from pebbles and water foam. This time, they came from deep water, from the reservoir and still pools along the bank of the river; and they came from stones in retaining walls and in foundations and walkways in the park. The stones cracked and the shells shattered and the dragons spilled out and unfolded their damp wings to dry and then flew away.

The older part of the courthouse collapsed one morning midway through June, when nineteen dragons suddenly hatched, one after another, out of limestone blocks in the foundation. Luckily it was a Sunday, so no one was actually in the courthouse, but several people at the outdoor tables by the café had to run for shelter when the building came down.

Mad didn't see any of that, but she heard about it. Everyone heard about it. By that time, the reporters and scientists had come back, and they discussed it endlessly. The scientists tried to capture dragons, mostly without success. The dragons were in the air so fast, and no one was going to catch any of these larger dragons with a butterfly net. So the scientists collected shell fragments instead, and shards of broken stone. They timed the sublimation of the nacreous layer within the shells, which was thicker in these larger shells, but still too ephemeral to analyze properly, and tried to find patterns in where and when the dragons emerged. The reporters were even more annoying than the scientists. They gazed earnestly at the cameras and mouthed empty phrases to hide the obvious truth that they didn't know anything, that no one knew anything. Mad carried her old television out to the garden shed and never turned on her phone.

Mad might have missed the excitement at the courthouse, but she saw the dragons that emerged. She could hardly have missed them. All nineteen of them flew past her house as they rose into the heights in a single spiraling line. One after another, like ballerinas performing a choreographed dance, she thought; not much like the random flight of birds. The spiraling flight of the dragons carried them past the bluffs below her house, out over the quarry lake and back again hardly twenty feet from her back deck, up and up into the vastness of the sky. They were the size of hawks, of vultures, of eagles, some of them. Some of them were larger than that. The last, pale as an owl, was the biggest. It had wings that stretched, she was fairly sure, farther from tip to tip than she could have reached with both outstretched arms.

It turned its head as it slid by Mad's high garden and the rickety back deck; turned its head and looked at her with eyes white as frost. Then its curving path carried it away again across the quarry. Its shadow drifted across the lake like milky emerald, until, as it neared the higher bluffs to the east, it tilted its wings and slid up in the sky after its fellows, up and up, until it vanished against the hazy light.

Mad set up her largest easel in the center of the deck and began to paint a spiraling flight of white dragons against sky and green water. She blurred the land beneath, veiled it in mist as it was sometimes veiled on chilly mornings. She blurred the dragons as well, made them ambiguous, visible and invisible in the pale light, there and not there amid the shadows of high clouds…they weren't really white, not even the palest of them. Not pure white. That last one had been a pale gold two shades darker than ivory, the undersides of its wings lavender two shades lighter than wisteria flowers. Its eyes had been true white, though, casting back the sunlight like the eyes of cats or foxes cast back headlights at night…she picked up a dab of chromium white on her brush and began to suggest another dragon, larger than the rest, pale against a pale sky. Then, far below the dragons, she delicately sketched in a tumble that might be broken stone and the shards of dragon eggs.

L ila had danced and whirled and barked at the dragons as they flew past, certain to the depths of her indomitable soul that she alone was responsible for protecting the deck and the house and Mad, sure that *she* was the one keeping them out of the yard and away from the hillside below. Mad smiled at her, five pounds of fluff, a handful of a dog who had never been frightened of anything in her life, all bright eyes and sharp-pricked ears and a plume of a tail. But she also looked thoughtfully at the open sky. At last she found Lila's collar and a leash.

"Just for today," she told her. "Just while I paint. I'm sure they're gone, I'm sure it's fine, but still."

Lila thought the leash was a wonderful idea. She thought it would be splendid if Mad stopped painting and did something more fun. She dashed toward the front of the house, uttering sharp little yips and dancing with excitement. *Come on! Come on! Hurry hurry hurry!* She was so confused and disappointed when Mad didn't pick up her keys and follow that in the end Mad sighed, took one last look at the dragons she'd begun to suggest in a sky that might or not might be the ordinary sky above Springdale. Then she put away her paints and brushes and went to town after all.

Everyone was talking about the courthouse, of course. "Did you hear, Mrs. James and her youngest were so close they were almost hit by falling shingles off the roof!"

Almost hit was as close as anyone had come to disaster. Someone had driven their car into a lamppost as they swerved; that was the worst of it. Of course part of the town square was cordoned off to keep people clear of the fallen rubble, away from the area where more debris might yet fall.

Naturally, boys kept ducking under the tape to grab souvenir shingles and chips of broken stone and, most coveted, bits of broken eggshell, though those were supposed to go to the scientists. Mad beckoned to Tommy when he ran up to pet Lila, and he gave her a piece of shell as big as her hand before crouching to let the little dog jump onto his knee. Lila stood up on the boy's knee, put her front feet on his chest, and licked his chin. Tommy laughed, and Mad gave him a handful of tiny biscuits and watched tolerantly as he sent Lila quickly through her repertoire—dance in a circle, jump through my arms, down! Up! Tommy was the only other person Mad would let work with Lila. Despite his well-deserved reputation for mischief, the boy had the intuition and focus to work perfectly with a quick little dog like Lila.

"I heard you got bitten," she told him.

Tommy gave a dismissive little jerk of his head. "That was ages ago. One of the little ones."

"Yep, that's what I heard. Better watch out—these aren't so little."

"Yeah! Take a finger right off, I bet!"

His enthusiasm made her laugh. She measured the curve of the shell fragment and decided the whole egg must have been about the size of a soccer ball, though probably not as round. She ran a finger across the iridescent interior. She fancied she could almost feel a faint chill as the unearthly layer of whatever-it-was sublimed into the air; almost see a faint mist rising from the shell. That was probably her imagination.

"Five hours and six minutes from hatching till it's all gone," Tommy said authoritatively. "If it's like the last piece I found. But this egg was bigger, so maybe it'll take longer. I'm going to see what happens if you spray it with hairspray, like you do to fix a pencil drawing."

Mad had taught an art class at Springdale's middle school. She'd thought Tommy had mostly noticed the hairspray as something to tease the girls with, but he must have been paying a little attention after all. She said, intrigued, "You could try it. But pencil doesn't sublime off paper the way this stuff sublimes off the rocky part of the shell…"

"I'll try it anyway! Next chance I get!" Tommy declared.

"If your mother doesn't want you taking her hairspray, you could use—"

"Madison Martin? It is Ms. Martin, isn't it?" asked someone behind her. "Can I call you Madison? Madison, can I ask you just one or two questions? How do you feel about—"

"Nobody calls you *Madison*!" Tommy said to Mad, indignantly.

Mad sighed. "Don't I wish." Turning, she raised her eyebrows pointedly at the woman who'd spoken.

It was the reporter. Of course. A pretty woman with a limpid gaze, not nearly as stupid as she looked, Mad thought. And certainly not nearly as friendly as she pretended.

"Not interested," Mad told her. Lila wiggled all over, wanting to greet the reporter; Lila promiscuously loved everyone, even reporters. Picking her up, Mad started to walk away.

But the woman darted after her, not letting her go, smiling and smiling a false, clichéd smile, pretending that they were friends, pretending that she had the *right*. "Madison! Ms. Martin! Let me just ask—"

"You're a reporter, aren't you?" Tommy asked with great interest, trotting after them. "Want to see my snake?" He brought one out of his pocket, a delicate little ringneck that curled around his fingers, and held it out toward the reporter, who shied away with a little squeak of surprise.

Mad ducked away, across the street from the ruins of the courthouse, into the gallery and out the back with a little nod for the clerk at the counter. Smart kid, Tommy Kincaid.

B ut after that, Mad had no wish to linger in town. Even so, she didn't go directly back to the car; as far as Lila was concerned, no trip to town was complete without a stop at the pet store for some of those jerky-wrapped biscuits and maybe a new soft toy to destroy. Lila liked dissecting the toys, removing the squeakers and leaving synthetic cottony fluff all over the room. When Mad was too sick of herself and her life to paint, sometimes she still had enough energy to stuff the insides back into Lila's toys and sew them up. It was a job that echoed life in so many ways: destruction took so little time and repairs were so tedious and so temporary. It hardly took any time at all to rip out even the most painstaking stitches…

Lila, oblivious to Mad's darkening mood, cheerfully removed every soft toy from the lower bin in the store and scattered them all over the aisle. She attacked a horrible purple-polka-dotted elephant with particular enthusiasm. Mad sighed and tucked that one under her arm. The elephant might be hideous, but not even the cutest toy looked like much after Lila had disemboweled it. Stitching this one up with big, sloppy Frankenstein stitches might even improve it.

Then a wary look out at the street—no lurking reporters, so far as Mad could tell—and back to the car and out of town, Lila standing up in the passenger seat so she could bark out the window at every person they passed. She barked twice as enthusiastically at her buddy Romeo, the Lindstrand's handsome pit bull, who pricked his ears and hauled little Rebecca Lindstrand halfway into the street when he heard Lila.

Mad waved to Rebecca, but she didn't stop. She felt a little guilty about it. Romeo adored Lila, though she bullied him unmercifully whenever they visited, and stole all his toys except one extremely heavy ball she couldn't begin to pick up. Even that she guarded fiercely and wouldn't let Romeo near. But Rebecca was obviously on her way to the pet store herself, and letting the two dogs play was difficult if they couldn't let them off leash.

So she turned left and left again, past the church and the cemetery and out of town, and up the long road that wound its way up among the limestone bluffs and around the quarry and finally led to Mad's mother's house. The shadows were lengthening by that time, the moon a translucent sliver in the pale sky although the sun was still well above the forested hills.

The house did look a bit worn from this angle. Mad usually didn't notice; it was too familiar. But Boyd's comment must have lingered in the back of her mind, because today she somehow couldn't help but study the house as she gathered up her purchases and beckoned Lila to join her. The afternoon sun showed clearly how the black paint meant to seal the foundation was peeling, how the stain was wearing off the logs of the house in uneven blotches. The screen of the porch was torn here and there, and the porch itself sagged at one corner, though it was safe enough if you stayed to the left as you went up the stairs. Last year's leaves moldered beneath and beside the porch, and some kind of determined vine with narrow serrated leaves and poisonous-looking black berries was slowly making its way up along one windowsill as though it were trying to find a way into the house. Wasps hummed—the nest clung to the eaves, but far enough from the door that Mad had never bothered to get rid of it. Paper wasps were not very aggressive, yet the drone of their activity somehow seemed ominous today.

Taken all in all...the house did look haunted. She hadn't been able to deny that to herself, not since Boyd had made that comment. It looked like a witch's house, the kind undisguised by gingerbread and gumdrops. It looked like the kind of house where the witch would be waiting for you inside, with her great cauldron and her bottles of heart's blood and infant's tears…

"I could paint that," Mad said out loud. But, though Lila yipped cheerfully as though to agree, Mad knew she really couldn't. She would never have the courage to paint this house as it should be painted. If she tried, she would feel the house itself looking over her shoulder disapprovingly. Or her mother's ghost.

Not that the house was *actually* haunted. Mad wasn't so weak-minded that she believed in ghosts. But it wouldn't matter. If she tried to paint the house, she knew she would have to stop before she even had the basic shapes blocked in. She would have to destroy the canvas and throw out all the paints and brushes she had tried to use, get all new ones, or she wouldn't be able to paint anything at all.

Mad wasn't blind, or proud. God knew she didn't have reason to be *proud*. She knew she didn't have half her mother's fierce, brilliant talent. But she had come to understand that she had a little talent of her own, something smaller and tamer but real enough. She knew she would never, ever be able to paint this house for fear she might see, mercilessly revealed in that attempt, its soul.

A dragon whipped by overhead, pearl and smoke in the afternoon light, and Mad unclenched her hands and made herself smile at the wildly barking Lila, who was tugging at the end of the leash, *so sure* she could catch that dragon if Mad would only let her try. *Lila* had no idea of her own tininess, her fragility. *Lila* didn't doubt herself, or fear that she might be about to hurl herself into a quest that was too big for her.

And since she didn't, Mad had to protect her from her own bravery. Picking her up, Mad went up the steps—carefully, on the left side—and into the house.

But the ghost of her mother seemed everywhere all that evening.

Oh, not literally. Of course not. But the creak of old

boards sounded a bit like someone moving about upstairs, in the master bedroom as likely as not. There almost seemed an echo behind the clanging gurgle of the hot water pipes, like someone calling out: *Mad, sweetie, I need you in the studio, come up here!* Not that there were any distinguishable words to that echo. Obviously not. Mad knew perfectly well that the summons echoed only in her mind and memory.

The house wasn't haunted, obviously. The only ghosts people ever truly saw were the ones they carried with them, in their minds and their hearts and their flinching memories. The departed disappeared as soon as they were forgotten.

Mad wished she could forget her mother. Though everyone else would remember her, even then. Mad's famous mother, who had been able, it was rapturously claimed, to capture in her portraits the very essence and soul of her models.

It wasn't true. Mad's mother had found it so easy to lie with paint. So easy to show her clients only the parts of their souls that they actually wanted to see. They ate that up, the shallow, posturing Hollywood celebrities, and the politicians who thought they were important statesmen but were really only a different kind of celebrity. They loved the flattering portraits Marissa Martin had painted for them. And too many of them also loved the portraits she had painted of her little daughter: nudes of Mad at five years, and nine, and thirteen. Disturbingly eroticized portraits, which critics called *edgy* and *sophisticated* and normal people knew actually skirted far too close to depraved.

Mad hated to think how many rich men and women had one of those portraits hanging in their homes. She had no idea how many her mother had painted. She tried never to think of it.

And she never painted people. She painted beech trees

leaning over water, trees whose reflections might possibly, if you looked closely, weave their way into a reflected faerie world; and she painted peach-colored roses whose color bled imperceptibly into the sunset until you couldn't quite decide if the roses were physical flowers or perhaps made of light; and she painted maple branches whose leaves might be fire above and water below. And when she painted portraits, they were of dogs, whose souls she could tell the truth about without fear.

Maybe Boyd was right. Maybe she should leave this house, sell it, let some contractor knock it down and build something else on the site. Or just open all the windows and doors and walk away from it and let the woods and weather pull it down.

But she knew she wouldn't. She couldn't. Anywhere she went, she would carry her mother with her. She didn't know how to leave her past behind.

The second emergence of the dragons gradually tapered off toward the end of June. A few of the scientists lingered, unobtrusive, but most of the reporters had passed on to other stories after the first week or so, and the other tourists left as fewer and fewer dragons unfolded from the stone of Springdale and spiraled up into the sky.

The days became hot and slow. Families brought picnic lunches up to the bluffs, and children swam in the quarry lake. The courthouse was repaired with stone prudently brought in from a distant corner of the state where no dragons had ever been seen, and the mayor of Springdale planted a tree in the courthouse lawn to celebrate. He planted a dogwood. Mad thought it should have been something stronger. An oak. A red oak, that would live a hundred years, with leaves that would turn to fire in the fall. She painted that tree, falling leaves that might be

flickers of flame and the suggestion of a great castle looming beyond it, that might be nothing but a chance jumble
of broken rocks. But she wasn't particularly happy with
the way the painting came out. It sold for a good price at
the gallery before she could decide what she ought to have
done differently.

Mad taught Lila the signal exercise from advanced
obedience, and the drop-on-recall—flashy tricks that drew
admiring comments when she took the little dog to the
park. Lila loved showing off and being admired, and Mad
liked people to pay attention to Lila because if they were
admiring the little dog, that meant they weren't privately
thinking about Mad and her mother and her mother's
paintings.

"Smart as a whip, isn't she?" was Boyd Raske's comment
when he saw Lila's drop-on-recall, which she performed,
as always, with flashy brilliance. She leaped into her recall,
hit the ground in a split second when Mad gave the down
signal, and whipped instantly back into the recall when
she got the signal. When she reached Mad, she leaped into
her arms, which wasn't part of the exercise, but Mad had
expected it and caught her without difficulty.

"She learned that in three days. It's a mystery how she
does it. A genius with a brain the size of a walnut." Mad
put Lila down so the little dog could dash to Boyd and
leap into *his* arms. The deputy caught her neatly.

Boyd held Lila up so she could kiss the tip of his nose,
then tucked her under his arm and strolled over to hand
her back to Mad. "Hot as blazes today."

This was more oblique than Boyd's usual advice, but
Mad deciphered it without trouble. "I was just about to
head over to the café to get her some water. And me some
ice cream." She clipped Lila's leash to her collar and they
both turned toward the east edge of the park, which gave
onto the town square and the café.

Boyd watched Lila dash ahead and dart back. "She'd

like ice cream too, I expect."

"And she'll get some. A dab won't hurt her. I don't even have to ask anymore; they always give her a sample cup of vanilla."

"Lucky she doesn't know what she's missing."

Mad grinned. Boyd was a rocky-road man. "You allowed to eat ice cream on duty?"

The deputy took off his hat and fanned himself with it. "On a day like today, it's all that keeps me in fighting trim." He hesitated, uncharacteristically. Then he added in an absent tone, "You know, we've got that reporter back in town. That one woman, you know."

Mad was sinkingly certain she knew exactly which reporter he meant. "Why? No dragons anymore."

"Yep, she's done with dragons, apparently. She's moved on to bigger and better things. She's doing a piece on famous people of the county. Over in Manchester, there's a guy who writes horror novels. And a woman in Barton who set some kind of hang-gliding record."

"And me. My mother's daughter." Mad tried to sound light. Unconcerned. Flippant.

"And you," Boyd said seriously, not for a moment believing Mad's light tone.

"Well, thanks for the warning. I'll set Lila on her if she annoys me."

"That should do it." Mercifully, Boyd changed the subject. "I liked that last painting of yours in the gallery."

Mad gave him a sidelong glance. "You didn't buy it."

"No. I liked it, but it wasn't quite right. I don't think it was something you really saw. Or wanted to see. I sort of thought you might have had something else in your mind's eye when you painted it."

Mad stopped dead.

"Or that's what I thought when I looked at it, but what do I know? I don't know anything about art."

"No," Mad said slowly. "No. You're right." He was

right, and she hadn't even realized it. Only, even now that she understood what had gone wrong with that painting of the red oak, she wasn't quite sure what image she ought to have painted instead. The oak itself…she didn't think that had been the problem. No. But she almost thought she saw, in her mind's eye, something else beyond the flaming oak: a looming shape that was neither a tumble of randomly fallen rocks nor a ruined castle. Something else. Something—

Lila yipped, then, knowing they were heading for the café and impatient for her ice cream, and Boyd made another comment about the weather, and the moment was past.

Mad never did quite figure out what the red oak painting had wanted to be. She couldn't paint after that. The blindness of her painter's eye blocked her; she couldn't see what she wanted to paint and so she couldn't paint anything. It felt to Mad like the house was laughing at her inability to sort out her own vision. She could practically hear her mother: *Painter's block is just the laziness of a minor talent, Madison. Real genius can't be blocked. Inspiration floods out of her like water through a broken dam.* And then her voice would change and she would purr, You're *my inspiration, Madison.*

Mad tried to block out the remembered voice. She got her paints out and stretched a canvas on her easel and then stood and looked at it for a while. Then she put everything away again and took Lila for a long walk in the woods instead, down the path through the woods to the quarry lake and back up the other way, along the base of the bluffs and up again, half a path and half clambering over and around jumbled rocks. She had to lift Lila over some of the rougher places, which didn't shake the little dog's confidence one bit. Lila always knew she could handle anything.

At the beginning of September, when daylong rains finally moved in and broke summer's heat and drought, dragons began to emerge once more. This time they were larger still. The smallest Mad saw was the size of a hang-glider, and the biggest looked large enough to carry off a cow. A good-sized calf, anyway.

This time, the dragons emerged from the bluffs to the north of Springdale, mostly. The limestone cliffs cracked and broke and fell and shattered, but that was better than dragons unfolding themselves from the foundation stones of homes or churches or public buildings in town. The mayor had signs placed at the campground: Danger: Falling Rocks. Mad thought anyone too stupid to figure that out on their own deserved to have rocks fall on their heads. Boys rode their bikes up to the bluffs below Mad's house, though, and dared each other to dash in and grab a fragment of shell. That was something else, and she worried about it.

"Tommy Kincaid says they can hear the cliff face start to go," Boyd reassured her when she asked him about that. He grinned at Mad's expression. "That boy got a map and stuck a lot of pins in it. He explained he's trying to figure out how to predict where and when the dragons will come out."

"He's a smart kid. Maybe he will." Mad wouldn't be surprised. "He showed you his map?"

"He hit me up for a box of colored stickpins, like cops use in movies to figure out where the bad guy is. He figured we'd have plenty at the sheriff's office."

Mad raised her eyebrows. "Well, did you?"

"Yep. I gave him a box. I didn't explain we mostly use

'em to post boring memos on the bulletin board and hardly ever to solve crimes. Naturally it's important to uphold the image of the sheriff's office."

"You're not worried he'll get himself into trouble, trying to track down these dragons?"

"Mad, to be honest, I don't think Tommy Kincaid's in as much danger as you are, in this house of yours up here on top of this cliff."

Mad stared at him. She'd never thought of that.

"I can't help but think of the way the courthouse came down," Boyd said apologetically. "I've been thinking maybe you should move to town. Just for a while. Until the dragons stop emerging. I mean, you never know. Better safe than sorry."

"I can't move to town," Mad said automatically. Then she paused, looking around. She knew it was true, but she wasn't sure why. It wasn't even truly her house. It was her *mother's* house. It wasn't as though Mad actually *liked* it. The house was too big and too old and most of all filled with too many memories. And it was a nuisance. The water pipes clanked in the summer and froze in the winter; the gutters had to be cleaned every fall and the roof patched every spring.

But it wasn't going to *stay* her mother's house, not forever. Mad was slowly making it hers. Maybe that was why she couldn't leave. Not until she'd finally found the courage to strip this house of the memories that were its ghosts. Not until she'd emptied it out and left it hollow and echoing, haunted by nothing but time and gradual decay.

They were both in the kitchen, where Mad spent most of her time. The kitchen in summer, the sunroom in winter, the back deck where she set up her easel when the weather was fine, the dining room which she had converted into a bad-weather studio by the simple expedient of giving the table and chairs and china cabinet and sideboard and all the china to Goodwill. Her bedroom was beyond the new studio, and she never went upstairs. She never needed to. She never wanted to. But someday she would go up there and clear everything out of her mother's bedroom and her mother's bath and her mother's studio. The studio would be the worst. She knew there were a good many of her mother's paintings still tucked away up there. Some of them would be childhood portraits of Mad. She didn't want to see them, knew she would not be able to resist looking at each one as she threw it on a fire. She *would* burn them. Once she gathered her nerve enough to intrude on her mother's realm.

She wouldn't give any of her mother's clothing to Goodwill. She knew that. She would burn all that, too.

"Maybe in the spring," she said out loud. "I'll do it in the spring."

"I'd rather you thought about moving now," Boyd said, not having followed Mad's train of thought. Or maybe he had, because he added, "Sometimes your past doesn't let go of you. Sometimes you have to reach back and amputate it, and I don't think it gets easier if you wait. Maybe you could at least look at apartments in town. Or houses for sale. There's a nice little place on the corner of Elm and Second, one of those new homes where the Seddon's hay-fields used to be. Big yard for Lila, big windows, plenty of light for painting."

"This really isn't any of your concern, you know."

Boyd affected surprise. "I just happened to notice that for-sale sign. Thought you might be interested. This house isn't good for you. And every journey begins with a single step, you know." He considered Mad's expression and added, "But better late than never. First thing in the spring, all right?"

Mad shrugged and promised him she would think about it, without exactly specifying what she would think about. But she couldn't imagine actually leaving this house. She couldn't imagine it would ever let her go.

She was actually watching at just the right moment one day, midway through September, when a dragon, lustrous green, emerged from the quarry lake. Drops of water fell like diamonds from the tips of its wings and scattered from its lashing tail as it climbed into the sky. Its claws and its spiky mane were transparent as water, its eyes lucent as pearls. Its wingspan might have been twelve feet, or fifteen, or twenty—Mad couldn't tell. But it was easily big enough to snatch up the Lindstrand's pit bull Romeo, far less a tiny dog like Lila. Surely the dragon wouldn't actually pluck a dog right off someone's back deck, but Mad picked up Lila and held the little dog close. The dragon didn't approach them, of course. It turned and turned again, spiraling into the sky.

"They never actually attack anything," she muttered, more to herself than to Lila. This was true so far as she knew, but the words didn't sound as reassuring in her ears as she'd hoped. Perhaps she needed to hear someone else say that. Someone like Boyd Raske, who had the skill of making anything he said sound like he was handing down the word of God engraved on a stone tablet. But he would probably ask her what she thought would happen if a dragon that size emerged from the cliffs below her house, and tell her again that she should move to town. And she didn't want to argue. She put Lila down again and turned toward the kitchen door.

"Yoo hoo! Madison! Ms. Martin!" called a voice from the front of the house, familiar and unfamiliar at the same time. Lila dashed past Mad, yapping with excitement and delight at the idea of a visitor, but Mad's heart sank even before she remembered where she'd heard that voice. Then she remembered.

"Why now? Why me?" she muttered out loud.

It was the reporter, of course. By this time, Mad had learned the woman's name. It was Brittany Silverstone, or so she claimed. That sounded like a stage name to Mad; like the name chosen by a woman with more ego than taste because she imagined it would sound good when she was anchoring the evening news.

But whatever the reporter thought of herself, it didn't matter. It *wouldn't* matter. As she walked toward the front door, Mad told herself, still out loud, "This is *my* house. I can tell her to leave. If she won't go, she's trespassing, so I can *make* her leave." Since this was true, it should have sounded decisive and firm. To her own ears, it sounded... weak. Like the helpless protest of a child faced with a demanding adult.

"Ms. Silverstone, this isn't a good time," she told the woman through the screen door. But this, too, sounded weak.

"Oh, call me Brittany!" chirped the reporter, oozing overfamiliarity and nudging at the door as a hint that Mad should open it. "What an adorable little dog! I've seen you with her in town. Did you train her yourself? She's so cute!"

Mad was tempted to declare, *She bites—you'd better stay out there.* But it was too late. Brittany Silverstone had already nudged the door open and was energetically petting Lila, who was standing with her delicate little feet on the woman's knee, her beautiful plume of a tail waving.

"What a splendid place you have up here!" cried Ms. Silverstone, with blatantly overdone enthusiasm. "With that road, I bet you must get iced in practically all winter. But the view from the back must be stunning." Giving Lila one last pat, she straightened and strolled through the door and toward the back deck just as though Mad had invited her in. Lila dashed in circles around her, bouncing with delight. Mad trailed after them, stiff with resentment.

"Oh, you're painting!" The reporter had stepped out on the back deck and was gazing at the canvas propped on the easel, her hands clasped over her heart in theatrical delight.

"*Trying* to paint," Mad muttered, meaning to imply that Ms. Silverstone was interrupting. But the other woman affected not to hear her, and Mad couldn't quite bring herself to be openly rude.

The painting was of Lila, sitting on a blue velvet cushion, one small foot resting on a mouse-shaped toy with a little bit of stuffing peeking through a seam. The painting captured a bit of the mischief that always glinted in the little dog's eyes. But it was a trivial painting. A cute little cliché. Something to keep Mad's hands busy while she tried to sort out the blockage of imagination that was stopping her from real painting.

She knew exactly what was wrong, of course. But she couldn't figure out what true idea she might be trying to express, so she didn't know what to do to unblock her mind's eye.

"It's wonderful!" declared Ms. Silverstone. "So darling! The apple doesn't fall far from the tree, does it, Madison? Your mother must have been so proud you followed in her footsteps. Well, not *quite* in her footsteps, of course. Marissa's work was so much more *cultured* and *urbane*, but this has such *simple charm*, I'm sure you must have many *local fans*."

"Cultured," Mad repeated tonelessly. "Urbane. Is that what you'd call my mother's work?" She wanted to shout, Don't you mean *exploitative* and *perverted*?

But Ms. Silverstone leaned forward earnestly, protesting, "Oh, but *your* work recalls a *simpler time*, Madison! A simpler, more innocent time! Your work offers such a wonderful *contrast* to your mother's work! That's my idea, you see, an article featuring your sweet little puppies and fairy tales juxtaposed with your mother's sophisticated nudes. And a show, of course! I've approached a *very good* gallery, they could do *wonderful* things for your career, and let me tell you, Madison, they're *quite* interested! We all *know* your mother had paintings she never sold. She always said she kept the best for herself! You could make those available. Just think of your mother's wonderful portraits alternated with your own pretty little—"

"Get out," Mad ordered. "Get out." She no longer cared whether she was rude or offensive.

But Ms. Silverstone's expression remained unoffended. In fact, instead of offended, she looked…confused. She was still smiling, that same wide, insincere smile, as though it were the only expression she knew how to wear, but behind the smile she seemed simply blank.

Then Lila, tired of being ignored, yipped and danced and waved her plume of a tail, and Brittany Silverstone looked down at her, and in that moment her smile became real. And Mad realized, as though her mind's eye had opened, that the other woman truly did not understand why her plan was so offensive. That she honestly had no idea what the problem was with Marissa Martin's paintings. That the silly young woman actually thought she was being helpful. She simply was not very bright, and she'd been taught to believe she was being chic when she admired perversion.

Nothing Brittany Silverstone thought or believed or suggested or mistook mattered. None of it had to matter to Mad at all.

Then Lila began to bark again.

But it was different this time. There was a new note to her high-pitched little yap. It wasn't the excitement with which Lila greeted every stranger, it wasn't the delight with which she met people she knew, it wasn't the predatory let-me-at-em yap with which she demanded Mad let her out to chase a squirrel that had gotten into the yard. This was different. Louder. Lila was backing up and turning in circles and barking, barking, barking, angry and frantically defiant.

And the earth trembled.

Without a pause for conscious thought, Mad scooped Lila up in one hand, grabbed Brittany Silverstone's wrist in the other, and ran for the door, off the back deck and into the kitchen, through the studio and down the front hall, dragging the other woman with her, not listening to her confused protests, which were half drowned anyway by the force of Lila's barking. Out onto the porch and down the steps and along the rutted driveway, past her own car and Ms. Silverstone's car beyond that, with Lila twisting to get free and barking fearless challenge at the house behind them, on another twenty feet, and twenty feet more…and the young reporter jerked herself free and cried like an offended child, "Hey! What's the big idea?"

Mad stopped, panting with terror and exertion, glad to use both hands to keep Lila safe, not caring a whole lot what Ms. Silverstone did. They were far enough away. She thought they were. Probably.

She could hardly believe the younger woman hadn't figured out what was happening. But then, she'd already realized Ms. Silverstone wasn't very bright. Certainly nothing like as sharp and sensitive and perceptive as Lila.

Behind them, the house…swayed. It actually swayed. Mad could see the patched roof actually *tilt*, one end dropping at least a foot, and then another foot. Loose shingles skidded and fell. The tip of a young pine near the house whipped back and forth, and the whole house started to slide toward the cliff.

Behind them, there was the crunch of car tires on the gravel driveway, and Tommy's young voice cried, "Mad! You're okay!"

It was Boyd Raske, who pulled his car over to the side of the driveway and got out, one hand firmly keeping Tommy Kincaid at his side rather than letting the boy dash forward. He was pale, and grimmer than Mad have ever seen him. "A little farther back," he told Mad and Ms. Silverstone, not a suggestion.

Mad moved to join them, shakily, walking quickly but not running. She didn't dare run in case she dropped Lila. Ms. Silverstone didn't follow at once: she was staring— gaping really—at the slowly toppling house. By this time, it was practically on its side, leaning way out over empty space. Mad couldn't imagine trying to claw her way out of disaster, if she'd still been in the house now.

It wasn't just the house, either. The whole cliff edge was going, and she suspected her car and the reporter's car were going to go as well. The whole cliff was breaking, stone cracking like gunshots and the ripping groan and crash of wood as trees fell. Even Ms. Silverstone was backing away at last.

"It was Lila," Mad said. Her tone sounded amazingly calm in her own ears. "I was so distracted by—by other things, if she hadn't barked, I don't know if I would have understood. Not in time." The little dog was quiet now, trembling in Mad's grasp. Though even after all that, she was trembling, Mad could tell, more with excitement than fear.

"For me it was Tommy," Boyd told her. "I didn't like the thought of you up here, but without Tommy's stickpins, I wouldn't have known a dragon was likely to come out right below your house, or when. And even so, I would have been too late."

"You're exactly on time," Mad told him. She stood with Boyd and Tommy as the house slipped at last irrevocably over the shattering edge of the cliff and disappeared, carrying with it all Mad's memories and all the echoing ghosts of her mother.

And the dragon rose.

It was enormous. The size of an airplane. Larger. The size of a roc, that could lift an elephant in each taloned foot. Its long elegant head and graceful snakelike neck broadened to muscular shoulders and vast wings, gold banded with sapphire, that seemed to blot out half the world. Its neck and body and long whippy tail were a rich iridescent color, like a golden pearl streaked with carnelian. Its eyes, each larger in diameter than Mad could have reached with both outstretched arms, were black as the starless sky.

But though it passed so close that the wind of its wings nearly made Mad take a step back, it didn't see them, or didn't care. The sheer indifference in its gaze did make her flinch and step back, but Boyd put an arm around Mad to steady her. She leaned against his side, staring up at the dragon that was climbing into the sky.

In Mad's arms, Lila barked defiance, perfectly certain she was the one driving the dragon away. She was surely too small for a dragon to notice, surely too sensible to run too close to the newly broken edge of the cliff, but Mad was careful not to let her go.

Then the dragon was gone into the heights. It had seemed to move slowly, but it was gone. And so was Mad's mother's house, and a big chunk of the surrounding bluffs. Mad looked around, feeling unreal, as though she might be dreaming. Behind her, the ordinary world, everything just the same as always. Before her, the gravel driveway ran out onto a new raw edge of the earth, and beyond that only sky.

"Mad! You didn't save *anything!*" Tommy said, sounding awed. "*Everything's* gone!"

"All the rest of your mother's paintings!" cried Ms. Silverstone, seeming to realize this for the first time.

The corners of Boyd's eyes crinkled with a hidden smile. "Every journey begins with a single step," he declared sententiously. "Or so they say. But I kind of think Ms. Martin was about ready to take that step."

Mad looked at Tommy, and then at Ms. Silverstone,

and then at Boyd, and finally at Lila, still cradled safely in her arms. "I saved the only thing that mattered in that house," she said at last. "Deputy Raske's right. If the rest is gone, that's all right. Let it go. Let it all be past and gone."

"But where will you *live?*" Tommy asked, a bit plaintive. "I mean, that was your *house.*"

"I'll find a different house. A new house, just built. A house without any past at all. I hear there's a nice one on Elm."

"Well, as long as there's a good yard for Lila," Tommy said authoritatively, and looked puzzled when Mad laughed.

Mad painted her mother's house broken at the foot of the bluffs. She painted the rubble, all splintered wood and broken stone, uprooted trees and shattered windows, surrounded by flaming oaks above and ice-green water below. High above the cliffs, the sky was commanded by the sapphire-and-pearl dragon. The unkind past lying in ruins below the wings of the unknown future, for of course no one knew whether there might yet be more dragons, or whether the ones that had already emerged might return. But the dragon in the painting did not seem interested in anything below.

The dragon drew the eye, of course. It was meant to draw the eye. But if one looked particularly closely at the wreckage below the bluffs, one might see a painting, upside down so whatever image it had held was invisible. Its frame was broken, and a twisted spike had torn through the canvas. In front of this, poised triumphantly atop the broken rubble, stood a tiny dog, five pounds of fluff and courage, not only proudly defending all her territory against enormous dragons, but completely unimpressed by lingering ghosts.

Mad had had offers for this piece, including, surprising her, one from Brittany Silverstone, and one from the gallery Ms. Silverstone had persuaded to be interested in Marissa Martin's daughter. But she knew she wouldn't sell it. She was going to hang it herself, in this new house. Somewhere she could see it, and be reminded that the past could after all be torn down and left behind, as a dragon left behind the stone in which it had incubated; and that a sufficiently indomitable spirit could face any challenge, however outsized, with glad confidence.

"You should hang it over your couch in the living room," Boyd said from the garden gate. He already knew she meant to keep this painting, although Mad hadn't said so and he hadn't asked.

He'd dropped by, as he did, just keeping an eye on Mad, almost the way he kept an eye on anyone else in town. But not quite. Just as he would let her pour him a cup of coffee almost but not quite as he would accept a fresh-baked cookie from Mrs. Kincaid.

Lila raced over from the far side of the yard, where she'd been hunting dragonflies, and leaped confidently into Boyd's arms. He caught her without fuss and told her what a fine fierce hunter she was, and smiled at Mad when he found her studying him.

"Maybe I'd like to paint you with her," she told him.

He didn't say, *But you never paint anyone's portrait.* He only said, "I think—or I hope—that I might like to see myself through your eyes, Maddie Rose."

Mad thought he might. She hoped he might. She thought she might like to see herself through his eyes, too. She didn't ask how he'd known her middle name, or why he'd suddenly decided to call her by it. She thought she might be willing to be called by a new name, now. She thought she might be willing at last to let him show her the world he saw.

DEATH OF A
YOUNG MAGE

A. E. McAuley

avin never expected his clan to be targeted by humans. He wasn't old enough to wrap his head around the idea that the tall horsemen who terrorized other elves near the cities could reach his desert oasis. They were shadows, like stories of ghouls on the other side of sand dunes. Zavin was getting too old to believe in monsters. He and his friends laughed when the younger elves shivered in fear at the mention of humans.

That was until he heard thunder rolling on the sand.

Zavin looked up from the knife he was sharpening, his small hands gripping it tightly as he watched his father's face go from focused to concerned.

"Bada?" he asked, his dark eyebrows knitting together as the thunder grew louder. "Do you hear that?"

His father's narrowed eyes were as bright as Zavin's, the sun making them look almost silver when the light hit them. "Where's your mother?"

Zavin opened his mouth but was cut off by a scream and an explosion of animal and man over the top of the nearest sand dune. The riders flowed over the crest like wild dogs, howling as their horses cried out at every crack of a whip. The wave of men flew toward them, but all Zavin could do was stare in shock, gripping a knife he didn't know how to use.

As the horses trampled over the first small tent, the caravan of elves scattered. They screamed and sprinted for weapons, but Zavin stayed rooted to the sand. Humans were too far away to be a threat. This wasn't real.

"Zavin!" His father grabbed him by the arm, pulling him toward their tent. "Move!"

He finally found his feet under him and managed to take a few running steps, his eyes still trying to catch his mind up on what was happening around them. The few who could work magic threw half-worked spells only to be cut down with long silver blades. An arrow landed with a sickening thud into an old woman trying to pry her granddaughter out of a man's arms. Blood, more blood than Zavin had ever seen on any hunt, spilled across the slick sand, only to be drank by the earth.

He was so caught up in the dark stains, he didn't realize they were in danger until his father jerked and fell, dragging Zavin down with him.

"Bada," Zavin screamed, hitting the ground hard, his sweat-covered skin making his long hair stick to his face as he struggled to get sand out of his mouth and eyes. "Bada get up! We need to find Mati."

When he peeled back his hair, he was met with his father's wide eyes staring at the sky and blood trickling from an arrow burrowed in his cheek.

Women howled; the humans threw nets over a few corralled children; somewhere a man spluttered curses. But Zavin could only hear the ringing in his ears that screamed over the rushing thoughts on how to save his already dead father.

Where had the arrow gone through? His cheek? He could get it out; he just needed to know what side the stone came out.

Maybe he could heal him?

No. He wasn't skilled enough for that. Where was his mother? She was better at that sort of magic.

Wait, hadn't the other conjurers been shot? Did that mean she'd been hit too?

If his father was dead, the elders needed to remove the tail of his twisted braid. The ancestors wouldn't accept him if the ends of his long hair were frayed.

A rope tightened around Zavin's neck and pulled him off the ground, snapping him out of his trance. He went wild, thrashing and yelling curses only to wind up slammed into a burlap sack and thrown to the ground. The air rushed from his chest, pain blooming across his back before he was lifted away again.

I'm going to die. The thought flickered between dry

gasps. *I am going to die.*

Another body crashed into him as it came hurling down into the sack. Air rushed into Zavin's lungs when an elbow hit his face. As the other elf child began to scream, the sound of thunder on sand picked up again, and the cries of his caravan began drifting away.

They rode in burlap sacks for days, occasionally dumped out to piss or have a sip of water. Sometimes for less time, if they were too loud. The degradation of being unwashed was enough to keep the older ones in the group quiet, but the littlest elves were constantly crying and clinging to one another. They were too young to have braids, and didn't understand what it meant for their hair to be so tangled and dirty.

It seemed the humans didn't either. Many of them had their hair cut so short, Zavin wondered what their ancestors must have thought at the sight of them. It was bad enough his hair was unbraided when they caught him, but to be held by those with so little self awareness at how disgraceful they looked—it made him sick.

He considered running, but after a young boy named Seff took off the first day only to be shot in the back, he knew he'd have to be smarter than that. If he wasn't, his soul would be left wandering the desert.

"How will the ancestors find him so far away from the elders?" Zavin heard one of the younger girls, Rachal, voice the same fears to her sister, but it was Pas, Zavin's sack partner, who answered.

"The ancestors can't see us in this place," Pas murmured. "They've abandoned us."

"Don't say that." Rachal's sister, Iza, snapped as she braided her long hair with trembling fingers. "They will tell our parents how to save us."

Pas didn't respond, but Zavin could see the question in his eyes that he felt in his own chest. *How could the dead save them?*

The group never spoke of Seff after that.

Zavin tried to push the dread away that first day. Now, on day three, he could feel it gnawing on the back of his mind again. There were only seventeen of them left. The youngest five, and the oldest, Pas, fifteen. Zavin knew his father was dead, but his mother and grandfather could still be alive, and the others were sure to have at least one surviving parent left. They would have to come. The clan leader always said the children are the shoulders who hold the future. They'd come.

Zavin believed that for the first five days. Every time he was let out of his bag, he stood to the north and murmured prayers to his mother for as long as he could before a human caught on and threw him back in the bag. She'd hear him. She always said they were connected by blood and magic. She'd know he was alive and find him.

On the sixth day, Zavin lost his first sliver of faith. The humans lined them up from oldest to youngest and yelled for them to stand straight as the largest of their group came over and stopped one by one in front of each of the elf children. Zavin watched, frowning at the man's eyes. They weren't the eyes of a monster. They were like his. With shoulders like a rock face and hands like slabs of meat, Zavin expected them to be black.

As he got to Zavin, the boy kept his eyes on the brown stains across the dirty tunic but refused to drop his gaze like the others had.

The man paused, grabbing him by the chin to force him to meet his scowl. Zavin was the son of a Wise Woman, the others would look to him for strength just like their parents looked to his mother for guidance. He wouldn't drop his eyes, not to this, or any man.

"You've got balls," the human said in the children's

language. "Are you a mage?"

Zavin jerked his chin away and glared, but stayed silent.

A heavy hand clapped the side of his head, making his ears pop. Zavin's knees trembled, but he stayed up, tears fighting to spill.

Bada never hit me. He tried to focus on that thought instead of the pain.

"Don't make me ask again," the human growled. Pas started to tremble on Zavin's left.

"Yes," Zavin finally answered.

"Let's see it then."

Zavin stared up at him, then looked back down the line, the others watching. "See it?"

The human crossed his arms with a nod, Zavin watching patience leave his eyes. "Do a spell."

Zavin swallowed, pushing his long hair from his face. He wanted to argue. As a novice, he wasn't allowed to work any magic without his mother's guidance, and this human wanted him to do what? Show off?

Besides that, spells couldn't be performed by a beginner without proper ceremony. How could he do anything with how unclean he was? And with his hair unbraided?

Shame grew in his chest as the human growled, and Zavin quickly put his hands out. He was breaking his clan's sacred rites just so he didn't get hit. He was a coward.

His fingers shook as he summoned whatever strength he could, fire flickering to life on his palms. The other humans dropped their hands to their swords, but the large man seemed unphased. His too-normal eyes watched with greedy interest, making Zavin's gut twist and the flames die.

"I'm still learning," he murmured, wrapping his arms around his sides as if he could cover the emotional nakedness from showing something so sacred to an outsider.

"Are there other mages here?"

Zavin glanced down the line and cast a mistrusting look at the human. "Yes."

"How many?"

"Why?"

Another smack on his ears. "How many?"

It was harder to stay on his feet that time, but he managed to lie. "All of us."

The man clenched his jaw, the muscles bulging along his face. He rose his arm; Zavin braced himself as the meaty hand fell on him again. This time, he found himself on the ground.

The world spun as Zavin stared up at the sky. A few of the younger children began to cry as he was pulled to his feet by his long black hair.

"How many mages?"

"Don't," Pas hissed. "He'll make them show—"

The human didn't waste time with smacking him across the ears. His open palm collided with Pas's face and sent him crumpling to the sandy ground. When he turned back to Zavin, any mercy he'd been pretending to show was gone. There were the eyes of a monster Zavin had been expecting.

"If I have to ask again, I'm going to have to guess, and that means I'll be starting with the littlest ones."

"Five," Zavin murmured, his head still spinning as the meat-hand man dropped his hair.

"Which ones aren't?"

He didn't answer. He didn't need magic to know they'd kill whoever wasn't a mage. It'd be better for them all to die than for him to sell out two of his own kind to save his own skin.

The man raised his hand a final time before Iza stepped forward.

"Me! I'm not a mage. I'll tell you."

Zavin shook his head so hard his tangled hair whipped at his back. "No!"

The human shoved Zavin back into the line and made his way to the slender elf girl. He stared down at her without pity in his eyes, and motioned to his men, "Bag 'em up. We'll separate them later."

"Iza!" Rachal screamed as they pulled the small girl off her sister. "Iza don't leave me!"

Pas was on his feet, lunging to help Rachal, but he was too slow for his human captor. The other children were gruffly thrown into their sacks as well, and the last thing Zavin saw before his own bag closed was the meat-handed man towering over Iza. He didn't think he'd ever forget the way she looked up at him, long black hair tangled, blue eyes on fire.

On the next break, only five of them were left. Iza was nowhere to be found.

Days blurred together as the desert turned to scrubland. Zavin kept a mental clock in his bag, each hour given an assigned task. From sun up to mid day, they stayed in the bags. When the sky was at its brightest, the humans let them out to relieve themselves and eat whatever scraps the humans had from their lunch, then they went back in till nightfall for dinner. The time in the sacks was the worst. The fabric made Pas and Zavin's skin itch, and their lungs ached for fresh air. They didn't talk out of fear of getting a firm elbow to the side of the bag, but occasionally they'd hold hands in silence.

The smaller three had it the worst. With so many of them gone, they were shoved into one sack. Every time they stopped, they smelled more and more sour, unable to hold their tiny bladders; their faces were always tear stained. The humans didn't seem to notice.

Zavin thought he hated them and their indifference, but he only learned the meaning of the word when the littles started dying.

Rachal was the first to go. She refused to eat and slowly wasted away. There was barely anything left of her by the time they finally left her in the desert to die. He stared at her body as they put him in the sack for the night, Pas's words ringing too clear in his ears.

The ancestors have abandoned us.

The broad-shouldered, meat-hand man who dealt out the punishments beat his men for not taking better care of them, but when the second smallest died, he simply chalked it up to the weakness of elves. The third smallest was shoved into their bag after that, but still Zavin tried to keep hold of the hope that it would be over soon.

When he finally lost track of the days, they found themselves in a forest. The others didn't seem to notice, all too tired, hungry, or beaten down to hold any wonder at the trees they'd never seen before. Only Zavin seemed to stare in awe on their midday break.

"They must be gods," he murmured, running a hand through his tangled hair.

"Not gods," Pas whispered. "Our gods aren't so loud. Just listen to the way they beat their arms together."

Zavin nodded, but suspected the older boy was losing his mind.

They're treatment since entering the woods hadn't been so bad, but one night Pas was ripped out of the bag and showed up to breakfast one morning with bruises on his slender arms. There was a look in his eyes that Zavin couldn't place. He said he had tried to run, but wouldn't talk about his punishment. Part of Zavin was glad he hadn't told him.

"No," he shook his head to chase away the image of a beaten Pas, "they're not our gods. But they still look powerful."

"Grab them up," the meaty man interrupted, smiling when Zavin met his eyes and scowled. "Still got some fire, huh?"

When he didn't respond, the man laughed again, wagging his finger at him. "I'm going to miss you when we hit the city tomorrow. Goddesses bless whoever buys you. They're going to need the patience."

Zavin opened his mouth to ask him what he meant, but Pas nudged him hard and shook his head. Zavin smiled at him, relieved to see his friend still acting like his overprotective self.

When they unpacked them for the last time, Zavin still didn't believe that anything they could do to him would break him. The building they were in when they dumped the sacks out was quiet, only one or two humans coming in to look them over before leaving. Not until a woman pulled out a small bag and handed it to the meat-hand man in exchange for the small girl, did the weight of the situation finally hit him. They were being sold.

Another group of humans came in, Zavin's heart beating hard. The meat-hand man motioned to Pas while talking to another human. The first pinch of fear stabbed his chest as he grabbed his friend's hand. Soon he would be alone for the first time in his life.

"Why here? Why sell us here?" Zavin whispered. It seemed like such a trivial thing to worry about, but asking *why* they were being sold was a question he didn't want to know the answer to.

"You'll live," Pas spoke with dead eyes. "I've seen it. Your body will live."

"My body?" Zavin swallowed, watching the human pass a purse to the broad man, but Pas didn't get a chance to answer. He was already in cuffs being lead away.

Zavin stared at his friend's back, his words ringing in his ears.

Your body will live. . . .

A sour knot twisted in his stomach. Pas hadn't been wrong. Not once.

My body?

Zavin jolted as the meat-hand man grabbed him and pulled him a few feet toward new humans. A well-groomed man clothed in bright blue stood with a woman covered from her shoulders to ankles in layers of flowing fabrics. They looked at the slave trader with distaste as he approached, and Zavin felt a prick of satisfaction through the unease. At least someone was as disgusted as he was at how dirty the meat-hand man was.

"He'll be good," the clean-cut man's tone rationalized as the woman stared down her nose at Zavin. "We need new blood."

Zavin glared at the woman till the meat-hand man grabbed his hair and forced him to look down.

"He needs a good wash," she huffed, shaking her head. "I don't want a dirty elf in my house; I don't care how young he is."

As they spoke with the meat-hand man, Zavin jumped as another human came and strapped a heavy metal circle around his neck and jerked him to his side with the chain attached to it. "Keep up," he growled in Zavin's language.

Zavin nodded, swallowing as he stared up at the towering sentinel. He wasn't human, he realized. He definitely wasn't an elf, either. Zavin had never seen anything like him before. At least a foot taller than the meat-hand man, he was built like a mountain, with a thick beard and pointed ears peeking out from greying shoulder-length hair. He'd heard stories of beings like him, giants that fought like lions and killed stag wolves with their bare hands, but he never thought he'd get to see one.

The giant pulled him along as the humans exited the building onto a bustling street. It was a good thing too. If the mountain hadn't guided him along, Zavin would've stopped to gawk. Occasionally, Zavin would get caught looking at something new and would be yanked back to attention, but after the third time broke the skin, he tried to keep his eyes to himself.

Everyone spoke in strange languages, dressed in colors more vibrant than he'd ever seen. No one bothered to look at him, especially not the few bald elves he spotted standing next to other humans, but he didn't take offense. He doubted they could do anything for him. He needed his clan. They would find him.

When they got to the house, Zavin was exhausted and starving, but he still paused to stare at the immensity of the building he was being lead to. Zavin had no words to describe the gardens and grounds they walked him across. Birds soared overhead; men and women worked on nearby fields full of trees and vibrant fruit. Even the air was sweeter here. This was where his ancestors would save him. How could any place so beautiful be as bad as the road to his new owner?

But when they made it to the house and the couple left him alone with the giant and three other men, Zavin's last bit of hope flickered.

"Sit," the giant said, motioning to a turned over bucket.

Zavin eyed the bucket and shook his head. "Why?"

"Time for your cutting."

Zavin frowned, his silver-blue eyes narrowed. "What cutting?"

One of the humans grumbled something he didn't understand before saying three words that made his skin go cold. "Grab him up."

Before he could move, they were on him. Zavin squirmed like a fire snake as they slammed him down on the bucket. His hissing and cursing only stopped as a set of sheers passed close to his face.

The giant just watched, his voice rougher. "Sit still or you'll get hurt."

Zavin gasped as someone grabbed his hair with one hand and held it out behind him so hard his back arched under the men holding him down.

"No!" he breathed. "Please!"

He couldn't scream; the sound of the metal slicing through his hair made him go cold. A weight was lifted as the remaining hair fell in front of his face, the giant's eyes focused on the fields.

"No," Zavin whimpered, trying to pull away again as they grabbed his head and sheared close to the skin. "Please. Don't."

"Other side," the giant said again, the other two snatching Zavin's chin so he could slice away every lock.

Zavin's willpower left him with each black strand that hit the ground. He broke an arm free and grabbed a handful of hair, holding it to his chest and staring ahead, the giant still not looking at him.

By the time they finished, he was empty. Zavin could only clutch the sides of his shaved head as the giant stood him up and dressed him in new clothes. There was still enough on the top for the humans to grab him, but he might as well have been bald. When the giant finished dressing him, he pierced his ears and attached a slender chain from the outside point down to the lobe.

Zavin didn't flinch at the stabbing pain when the giant gave them a pull to walk him back to the house.

"Let's go, elf."

When Zavin still didn't move, the giant dropped his hand to his shoulder to guide him instead. Once they were alone, the giant stopped him and crouched to his level, but Zavin couldn't raise his eyes from the floor.

"This is your life now, little elf," the giant said, the gentleness of his voice not reaching Zavin. "It'd be best if you got used to it."

Zavin wasn't sure he could speak, so he stayed quiet. If he opened his mouth, he might scream until there was nothing left.

THE SACRED COAL OF ZATTFU MOUNTAIN

Abigail Pickle

I

The firepot wrapped its small, pottery shelter around the single coal, the seed of last evening's fire. In vain, the darkness pressed all its black weight over the closed, round form, straining to invade through the two tiny holes in the lid.

But the nested coal breathed on in silence, speared the cloud of darkness with two sliver-splinters of light.

The man awoke, open eyes submerged in black. The warmth of the fading campfire lapped at his cheek. Soon but slowly, the silent solemn light of the coals waded into his eyes and cast out the tyrant dark with a single touch.

The man looked. He saw a dome of mist-ink, painted char-orange and red with the low embers. A dome of darkness with a ceiling less than five feet from his nose. Birdsong came in chorded dance to his ears. He smelled grass growing and flowers opening their silk jars of perfume. A small wind wandered over his left side to brush the sunken fire. The radius of light retreated, then again breathed out.

By the warmth of that wind, he guessed it must be late morning.

The man rolled from his back and pushed up to his knees. He reached beyond the dome of darkness, saw his hands disappear. Grass ribboned his calloused palms with cool softness as he groped for his pack. Coarse burlap met his hands, and he pulled the traveler's backpack into the dome of illumination.

As sleep fell from his mind, he scanned the gray ground of that dome, the gray grass, the gray bedroll, the gray backpack. His eyes snapped a sharp blink; his gray hands dove again into the darkness. He searched the dark with quick, frantic touches to the ground.

His hands sank into the fabric of his cloak. His breath stopped as he felt through the sturdy folds. Then a round clay form spoke its warm solemnity to his hands, and his shoulders sank down with a sigh.

Though the firepot would fit in his palm, he took it in both hands and brought it carefully to his chest. Against the gray of his hands, the henna-colored clay hummed like music from a distant tavern. The man held the vessel before his face. Its details blurred. He adjusted the distance—away, closer, away—until his eyes focused. Then he turned the firepot slowly, scrutinizing every divot and freckle for the beginnings of a crack. Gradually, the clay's hale surface allowed his tense body to relax.

He placed the firepot gently between two of the stones sheltering the low campfire. The little round vessel constantly drew his glances as he donned his cloak, rolled and stowed his sleeping mat, and shouldered his pack. His mouth and eyebrows tightened into a pained grimace as he gazed at the ground where the mat had been lying.

A black stain marked that earth. A heavy, black blot, with edges like twisted roots, like old knuckles clutching too hard. The ember light penetrated the stain with its red-orange touch. It showed the shriveled forms of the grass and weeds of that spot, stems withered as if at the hands of a three-month drought.

"Forgive me," the man whispered.

His face settled from the grimace into his constant frown as the firepot again pulled his gaze. He squatted by the old embers and removed the vessel's lid. The nested coal breathed the red-orange spectrum into his wide pupils; a promise in tangible form.

The old woman's words played in his mind, *Carry the fire to the cave of Zattfu Mountain.*

With a rock and a short metal rod from his pack, he brought two coals from the pile of embers to join the nested coal of the firepot. Then, returning the lid to its place, he wrapped the firepot in cloth and placed it in the double-lined hip-pocket on the inside of his deer-hide cloak. Lighting his torch in the embers, he banked dirt over the old fire, and, checking his compass, started walking northeast.

The darkness followed him.

His sphere of light shrank so that he could not see his feet without lowering his torch. He paused to check the ground between every other step. Soon his walk became methodical and his thoughts began to move.

Like a tongue's relentless return to the gap of a missing tooth, his mind worried into pitch black vaults and strove in vain for a single specific memory. He reached for faces or names of family or friends, but found only vague, gray mist. He searched for any memory of a day in his old life—if there was an old life—a day without the darkness.

Nothing.

He tried to remember yesterday and met the same void.

He tried to remember his name.

Nothing.

The man shook his head at himself and yanked his mind out of that abyss. His focus landed on the crackling colors of the torch. With those colors, he remembered the coal in the firepot. With the coal, he remembered the quick, cocked smile of the strange old woman.

His torch had cast the gray dome forward. He had stepped in the gray light and seen a short figure with its feet planted wide-stanced in his path. The figure threw back its hood, revealing the face of an old woman. She scrutinized him with an upward stare.

The man turned his face away and averted his course to walk around the stranger. Her arm darted up like a snake striking, and she caught his wrist in her grip. The man halted. He returned her gaze with his constant frown.

"What is your name, traveler?" the old woman asked.

He dredged his strained voice up from long silence, "I don't remember."

She nodded once. "Where do you come from?"

"I don't remember."

"They drove you out from your village," she stated.

"Probably… I don't know." He reached with his thoughts into the black void of lost memory. "I may have left on my own."

"Where are you headed?"

"Nowhere."

The left corner of her lip quirked up and made chasms under her eye. "Nowhere's a poor heading for a young traveler."

"I'm not young."

"You can't remember your name. I'm quite certain you can't even remember yesterday."

"I don't know how old, but I know I'm not young."

Her eyes became less piercing as they moved to study his face. "You look about forty years. That's young. Don't argue with me."

The man passed his gray-light torch to his other hand.

The old woman folded her arms. "You swallowed an ophidian jewel."

The man stared.

"You're not the first."

"I'd rather I was."

"Don't rather that. If you were the first, I wouldn't be walking straight up to you with a remedy."

His eyes widened and his hand sank to his side with the gray torch.

"I see what you mean though." The old woman softened her voice and her brows. "It's a loathsome plague… You're right to keep moving. You doom any place you stay."

"You said remedy."

"I did. Though it is not an easy task."

"Please."

"Peace, young traveler. I'm not speaking in vain." She took a clay pot from her satchel, slowly lifted the round lid. A red-orange glow crowned the opening mouth.

The man gasped. He nearly dropped his torch, but clutched it fast in a bolt of reflex.

The old woman nodded. "You've forgotten color."

The man could not speak.

"This fire has a power against the darkness that pours from you. You must not let it go out. Carry this flame to the cave of Zattfu Mountain. There you will find your remedy."

"Where is Zattfu Mountain?"

The old woman held the firepot out to him. "Light your torch with this fire."

Frowning, he stepped closer and lowered his torch, eyes fixed upon the pot's colored halo. The glow caught the torch's gray flames with a hiss; red and orange light came to bless the small sphere of his gray world.

"Now," the old woman said, drawing another item from her satchel. "Take this compass." She passed him the small circle. "Follow it northeast. When the land begins to rise steeply, keep careful watch. There is a path up the mountain into the cave. This path is marked with white stones that bear a small oval carving. They will glow white in the light from this fire. Their glow will guide you."

"How far is it?"

"Is there a distance you will not go? Know that your journey has an end. It will do you little good to number its steps."

The man frowned but nodded.

The old woman closed the firepot and cradled it in one arm. Stepping close, she opened his cloak and searched with her eyes through his clothes.

The man shied back. He stared at her with limbs tight and pained as a decade-old knot in a weight-strained rope.

"Do you have a pocket?" the old woman asked. "I mean to give you this fire and the vessel to carry it."

The roots of his teeth strained as his jaw clenched. But he turned out the left side of his cloak and held open the largest pocket.

Again she stepped close. The man held himself rigid as, gently, she nestled the firepot into the pocket of his cloak.

"Take this flame," she said. "Follow the heading. Follow the stones. Carry the fire to the cave of Zattfu Mountain."

The man stared as she stepped back. "Who are you?"

She gave him a smile that pulled the light and shadows touching her face into a glorious game. "After you find your remedy, come back here and speak your name. Then I will tell you what they call me."

II

One day—not the next, for the earth now smelled of storms and early summer—the man heard the rumbling from the sky and felt the sudden gales of cool, wet wind. He began keeping watch for a shelter. Sometimes he could find a bridge, or an overhang of rock, or even an abandoned hut.

Now, as he walked, his flame-blessed sphere passed over a cobblestone path. He paused, listening for voices or footsteps. He heard the wind chasing through tall grass and the nervous moan of a cow in the distance. But no sounds of humans on the road.

The man stepped onto the cobblestones and followed the path at a brisk pace. It carried him east but soon began to wind southward. A gust of wind caught his hood and snapped it from his head. Thunder thrashed the air. The man raised his pace to a jog, half-crouching to hold the torch low and see the ground.

A scream knifed the darkness ahead of him.

The man halted.

"What is it?" a voice shouted.

"There's an evil coming with this storm," came the faint answer.

The man turned around and began retreating along the path.

Then he heard a bowstring and a quick whistling with the wind.

He darted right and sprinted from the road, fleeing with his feet in the darkness. A thick raindrop struck the back of his head. As he sprinted, the sky sucked in its breath.

A quick scatter of drops assaulted his shoulders. His torch hissed with snarl-curled flames. The man clenched his teeth and, hunching forward, pulled the torch close to his chest to shelter its fire. He forced his legs to keep running.

Smoke from the torch bit his open mouth. The rain rose into a steady roar.

The ground dropped.

His pound-step fell, fell, and he tumbled forward. Rock bruised his shoulder. His hand flinched open, dropping the torch, and he rolled downward out from the sphere of light.

Darkness.

Flat rock halted him two bruises later.

The man groaned and fiercely pressed his fingernails into his temples to curse his own foolishness. Rain pounded, drenching his hair and drumming his cloak with rapid percussion.

Suddenly, the smell of smoke sliced his heartbeat in half. A burning horror gnawed into his hip. He struggled out of his cloak as the color of flame pushed back at the darkness.

His hands dove into the infant fire tongues, into the sacred vessel's pocket, and met broken pottery and a searing white-hot pain. He yanked back from the fire's bite and slapped his palms to the water-pooled rock. Too many seconds, he stared frozen as the flames sputtered in the downpour, chewed out on his cloak, sputtered lower.

He shook himself and leaned over the struggling red-orange life. The fire sounds shifted from snapping pops to a dragging hiss. But though the little flames lifted their heads, they began to wane into the drenched leather.

With desperate grasps, the man searched through the folds of his cloak beyond the fire. The rain mocked his hands with drilling cold, penetrating in an instant, the single dry patch of cloak he found. His voice made a wet, strangled sound as he twisted and saw that his pack was no longer on his shoulders.

He squinted to scan the ground as the fire's small sphere of light flickered and sank. Straining to keep his chest over the weakening flames, he reached out into the darkness. His hands met only the wet rock.

The light sank again, and the darkness enveloped his face.

The man cried out. He dropped one hand near the fire's warmth and continued searching for his pack with the other. With its continual roar, the rain drove cold furrows into his back. As his seeking hand splashed on soaked fabric, the warmth beside his still hand faded to an old shadow.

He brought the pack to his side and delved inside. But here again, he found no dry haven, only rain-conquered food and fabrics and metal tools that would not burn.

Cold seeped and settled deep into his bones and stiffened his muscles. The man felt in his cloak for the fire, for the warmth of the coal, but he met only cold, drenched darkness.

A shard of pottery sliced his palm.

The man let his body slump.

The rain made weeping rivers in his hair, down the bridge of his nose to the sockets of his eyes, down his cheeks and over his mouth to his chin, over his collar bones and sagging shoulders.

He did not move.

His face, his limbs, even for a time, his breath: all still as wet ash.

The cold damp darkness soaked into his expression, deep under his muscles, into his heart. His heart pumped the chill through his blood.

As if across a vast, gray distance, he felt, as always, the bitter prickling of the darkness pouring from his back. And he felt his body weeping.

Time faded from his senses.

His weeping body stilled, sank half-crumpled to the rocky ground.

Broken pottery in the rain-pounded darkness.

The rain left him behind.

Delving blindly through his black existence, sun-warmth touched his shoulders, limply pressing away cold. But soon that short warmth sank down and left him damp in the deepening cool of night.

His teeth chattered and his body shook with chill.

Night bugs sent their layered drone into his darkness. His mind flickered out in that gentle music and came at last to sleep.

He woke in the noon heat. Rising from his damp cloak, he looked into the darkness, and waited.

Waited.

But no sacred flame came to battle his blindness.

He shut his eyes and lowered his head. His mind reached into memory. He gasped as he saw the firepot in the old woman's hand, as he saw the red-orange halo.

"Carry this fire…. Zattfu Mountain… There you will find your remedy."

The man set his face and opened his eyes to the blackness.

He needed light, a new torch.

First, he spread his cloak and his clothes and the contents of his pack on the rock ground to dry in the warmth of the summer-bent day. Then he set to the old, gray way of starting a fire.

With one hand on his cloak, he reached out to search for kindling.

He searched in utter darkness.

To his left, the ground sloped up; he felt mostly rock with dirt in its seams. To his right, the rock ground made a short drop to muddy earth.

A nest of briars gnawed at his arm. He grimaced, gripped, and pulled until, with a brittle crackling, a few of the vine's dead branches broke free in his fist. He broke the briars into short lengths and pyred the sticks on the dry rock beneath him.

Again, he reached out from the edge of his cloak. He would need a branch for a torch.

He searched in utter darkness.

His hand met only rock and brambles and grass, no sturdy stick or length of wood.

The man let out a shaky breath. He half-rose and took a trembling step down from the rock.

Away from his pack and his clothes, he stepped out in a straight line.

He searched in utter darkness.

Chipped rocks and brambles bit his bare feet. An insect collided with his bare chest.

He shuddered, stepped, searched in utter darkness.

At last his wrist knocked the prickly bark of a scrubby bush. He grasped a branch and strained until it split from its short trunk.

He withdrew his steps, retreating in the darkness, carefully stepping backward until his heel hit the side of the flat rock. He turned and felt for his cloak.

At the touch of the damp leather, relief flooded his veins with warmth. He climbed back up the rock and began stripping the scrub bush branch of its leaves and twigs. Finished, he felt around for his shirt. The fabric's now faint dampness cooled his fingers. He found the seam at one of the sleeves and, pausing to fix his grip on both sides of the cloth, ripped the sleeve from its home.

He wrapped the fabric around one end of the branch. Setting the branch beside the pyre of bramble-sticks, he searched for three precious items from his pack: the bottle of oil, his knife, and his flint.

He dripped the oil on the fabric that wrapped the branch and set the ready torch at his side. Then he took the flint and the knife and, in solid darkness, struck by the old habit in his arms. Struck. Struck.

A gray spark leapt into the darkness, dove for the pyre of sticks. Smoke smoldered up to the man's face. He squinted and watched a tiny nub of gray light rise. He breathed a gentle exhale on the light. A furious grumble of smoke filled his eyes and nose with acrid sting. But the little gray light expanded. He breathed again on the flame, and soon it claimed the pyre with quick-crackling gray light.

He presented the torch to the young fire and the gray light spread.

Gray light.

His frown deepened with an ache for the orange fire-light that breathed in his memory.

Zattfu Mounatin.

The man dressed into his still damp clothes and cloak.

He gathered and stowed the scattered contents of his pack, put his arms through the straps, took up the torch, and, checking his compass, started off: northeast.

III

He did not count the days; he did not count the steps. After flatlands broken by hills and rock outcroppings, the ground began a sudden, steep rise. Now he searched with every step for a stone with an oval carving.

His hollow stomach growled. He stopped to look through his pack. No food. He tried to remember eating and could not. His only memory spoke the old woman's voice. *"When the land begins to rise steeply, keep careful watch."*

The man stepped up the slope and searched the ground.

He climbed and searched until his hands became a constant complaint of raw skin and aching joints. Until his whole life became a single search and a single echo. A single search for a rock with an oval carving, a rock that would not glow in his gray light. A single echo: the memory of the sacred red-orange fire, the nested coal, lost to his eyes and yet breathing life in the black, ruined halls of his memory.

The man climbed and searched. He stopped suddenly, blinking away his daze. His hand rested on a small, round rock. His eyes focused, and he saw the oval carving in the rock's smooth side. He clutched the rock with fresh fierceness, as if the mountain itself would snatch the treasure away into the darkness of lost memory. Clarity seeping back into his mind and his hands, he searched the ground just up the slope with the gray sweeps of his torch.

He found a narrow path of chiseled stone steps.

His voice broke from long silence to laugh, two broken

notes. The man straightened his cloak, gripped his torch, and followed the narrow steps.

The path wound back and forth along the steepening side of the mountain. The man searched the sides of the steps and found the oval-carved stones at intervals. Gusts of wind battered the gray flames of the torch. He half-crouched to shield his gray fire in his cloak and to see the ground as he climbed.

His ears popped with altitude as the path turned into the mountain. He stepped forward. Soon he felt the shelter of cave walls as the wind roared behind him. His footsteps echoed. From both sides, and above, and deeper into the mountain.

A voice came from the darkness ahead of him. "What is your name, pilgrim?"

The man stopped. "I don't remember my name." Speaking pained his throat. He looked down at his gray hands and gray cloak, up at his gray torch. Facing the voice, he knelt on the ground, laid the torch at his side, and forced his words to move. "An old sage met me when I was lost. She gave me a fire and told me to carry it to Zattfu Mountain. I…" He swallowed and fisted his hand in his knotted hair. "I have let the fire go out. Even so… I seek a remedy against this black poison that haunts my existence."

"Do you remember the fire?" The voice struck into the man's gray sphere with notes like clear sunbeams.

"Yes," the man said. "It is my only memory… my only thought."

"Then you have carried it," the voice said, drawing nearer. "And it has not gone out."

A white glow came and washed the gray sphere free from every rumor of death; it filled the gray with a new breath that transfigured it to the grey of dawn's first whisper.

A young man stood holding the white glow. His eyes,

white and potent as lightning, smiled through his grim expression. "I am Zehreph." He crouched to level his face with the man.

Zehreph stared a long silence.

The man returned the strange stare of the glowing, pale irises, then looked down to the brilliance in Zehreph's hands. His eyes watered in the pain of the radiant blur. For a timeless moment, he saw only white—white ringing high in his eyes like the cry of a gull.

Then his vision settled. He saw an olive branch in Zehreph's hands. The white light poured from the ripe, oval fruit.

"Good." Zehreph broke an olive from the branch and held it out to the man. "Eat this."

The man straightened sharply and frowned at Zehreph's face. "The old sage I mentioned before, she said my curse came because I swallowed something."

"Yes," Zehreph said. "An ophidian jewel."

"And what is that you want me to eat?"

"An olive."

"No it isn't."

"It is an olive that grew from a tree with its roots in the veins of this mountain."

"And what will happen if I swallow it?"

Zehreph looked at him steadily. "You will die."

The man snatched up his torch and stood. "I can die anywhere. If there's no remedy here, I'll leave and keep looking."

Zehreph gazed up from his low stance. "If you were to die alone, apart from this power, your darkness would bleed into the land and spread."

The man glared down at the white light touching his grey boots. "Is there nothing else I can do?"

"The darkness is inside you," Zehreph said. "If this light is to dispel the darkness, it must enter you also."

"Am *I* the darkness then?" The man clutched the rough

bark of his torch.

"The darkness has bound you, yes," Zehreph said. "And you have bound yourself to the darkness."

The man sank again to his knees. "If that is so, then it is right that I should die."

"Child." Zehreph laced his voice with admonishment. "Look at this light."

The man started and looked up with one brow raised.

Zehreph met the expression with a spark of laughter in his eyes. "You thought you were the elder?"

"Well you look…"

"Oh…." Zehreph's gaze wandered to the invisible ceiling. "That's right, humans often see only appearances. I forget sometimes."

"You're not… What are you?"

"I am the appointed keeper of this mountain." Zehreph's eyes returned and fixed sternly on the man's face. "Listen, child, you are very young on the scale of the earth. But even so, even with your human sight, you are not wholly blind to the will of this power. You saw it before. Look again."

The man looked at the glowing olive in Zehreph's hand. The white light sang in his thoughts. And for a moment, he saw in its song—as if through the feather edge of prism mist—he saw all the colors once black-blotted from memory. His chest pulled a deep, slow breath. He heard in the white light a familiar voice. He chased the voice into the wasteland of memory, but he could not catch its name.

"Alright," the man said. The familiar voice faded as his eyes moved slowly from the olive's glow to Zehreph. "I'll do it."

A flicker of a smile broke Zehreph's grim expression. He passed the olive to the man's hand, then stood and strode back into the cave.

The man stared at the white olive, again chasing memories he could not catch. Finally, he pressed the light into his mouth. He chewed through a magnificent, quiet-earth taste. Chewed to the hard stop of the pit. He shut his eyes. Swallowed.

Pain. As if, in every corner and layer of his body, deep-clinging claws were digging in, even as a quench-less gale tore them away.

The gale wrenched.

The man screamed with the pain of ripping flesh. And then his breath stopped.

Darkness snapped, and the man's whole being and whole world submerged in light. He drifted in the eye of the sun.

Again, but clearer, he heard a familiar voice. And he knew it was his mother, calling out from the edge of the herb garden, a long, long time ago. *"Caraway... Caraway come home for dinner."*

Caraway sucked in air and sat up.

He saw Zehreph sitting across from him. Late-afternoon sunlight drenched the cave walls in hues sweet as honeysuckle. Caraway looked over his shoulder and nearly choked on the blue of the sky. He looked back to Zehreph. His glowing white eyes sang in celestial contrast to his dark brown skin.

Zehreph smiled and handed Caraway a drinking skin, a bowl of steaming vegetable stew, and a half-loaf of bread. Caraway watched his own hands as he accepted the gifts. They were pale brown and weathered with red cuts and yellow calluses.

Caraway shut his eyes, put the drinking skin to his lips, and took the water in swift draughts. "Thank you," he gasped when he finally stopped for breath.

"There's wine," Zehreph said. "If you want it after you've eaten."

Caraway laughed. "Yes, I'd like that." He took a bite of the stew. Sighed and shook his head in the tide of pure delicious. He swallowed. "Zehreph, my name is Caraway."

Zehreph gazed up for a moment, then grinned. "Like the plant."

"My mother loved it," Caraway said. "The seeds… they taste like licorice. She used them to make medicine."

"Do you remember, Caraway, the ophidian jewel?"

Caraway grimaced. For a long moment, he glared at his hands. "There was a plague in my village. People were dying. None of the remedies my mother made could help. I had heard from a traveler of a place of power nearby. I went. A creature met me. I do not know what it was, for darkness swarmed about its form. I asked it if it knew of the power. The creature told me it owned the power and would grant any wish. I said I wanted the power to heal my neighbors. The creature gave me a black jewel and told me to swallow. I did. And there I became a plague rather than a remedy." Caraway fell silent and answered his sudden exhaustion with three spoonfuls of stew.

Zehreph stood, walked to the back of the cave, and returned with a bottle, clay cups, and a bowl of stew for himself. He poured the wine and passed a cup to Caraway.

Caraway flicked a smile as he received the wine. He stared into the dark red drink. "I do not know what became of my village." He paused there, then sipped a red melody of warmth and sharpened life.

The taste snatched Caraway's voice into a cry of joyous shock.

Zehreph's lips lifted from a heavy expression. After taking a bite of his own stew, he untied a pouch from his belt. "I have a task to give you, Caraway," Zehreph said.

"A task?" Caraway dipped bread in his stew, chewed, then took another sip of wine.

Zehreph held out the pouch to Caraway. "These are seeds from the olive tree that has its roots in this mountain. Go back and wander the world. Wherever you find a black stain, plant a seed."

"I will." Caraway took the pouch and put it in the

inside pocket of his cloak. "And I will go back to the place where I swallowed this darkness. I'll find the deceiver and destroy him."

"No." Zehreph's face became rigid and stern. "That task is not for you."

"The woman who sent me here said there were others before me. More will follow if we do nothing."

"And was it your power that purged the darkness pouring from you?"

"No… I could carry this power to that place."

Zehreph smiled and shook his head. "Plant these seeds. Who can say what good their roots will work beneath the earth?"

SONATA
FOR SNAILS

Michael Hustead

Teppo sat on his front porch in the grey, pre-dawn light, eyes fixed on the eastern horizon. His eyes burned from lack of sleep and his shoulders and back ached from the hard wood of the porch, but he refused to go inside. He had not missed a sunrise since his beloved Kirsi died, and he wasn't about to miss it now. Kirsi loved the sunrise...had loved it. Somehow, in the morning sun, Teppo could almost feel her with him again.

The sun slipped above the horizon, its first rays casting golden light over Teppo's garden. Teppo closed his eyes, feeling the sun warm his weathered skin, and inhaled deeply. Without looking, he reached for the battered wooden flute at his side, lifted it to his lips, and began to play.

The melody was spritely and joyful, an ancient harvest tune of the village. As the sun rose, Teppo played of life and abundance, tears rolling down his face. The song ended, but he played on, moving seamlessly into a hymn, solemn and beautiful, praising God for another day.

He didn't notice when the singing started, couldn't have said how long it had been going on. It was only as the hymn reached its crescendo that he noticed the delicate accompaniment of the voices. Teppo faltered and stopped playing, the flute poised at his lips. The singing continued, voices rising and falling in hypnotic waves.

Teppo surged to his feet, the flute falling from nerveless fingers, peering around for the source of the music. There was no one in sight. Hands trembling, Teppo scooped up his flute, and, brandishing it before him like a sword, stepped gingerly off the porch. A glance showed no one hiding beneath the steps. He poked cautiously at the wood pile and yelped as a mouse, startled from its nest, darted between his legs.

This is it, he thought, scratching at his short, grey beard. *I've gone mad.*

Still, the music continued unabated, voices raised in

joyous song as the sun broke fully above the horizon. And then, without warning, the music stopped. Silence settled over the garden. Teppo waited anxiously, his ears straining for any hint of the voices, but there was nothing. At last, he lowered his flute and headed back to the house to fetch his tools, muttering under his breath.

Teppo worked on his hands and knees in the garden, weeding and pruning his way down the rows. He did not sing or hum as he worked, praying fervently instead. Teppo was not an educated man, but he knew hearing voices was a bad sign. He had prayed often for death since illness took Kirsi, but he had hoped for something a little simpler than a downward spiral into madness.

He tossed and turned that night, unable to relax, and it was with some trepidation that he poked his head out of his front door in the cold hour before dawn.

Nothing moved.

Teppo shook his head, rubbed at his eyes to drive the last vestiges of sleep away, and stumped out onto his porch, his flute clutched firmly in his hand. He considered the garden with suspicion before turning and going back into the house. He returned a moment later with his axe in hand. He leaned the axe against the porch rail and settled onto the stoop to await the sun.

As the sun rose, he lifted his flute and played. The music came timidly at first, but as he finished the first chorus, the comforting routine dispelled the fear of the previous day and his sleepless night and he played with more vigor. This time, however, he listened carefully as he played, and so he noticed the moment the voices started.

They joined in effortlessly, picking up the thread of his song as though born to it. Teppo stopped playing immediately, and the voices stopped as well. After a moment, he lifted his flute to his lips and took the song up again. He finished the verse without incident, but as he started the chorus anew, the voices came in as well.

Teppo leapt to his feet, fumbling for his axe. He half fell off the porch in his haste, nearly severing his leg as he struggled to juggle his flute and the axe. Cursing, Teppo shoved the flute through his belt and took a firm grip on his axe. The voices continued undeterred as Teppo approached the garden, axe raised over his head. He tiptoed down the rows, stopping when he reached the lettuce. The sounds came from here; he was sure of it. He reached out and delicately poked at one of the bushy plants with the head of the axe. The voices cut off instantly.

My lettuce is singing to me, he thought. He had always been proud of his lettuce, but this was taking things rather too far. He shoved at the offending vegetable again with the axe, but nothing happened. He turned to go but had not taken two steps before the singing returned.

Teppo bellowed and spun, bringing his axe down upon the lettuce. The blade split the plant in half, embedding itself into the soil between a group of snails clustered beneath the leaves. The singing cut off with a startled squawk as the snails stared fearfully up at him. Teppo screamed and fell backward, landing with a thud on his rump. The snails screamed and...shifted slightly as they attempted to scatter and flee. Teppo stared at the retreating snails, trying in vain to make sense of what he was seeing.

"Not my lettuce singing after all," he said. "It was the snails." He didn't know what to make of this new development, but the sinking feeling in his belly told him a snail choir was only marginally better than a lettuce one.

He sat there in the dirt for a long time after the snails had disappeared, unsure what to do next. He didn't do any work that day. Every time he tried to focus on his chores, the image would drift up, unbidden, of the snails singing, and he would have to go lie down.

"Snails don't sing," he told himself for the hundredth time. "Snails don't sing, lettuce don't sing, and God help me, but the rutabagas don't sing neither."

By the time he went to bed, he almost believed it.

He didn't play his music the next morning at sunrise, but it had nothing to do with the snails—he was just getting too old to be up before the sun every single morning. A body needed rest after all. No doubt it was simply exhaustion that had led him to imagine a garden full of singing snails. He went about his work that day with stoic fortitude, glaring at the garden occasionally as though daring it to produce any unsolicited music. The garden remained silent, as gardens typically do.

Teppo didn't play the next day either, but on the morning of the third day, he awoke just before sunrise with an ache in his chest. He missed his music. Without it, he could feel Kirsi slipping further away from him, and somehow he knew that if he continued as he had the last two days, he would lose her forever.

He dressed quickly and rushed out onto his porch with his flute in hand moments before the sun rose. He raised the flute to his lips and played frantically, the music filling the air just as the first rays of the morning washed across the land.

Voices burst gleefully into song right by his ear, and Teppo jumped half out of his skin. More than three dozen snails had arranged themselves in orderly rows across his porch railing; their heads lifted high in song while their antennae waved in the morning breeze. Teppo stared, dumbfounded, his flute frozen halfway to his lips, as the snails finished the harvest song and moved softly into the hymn.

Teppo glared at the snails, but they ignored him, their song continuing unabated. After a moment, Teppo began to play again. The snails shifted seamlessly into a subtle harmony, letting Teppo take the lead. Unable to believe it, yet unable to stop, Teppo played as the snails sang and the morning passed unnoticed.

"Good day."

Teppo turned at the sound, and his breath caught in his throat. His neighbor, Jormun, who farmed the field across the creek stood in the lane before Teppo's house, white-knuckled fingers clutching a basket.

"Preita sent me with some things for you," Jormun said. "I didn't mean to intrude, but I heard voices..." Jormun craned his neck to see onto the porch.

It was only then that Teppo realized the snails were still singing, unaware perhaps of the farmer's presence. Teppo glanced frantically over at the snails and hurried down the porch, but it was too late. Jormun's gaze fastened over Teppo's shoulder at the snails. His mouth worked silently for a moment.

"Are those snails... singing?" Jormun asked.

"Well—" For a brief instant Teppo considered lying, but frankly, he couldn't think of anything remotely believable. He could hardly deny it. There the blasted snails were, singing away for all to hear. "Yes. I suppose they are."

"Snails don't sing," Jormun replied, his eyes still fixed over Teppo's shoulder.

"Well..." Teppo said again, rubbing at his hair. "They don't normally, but these seem to be a mite unusual."

"Snails don't sing," Jormun said again, more firmly this time.

"Yes, well, I suppose you could try telling *them* that. They might listen to you. God knows they didn't pay any mind to me when I told them."

Jormun continued to stare, his mouth hanging open until Teppo shifted to the side to block his view. The farmer blinked, his eyes focusing in on Teppo at last. The color had drained from his face, leaving him pale as a ghost.

"Demons," he said, at last, the word hanging in the air between them.

"Don't be a fool," Teppo said, moving to take Jormun's arm.

"No," Jormun cried, shoving the basket between them like a talisman. "Stay back!" Teppo reached for him again, but Jormun shrieked and threw the basket in Teppo's face. The basket burst open, covering Teppo from head to toe in mushroom soup. While Teppo struggled to clear his face, Jormun turned and ran full speed down the lane and out of sight.

Teppo stared after the retreating farmer and heaved a sigh. He glanced down in disgust at the soup dripping from his clothes and cast a rueful glance back at the snails who had fallen silent at last.

"This," he said, "is not going to be good."

Teppo spent the day in a frenzy of work in an attempt to keep his mind occupied, but to no avail. The image of Jormun's face and his shrill scream of demons remained plastered across his mind. Trouble would come of it, and Teppo kept waiting for something to happen, but nothing did until the day was nearly spent. Teppo straightened from chopping wood, feeling his back pop as his tired muscles stretched and his tired eyes strained to see a crowd coming down the lane toward his cottage. He blinked sweat from his eyes, glowering at the figure of Jormun in the lead, and moved to intercept them with his axe in his hands.

"What's this, then?" Teppo asked.

"You know why we're here," Jormun said, his voice tight with strain. "I told them about the demons."

"You're wasting your time," Teppo spat. "There are no demons here. Surely you people have better things to do than listen to this man's ravings."

Behind Jormun the crowd muttered and shifted uncomfortably. Jormun glanced back, sensing that he was losing them, and wilted for a moment before gathering himself and turning back to face Teppo.

"They're here to do their duty," he shouted shrilly. "Everyone knows you've been strange since Kirsi died.

After what I saw, maybe folks are starting to wonder how exactly she did die."

Teppo roared and jabbed with his axe, smashing the butt of the axe into Jormun's gut. The air wooshed out of his lungs and he doubled over. Teppo kicked out, planting his boot in Jormun's chest and sending the smaller man sprawling into the dirt. Teppo snarled and strode forward, axe lifted, to stand over Jormun.

"How dare you come on my land and speak about my wife. You can accuse me of witchcraft, or square dancing, or any other fool thing you please, but if you bring Kirsi into this, I will kill you."

A stunned silence fell over the crowd, broken only by Jormun's panicked whimpers. A stirring came at the back of the crowd and a deep voice boomed out, "Now then, now then, make way there. Let an old man through."

The mass parted, and a squat, barrel-chested man in a coarse, black cassock pushed his way to the front. He spared a glance, taking in Teppo, Jormun, and the raised axe in an instant. He turned around to face the villagers and waved his arms for silence.

"Go on home, friends," he shouted. "There's no need for a mob. I will take care of this."

They lingered for a moment longer, reluctant to leave, but the priest glared and clapped his hands together and the mob drifted apart, dispersing back to their homes.

"And you," the priest said, casting his gaze down at Jormun. "Get yourself on back home before there's real trouble here."

"Father Armas," Jormun stuttered. "This man has been consorting with evil spirits. I saw it myself."

"Then you should have come to me," Armas said, leveling a finger at Jormun. "Witchcraft is the domain of the Church, not a matter for mobs. Go home, fool, or I'll have you doing penance until the new year."

Jormun scrambled to his feet and beat an undignified

retreat down the lane. Armas stared after him until he was gone.

"Imbecile," he muttered under his breath, spitting in the dirt. The priest sighed and turned around, crossing his arms over his chest. "Well, Teppo. What is all this foolishness about?"

"It's a mistake," Teppo replied. He turned and strode back to his porch, leaning the axe against the railing. "I was playing my flute for the snails when Jormun happened by. He accused the snails of being demon possessed and ran off."

Armas stared at Teppo for a long time without saying a word. Finally, he exhaled and uncrossed his arms, rubbing at the furrows in his forehead. "Playing your flute for the snails. Teppo, I took the position as priest to this parish because I wanted someplace quiet to finish my career. Someplace peaceful." He thrust his bony finger into Teppo's chest. "You and your flute are ruining my peace. I don't want to hear any more nonsense about demon snails or witchcraft—is that clear?"

"You have my word," Teppo said, bowing his head.

"Good," Armas grunted. "Keep your head down for a few days and mind your business. I'll try to talk some sense into that idiot Jormun. He's an excitable fellow, and the last thing we need is him getting folks all stirred up." Armas clapped Teppo on the shoulder and left without another word.

Teppo deflated as the tension of the moment passed. He reached for his flute and then thought better of it, setting it on the porch railing. Teppo sank down to the porch, burying his head in his hands, and took deep, shuddering breaths. What had he gotten himself into? He had nearly killed Jormun. He sat there until it was fully dark, and then finally took himself off to bed, leaving his flute behind.

The sound of a floorboard creaking jolted Teppo awake.

Torchlight filled his room, and he could dimly make out dark shapes crowding into his doorway. He opened his mouth to scream, but someone punched him in the jaw, snapping his mouth shut. He bit his tongue and groaned as the metallic taste of blood flooded his mouth. Rough hands grabbed him and dragged him from his bed.

Teppo struggled futility for a moment and then lunged, sinking his teeth into the hand of one of his captors. The man hollered and let go, snatching his hand out of reach. Teppo surged to his feet, flailing madly. He grabbed one of his attackers and shoved him forward, using him as a battering ram, and scattered the shadowy figures from his path. Something struck him across the back of his head; he staggered for a moment and then fell to his knees. A second blow drove him to the ground, and his vision blacked out.

Teppo rolled forward, blindly tangling himself in the legs of one of the assailants sending the man crashing down.

"Go," someone shouted. "Get out of here, quick."

Teppo pushed himself up and forced his eyes open. His head swam, and he retched, fighting down bile. Flames cracked from a falling torch, spreading quickly across the floor and up the walls. Smoke filled the room. Teppo coughed and stumbled out of his room, feeling his way through the house. He half fell through the front door and tumbled down the steps.

He wiped blood from his face and stared around wildly. His home and garden were engulfed in flames. Smoke hung in the air, searing his lungs.

"Help," he cried out. "Somebody help!"

Something slammed into him from behind, and his legs flew out from under him. His axe hit the ground in front of his face; blood splattered on the butt. He heard feet pounding on the dirt and shouts that quickly faded into the night. He tried to rise, but his body refused to obey him, and he slipped blissfully into unconsciousness.

When Teppo came to, it was nearly morning and the horizon was just beginning to lighten. He groaned and pushed himself to his feet. His head exploded with pain, and he reached around, probing with his fingers. His hand came away sticky with blood. Smoke drifted lazily through the air, making his eyes sting. He coughed and looked around, taking in the damage.

He walked woodenly toward the house, unable to believe what he was seeing. The home he had built with his own hands was little more than a blackened husk. All of their memories destroyed in an instant.

His feet knocked against something, and he glanced down, staring for a moment. It was his flute. Teppo bent down and picked the instrument up, brushing the dirt off it. It was blackened from smoke but otherwise seemed unharmed. He lifted it to his lips and tried a few notes. Miraculously it still worked. Teppo sank to the ground before the ruins of his home and began to play. Next to him, a soft voice rose in song.

Teppo stopped and looked down, unable to believe his eyes. A single snail perched on a rock next to him, facing toward the east and singing expectantly. Teppo smiled as tears ran down his face, and he lifted his flute again.

Together, Teppo and the snail sat before the ruins of his home and played and sang as the sun rose above the horizon.

THE VAMPIRE

Madelin Pickett

"From what I could tell he was a vampire. The way he hated being in the sun, his pale skin, even his incisor teeth were really pointy. I'm not sure where I went wrong." I inhaled deeply, images flashing through my head of the previous month, trying to find the exact moment I screwed up.

The only friend I made would probably never talk to me again.

"So, start from the beginning."

And I did.

It was late September in Florida, which meant we were still in the heat of the summer when Derek started Beechworth High, but I remember watching him as he stepped out of his black convertible wearing long black jeans and a black leather jacket. He wore dark sunglasses to shade his eyes. His pale skin stood out against his black clothing.

But what caught my attention most was that he was speaking to *me*.

I'd been cast aside as the school laughing stock, always lugging around encyclopedias of vampire lore. I'm not sure when or why my obsession started, but it did.

I guess that's why I'm here talking to a shrink.

Anyway, here he was asking me for directions to the office.

"Do you know how I can get to the office from here?" He asked, squinting through his sunglasses. The sun in Florida was intolerable, but if you've lived here long enough you can get by without wearing sunglasses or squinting, which was my first clue.

"I can show you." I said. He could have found it himself, but this gave me an excuse to question the new kid, the new guy that was willing to approach me. I lead the way through the double doors of Beechworth High. "First day?"

"How could you tell?" He grinned his pointy teeth at me. In that moment I immediately thought 'vampire.' All those years reading novels, studying myths and legends, and, finally, here was an actual vampire.

I've met a few people in my life with pointy incisor teeth, but his could break skin; his could draw blood.

I could feel my heart leap with excitement. A normal human might be scared, but I felt as if I was on the brink of a discovery.

As if this world I lived in was capable of being more than ordinary.

"Your attempt at hiding from the sun?" I joked as I gestured toward his ensemble and hoped he would get that I knew his secret and was on his side.

"Yeah, I burn easily." He rolled his eyes. "I tried talking my parents into moving somewhere with less sun, but Florida was it."

"It can't be that bad." I said, hoping to gain his trust and possibly his friendship.

"I seriously can't be out in the sun longer than fifteen minutes without burning." He gritted through his teeth.

My eyes went wide. I checked off another mental tick by 'can't be out in the sun.'

"Well, we are here." I stopped in front of a wall of glass that peered into the front office. "I'm Donna."

"Derek." He took my hand. I let out a small gasp. "Yeah. Sorry about that, my parents believe I have some sort of medical condition that prevents me from being warm."

An excuse.

I pulled my hand from his grip, slipping it into my pocket hoping to regain the warmth that was stolen from it.

"I know this might seem odd, but would you like to come over to dinner tonight?" I nibbled on the hanging skin from my lip. I was nervous. Here I was asking a vampire to dinner.

To him it could sound like I was offering myself as his dinner.

"Sure." He replied before disappearing into the office. I couldn't help but stare after him with a ridiculous grin on my face. There before me had stood a real, live vampire.

"So you're telling me you really thought he was a vampire." A woman sat in a chair across from me as I lay on the couch retailing every moment I could possibly remember from last month.

"The signs were all there," I stated flatly, still holding on to the idea that he was a vampire.

"But you know it's just a myth."

"There a lot of things that people believe that others don't, does it make it not real?"

"That is true. But do you think if vampires existed we wouldn't know about them?" The woman waited for my response.

"Not if they were killed."

"So, you still believe this fabrication you've latched onto?"

I nodded hesitantly. How was I supposed to change my mind?

I haven't seen Derek since that night. No one has told me whether or not he was okay, which to me meant he was more than okay.

I'm here to tell my side of the story, even if some therapist doesn't believe me.

"He came over for dinner that night, " I explained.

opened the door after smoothing out my dress. I'd never had a guest over, and my nerves were fried.

I opted for something more formal but felt silly after seeing Derek standing on my front porch wearing the same clothes he wore to school.

"Thank you for coming, Derek." I didn't think he would show. Surely by now he's heard the school rumors calling me a freak; its enough to steer the whole student body away from me.

"Aren't you going to invite me in?" He looked at me questioningly.

"Of course. Come on in." Derek took one step in and made it past the threshold.

I felt my smile go even bigger: *Asked permission to come in? Check.*

"You must be Derek!" My mom exclaimed, stepping out from the kitchen and holding her hand out. Derek took it. "Cold?"

"My body temperature is below average." He replied.

"Well my husband is making steak, how would you like yours cooked?" She asked, looking between the two of us.

I don't think my parents had believed me when I told them I invited a friend over.

He laughed. "As rare as you can make it."

"You and my husband like the taste of blood." My mom shook her head in disgust as she headed out onto the back porch.

"Can I get you something to drink?" I wanted to come out and ask him right away, but I needed to wait. I needed Derek to believe he could trust me with his secret.

"Water is fine." He took a seat at one of the bar stools.

I pushed the cup across the counter, letting our fingers graze carefully. I could feel my heart trying to take all this information in.

"Where are you from?" I asked.

"My mom's from Ireland; my dad's from Russia. They both moved here when they were young. They met, married, and here I am." He looked around the kitchen, taking in the various oddities that hung around the house. Like cartoon pictures of teeth because my dad's a dentist, or figurines of mythical creatures because Mom and I both love things of fantasy. And here is one standing directly in front of me.

I followed his eyes to a particular figurine.

"You like?" I asked.

"I saw you carrying around books earlier. Is there a reason you like vampires?"

"What's not to like about them?" I smiled brightly at him. "They hide in the night, can go anywhere in the world, and they live forever."

"Would you truly like to live forever?"

"Yes." I might've replied a little to quickly.

"I wouldn't."

The rest of the evening went on as normal as you could make it. Derek was polite to my parents. I watched as he slurped down his bloody steak, and as soon as he left the threshold I ran up to my room to jot everything down.

"So you kept tabs on Derek."

I nodded in reply to the lady. What scientist wouldn't?

"My dad's a dentist, he takes notes on all his patients, and my mom works at a lab. So, I guess I'm trained to take notes." I explained, sitting up and facing the lady. "You think I'm insane, don't you?"

"I do not." That's all she said as she continued to write in her tablet.

"See, you take notes as well." I pointed out. She looked at me briefly before looking back down at what she had

The Vampire - 137

written.

"Tell me, Donna. At what point did you think what you were doing was crossing a line?"

Now she was asking the tough questions. Because if I'm being honest, and I am, it was the night I harmed Derek.

"Your secret is safe with me!" My voice echoed through the night.

I was growing too impatient. A month of keeping a journal of his characteristics, giving him my trust, and yet he still stood in front of me confused. What would it take to get him to tell me his secret?

Derek and I were standing on the street. I couldn't wait another moment for him to admit it all to me, so I just blurted it out.

"What are you talking about?" He was still keeping up his façade.

"I know you are a vampire."

There. I said it. I shouted it to a couple of streets over and back. No one was out this late, but here we were alone on the street with houses decorated for halloween.

"You're serious aren't you?" He looked bewildered, as if he didn't know who I was anymore. "I'm your friend, Donna."

"Which is why you can tell me." I pleaded.

"I have nothing to tell." He started walking home. "When people at school told me you were weird, I didn't listen. Maybe I should have."

"Derek, please."

I could feel the grasp of this thing slipping away. I followed him for a few steps, gripping a wooden stake Derek hadn't noticed, long as a railroad spike and sharp as a pencil.

"If you weren't a vampire, then I wouldn't be able to do this!" I lunged forward, with his back toward me he didn't see it coming. I stabbed my weapon into his back—but not where his heart was. I didn't want to kill him.

I just wanted to prove to him that I could be trusted and that I wouldn't stop until he told me the truth.

But as blood poured from the hole, I could feel the doubt rise up in my throat.

His blood drenched my hands. I stepped backwards pulling the stake out. He would heal.

Derek cried out in pain. His scream pierced the night that was turning colder by the second.

"What the hell?" He looked back at me, and I could see the tears soaking his face as he tried to crawl away from me, falling in pain with every movement.

"Y-you should start healing soon." I stammered.

"Stay…just stay the hell away from me!" Derek had fear written all over his face as he hobbled away from me.

"Please, Derek." I begged, wanting to prove this wasn't for nothing.

"Help!" Derek cried out in pain as he ran from me now. "Get away from me!" He fumbled for his phone in his pocket and quickly dialed the police.

I looked around frantically as porch lights started to turn on.

"Derek, please. Just show me, tell me." I could feel my heart kick into overdrive as he talked to the operator on the other line.

I stood in the poorly lit street, watching as Derek waited far away from me, cringing in pain.

I could now hear sirens in the distance.

My feet were cemented in with the road, not letting me move.

Derek collapsed from the pain, blood pooling around him.

Derek wasn't a vampire, and reality was setting in.

Seconds passed and nothing healed. Minutes passed and ambulances were whisking him away as I was being loaded into the back of a cop car, tears rolling down my face.

I rocked back and forth, questioning where I went wrong.

"You're not sure where you went wrong?"

"I shouldn't have stabbed an innocent boy." I shrugged. "But you're telling me if you saw all the signs of a vampire, you wouldn't have tried to unveil it somehow?"

"Donna. You have a hard time distinguishing between reality and fantasy. Which is why I've decided we are going to hold you for a few days." She shut her tablet, stood up from her chair, and walked toward her desk.

She buzzed in doctors.

They took me away from her and put me in a room.

For the first time ever, I was alone.

That night I stayed awake, trying to convince myself what I saw this past month wasn't real, that I made it all up in my head.

As I rocked back and forth on the thin mattress that was to be my bed for the next couple of days, I heard my door creak open.

"Derek?" I called out to the figure standing in front of me.

A wide grin spread across his face as he stepped out from the shadows.

"But how?" I saw him bleeding. I saw the open wound. I saw the ambulance take him away.

"Not everything you read is accurate." He laughed. "It takes us more than a few minutes to heal."

"Are you here to kill me?"

"No, dear. I'm here to drive you further into insanity."

He vanished before me, and I felt two pricks in my neck. "Girls taste better when they are crazy."

AN
INCONSEQUENTIAL
MISCALCULATION

E. S. Murillo

No one was certain where the Seers had come from, or why they had chosen these four cities to cheerfully lay to waste over the years. They claimed there was a girl (as these things go), that she was missing, and that they wanted her. What they wanted her for they were never clear on, but after the first city unceremoniously blew up, the last three took notice.

The four cities on four hills had been settled during darker ages, but managed to live near one another in peace since as far back as the proverbial stories went. Travel between them was common and word spread. The curse had been clear to each: Give her to us, or else.

North had the least warning, and had taken the threat the least seriously. The Seers arrived in North at midnight, sometime in the late fall, and asked to be taken to the city's finest alehouse. The guards had neglected to ask the obvious—and in retrospect, necessary—questions. For example, "How did four old men in robes climb a mountain in the dark with no discernible light source?" Or perhaps, "Say, that's a neat stick you're holding there. Why is the top smoking?" They had sent for the city's finest alcoholic (lawyer) who took it upon himself to parade the Seers down North's own version of The Row until they reached his favorite watering hole.

There were four Seers, each tasked with cursing a different city. North's doomsday declaration was given by the oldest-looking one. Grey-headed and gnarled, he, despite his advanced age, climbed on top of the bar with ease. He held his arms open wide, waved the aforementioned stick around, and declared that if the girl with the lavender eyes was not handed over to them within five years of this pronouncement, the city of North would be consumed by both fire from above and fire from below.

The men had started to snicker at the sight of Knobby Knees mounting the plank of wood and were incapacitated with laughter by the time the whole business with the lavender eyes and the unearthly fire came about. The people who settled the Four Hills had been a practical, no-nonsense group of travelers (Dutch), and if any of them had seen or known of magic in their old lives, they were careful to leave it behind. Magic had not been one of the crafts passed down by the families of North, and common sense had not been one of the virtues passed down to the patrons of the tavern. It was fortunate the Seers elected not to turn them into bar gnats on the spot; though, in the long run, North might have been better off for it.

The Seers were ushered out of the gates with the utmost decorum and spirits for the road. As they turned their backs to go, it occurred to one of the guards to ask how they might find them should a girl with lavender eyes turn up. Knobby Knees responded with, *"We'll* find *you,"* and, as anyone who has performed poorly on a job interview knows, this did not bode well for the townspeople.

Some effort was made in the beginning to find the girl with lavender eyes. Fliers were hung around town, and the census keepers teamed up with the opticians and spent a six-month period going door to door looking in the eyes of every woman in North. This was done mostly out of curiosity. By the second year the story had become tavern gossip, by the third it was relegated to the chatter of bored housewives, and by year four it had all but died. As late fall approached in the fifth year, however, the city found itself becoming restless, and people began to talk again about the Seers and their curse. A few of the more cautious families (actuaries, morticians) found pressing reasons to visit West for the month, but for the most part, the people of North stayed put and slept soundly.

They were never given the opportunity to be surprised by their fate. Five years to the morning after the Seers' pronouncement, the mountaintop previously hosting North dawned silent, and underneath about six feet of ash.

Needless to say, at midnight that evening, when the

city guards of South found themselves in possession of some old men in robes, the walk from the city gates to the requested tavern was a little more macabre.

The Seers decided to streamline the incineration process. South and East were both put on lockdown following their curses. The Seers warded the walls and the gates, and when their time was up, there were no survivors. South produced seven feet of ash—its city engineers having designed taller and more spacious buildings than in North—and East only four feet, as it had the fewest people. Each time, the city was given five years, and each time, the interval expired with no girl.

The night following the fires of East, the taverns in West were crammed full of people, and the city guards stood on high alert. The barkeeps had overstocked their wells, but they should not have bothered. The people of West would never again be as sober as they were that night, sandwiched two to a bar stool.

Weeks passed, and just as the city leaders began to unclench and the populace ramped back up to their usual level of intemperance, their unwelcome midnight visitors reemerged on the scene.

The leader of the Seers was the youngest by far. He might even have come into being within the current age. When he arrived at the gates, his weakened companions dragging behind, the captain of West's City Guard was the first to ask for his name.

"What should we call you?" he had ventured, while leading them down the dusty streets. The young Seer contemplated this for a moment.

"Mortals know me as...Steve?"

"...Steve..." the captain rubbed his chin. "Isn't that an Old Norse name?"

Steve nodded, pleased. "Sure."

This time there were notable changes to the party line. "Firstly," Steve intoned, "we know she's here. Secondly, we know she's being hidden. Thirdly, we're feeling generous, and we think with extra time you will see things our way. You have ten years."

The Seers would not accept any spirits for the road this time. They had actuaries of their own.

Jai sat slumped over the thick plank of wood while the person tasked with standing behind it and turning his thoughts into something a little more palatable wiped down the glasses.

"How do you fight fire and magic?" he mumbled into his arms, and the bartender patted him on the shoulder. The gesture was laden with affection—the bartender being intimately familiar with both the shoulder and the conversation, having maintained each for many years.

"I need you to drink some water."

"I need to figure out how to beat this curse."

"Man cannot live by liquor alone."

"Wrong curse."

Remy grinned at the top of his head. The situation was dire, but not so dire, she felt, as to warrant this level of melodrama. She turned back to continue cleaning the glassware and allow him more time to stew in his brain. The greens, blues, greys, and yellows in the glass bottles lined up on the shelves behind her twinkled in the setting sun; he sat up and watched their reflections flicker across the old wood, covering his hands and his scars and his drink in a rainbow of delicate colors.

Closing time was nearly upon him. The oil burning in the lamps smelled like springtime and purple, compounding the haze inside his head. Remy's tavern was the most popular on The Row for men who wanted to be alone with their demons (and were willing to wipe their boots on the metal grating outside). Comparisons of Remy to the girls in the favored oldest profession down The Row crept in through the cracks by way of jealous wives and owners of less lucrative taverns, but did little to affect her business. The tavern her father passed on to her came equipped with an anti-conflict system consisting of one boy next door and one silver wolf.

The boy—now a man, or something at least man-like, Jai felt—was sitting at the bar, and the silver wolf, who was known for dining on the bodies of Remy's more aggressive competitors, was curled up under his boots.

Drooling.

Remy peered over the bar at her fearless protector. "Aya does not seem too concerned about it."

"She'd be the only one, then."

Remy looked around at her near-empty tavern. She could sense the mood there and everywhere else in the city becoming heavier with each day that passed. The younger generation had little memory of the world before the curses began, so at the age of twenty-five, Remy was accustomed to the taste of city-wide grim indifference. In the midst of this bleak atmosphere, however, her father had passed down the family craft of boozy hospitality to his daughter.

At this particular moment in time, Jai had the entire bar top to himself. He killed his yellow drink and gave Aya a scratch behind her ear with the heel of his boot. She let out a big wolfy smile, and he tried not to think about the fact that she and Remy were the only ones left in the city smiling at him anymore.

Remy made last call just after sundown, and Jai locked up the tavern. Remy extinguished all the lamps but one. Reaching up to remove it from its place, she took it with her as she and Jai made their way to the back, where heavy double doors opened into the passageways leading to The Row houses. They left the tavern's scrubbed and polished wood for the dank, rat-infested tunnels behind it. Jai stifled a sigh and held his breath. If by some miracle the city made it to next year, rebuilding The Row passages needed to be the first thing they put their waning and wasted energy into.

The other folks who worked and lived on The Row shuffled past on the way to their chambers. City curfew—enacted after the curse to prevent the "for tomorrow we die" criminal types from getting carried away at the expense of the "for tomorrow we die" depressive types—meant the passages were full and difficult to navigate after dark.

Passersby gave the deep orange light of Remy's oil lamp a wide berth. Jai took her hand and led her through the crush and up the narrow stairs, while Aya brought up the rear. Jai didn't carry weapons; he didn't need to. His compatriots had long made a habit of staying out of his way.

The two of them often left much unsaid in the way people who have shared a bed long enough do. While Remy assembled the herbs for tea, Jai built a fire and sat down in the larger of the armchairs he had carved for her.

"Pick your poison."

"What do you have that will help see the future?"

"You know I'm out of those; they are out of season."

"The real future, Remy."

"Can't imagine why that would interest you, love."

He leaned his head back and chuckled at the ceiling. He knew before the kettle hit the flame that she had made him something for sleep.

Ten years prior, on the night the Seers arrived in West, Jai's father had charged him with guarding Remigius's tavern. Jaival, the Captain of the City Guard, had struck a deal with his buddy years earlier to allow Jai to exercise the family craft of being large and scary-looking in a less hazardous environment. It turned out to be a mutually beneficial arrangement—Remigius gained an extra set of muscles to preserve order, and, in exchange, Jaival didn't lose a whole lot of sleep over the well-being of his only son.

Jai stood in the tavern doorway every night as a tall, dark, and effective idiocy deterrent. His stature discouraged fighting, though he did throw out the occasional drunken farmer. On slower nights he played chess with the tavernkeeper's teen-aged daughter. By then, Remy had already become well known for drying, mixing, and selling herbs no one else could identify (much less put to use without her meticulous instructions), and Jai was well known for standing near her.

Several weeks after the two of them had watched East burn slowly to the ground from their rooftop, the townspeople of West felt able to breathe again, despite the amount of ash still permeating the air. But Jai was still on edge. Had he not been, it might have come as more of a shock when he looked down The Row from his spot in the doorway and saw people darting out of the dusty streets. If he were a lesser man, he might have choked on his fear at this development. But not Jai. When he saw his father leading the Seers toward Remigius's tavern—the sight of their robes colliding in his brain with the sound of Remy's triumphant laughter as she took his Queen—it was without a doubt the dust he choked on. Not the fear. Definitely not the fear, he told himself.

He turned to Remy because that was what instinct told him was necessary, but Aya was dragging her towards the passageways by her arm before he had time to curse. Men all over the tavern stopped what they were doing and listened to Remy's howls of frustration as they grew further and further away.

Remigius spat tobacco at the ground when she was finally out of earshot. "Don't move, son," he told Jai calmly as he reached under the bar for the old blade with no handle he had kept rusting there for the past fifteen years. He laid it across the wood in plain sight, and waited. Jai was no fortune teller, but he was getting the sense that things were about to get a bit dicey.

Remy's signature smirk appeared on her father's face as he looked at the young man. "And so it goes."

By the time the group reached the door, the whole tavern had gone silent. Remigius stood motionless behind his bar while his friend led the Seers inside. The two men faced each other for a long moment. One corner of Jaival's mouth turned up ever so slightly, sadly.

"They requested the finest alehouse."

Remigius had always had a taste for crazy women.

Not that there were not some great home-grown options available to him in West. The Dutch lineage boasted plenty of fair drinkers and live tempers among their female companionship; though one had to wade through a lot of broad shoulders and strong opinions on minutiae to find them.

An evening out, and then in, with a sorceress was more than he had planned to undertake, but it felt worth it at the time. She had liked his smile and he had liked the promise of a challenge. It would have remained the ultimate tale of bragging rights had he not, some ten months later, come home to find a baby rocking smack in the middle of a nursery that had not existed when he left for work that morning. Aya lay asleep under some type of rocking crib (the thing appeared to be moving itself, magic certainly afoot) looking full and pleased. Closer inspection revealed his lady friend had not bothered to use magic to get around his fearsome wolf beast; she had deposited fresh deer bones in a pile by the fireplace, and

Aya had found it in her best interests to look the other way.

Later he barely recalled almost breaking down Jaival's door in a blind panic. Jaival came at once to help make sense of the situation, and even brought his eight-year-old son to frolic with Aya through what remained of the bone pile. Amongst the cleanly picked cartilage, the boy found a bone shaped like a slingshot. He stood in the window and pretended to shoot the people walking down The Row, half listening to—and not caring at all about—the squeaks of the new baby in the new room. Aya was ever pleased to share her spoils with someone who was interested in creating weapons with them.

The men inspected the construct while the baby inspected the men. The nursery had four walls, a floor, a roof, and a window overlooking fields of Morning Glories where, architecturally speaking, no exterior window could have been and no Morning Glory fields existed. The baby had a pile of dark hair, a turned up nose, and grey eyes like her father. As soon as she opened them and looked at both men with something twinkling there, bordering closely upon entertainment, they knew who she was. Remigius made a strangled noise like a man who had just watched the rest of his life flash before his eyes—it contained quite a few more daisy chains than previously accounted for—and Jaival did what any true friend would do in this situation and had a good laugh at Remigius's expense.

Laughed quite a lot actually.

Remigius rather felt the laughing went on longer than necessary, given his distress.

He had not known what to do with this plot twist in his affairs. On the one hand, having a child to pass down his knowledge and livelihood to without the pesky hassle of a wife to deal with had a specific kind of appeal. On the other hand—

The nursery dweller stretched and blinked at him. She

smiled. Were babies that small even supposed to smile? He never did find out.

One thing he was sure of, however, was that he had known a woman with lavender eyes once. Well, not exactly a woman, but in all probability the woman the Seers were hunting for when they started burning down cities just as Remigius had made his peace with the prospect of the daisy chains.

Perhaps it was ungentlemanly of him not to suggest to the powers that were, or even to his best friend, that he might have an idea what all the histrionics were about, but Remigius had never desired to be a gentleman. It seemed practical to keep his mouth shut and hope for the best. Besides, he told himself at four a.m. when the blue stuff wasn't cutting it and doubt took over, he didn't have any idea where the sorceress was. Whatever the curse had to do with him, he suspected he was not going to like how it ultimately went down in the end. He was not wrong.

Jai slid his hand between her thighs in his usual manner. Remy was used to being awakened this way. The night air on The Row was stagnant, but the breeze blowing in her window off the sleeping Morning Glory fields cooled the room and made the hairs on her arms prickle. She opened her eyes, taking in the faint grey slope of his shoulders in the moonlight, black ink intertwining over the top of them, before drifting back to sleep to the sound of his rhythmic breathing. The world beyond the window smelled like rain, as it had so often in recent nights.

They took their coffee black. Jai had long wondered if the beans came from somewhere beyond their bedroom window rather than the adjoining hillsides, but, as he was unable to function without the caffeine in whatever earthly or unearthly form it came, he had opted not to question it. It was not until trade in and out of the city ceased with the pronouncement of the curse and he still had all the coffee he cared to drink that Remy confirmed his suspicions.

"Is this coffee?"

"Yes."

"Still?"

"Yes."

"I love you."

"You had better."

Jai left after breakfast to check in with his father at the Guard. Remy watched him pull on his boots—each worn thin in the middle from age and overuse—first the left, then the right. His movements were more familiar to her than her own.

She took this time in the mornings to drink her second carafe of coffee downstairs in the tavern and to water her domesticated plants before the shutters were opened and the spell was broken for the day. Few know that if you sit at a bar top just as the sun is rising you can get a sense for the mood of the city before it has fully awakened, but Remy was one of those people. If she paid attention, she could tell by the hum outside on The Row whether it was going to be a grey or a green drink kind of a day.

She was not used to finding company. The Seer startled her into dropping the carafe, glass and coffee exploding at her feet.

He stood with his back to the door and did not speak. Remy felt an irrational level of annoyance at the intrusion. The Seer pulled a small leather-bound file from some best-left-unknown fold in his robe, and she could tell each movement came with great effort. He checked the file and cleared his throat.

"Remy Aime. Local tavern keeper and resident...if I am reading this correctly, in your common tongue...'herb-alist...'" (here the Seer used air quotations, which were most unbecoming for a man of his apparent age). "Father dead, mother unknown." He raised an eyebrow at her. "Drug dealer? A strange use of near limitless power. To each their own, I suppose."

Remy could smell the coffee-soaked wood under her feet. It kept her from stooping to press her fingers on the broken glass, to verify she still stood in a world where she could bleed. The Seer rifled through the pages in his file until he found what he was looking for.

"You are married to the Captain of the Guard's son." He attempted to pull a smile. "Kind of cliché, don't you think?"

Remy knew he was trying to provoke her, but she had already heard every whisper and averted gaze in the city on this topic. She waited, arms folded, for him to either smite her or come to his point. Her hands were growing warm, and she wondered where her useless dog had gotten to. Behind him she could hear the city waking up at last and knew this morning it was leaning grey.

She did not like his face. Something lurking beneath it tipped his hand to his cruelty even before he did.

"Your mother's memories did not do you justice." He tilted his head. "We've come for you."

Remy lurched and the Seer's elderly leer widened.

"Were you not aware that this was your mother's land? There is magic on these hills no one knew of; it is what drew your father's people here without their knowledge or consent many lifetimes ago. The magic is in the land and transfers to those who dwell on it; strengthens the blood, strengthens the blood lines."

Remigius had never talked about her mother, aside from the occasional tired joke about Remy being the only woman in his life he could handle, but she was smart enough to guess she had not been a normal woman. Windows that lead to the tangled world she had been tromping through since she was a child were far from a standard amenity on The Row. Still—

Jai snapped the Seer's neck cleanly, and he crumpled to the floor. Jai did a little hop backwards and started laughing.

"You know I was only about thirty percent certain that was going to work." He grinned at Remy whose eyeroll threatened to snap her own neck. "Convenient that he stalled just long enough."

She murmured something about men feeling compelled to over-explain everything and leaned a hand on the bar to steady herself. She was in need of something decidedly blue to drink.

Jai poked the body with the toe of his boot as Aya sauntered through the door he had eased open a few critical moments before. She sniffed the Seer with delight. Magic bones were her favorite bones, and it had been too long since she'd indulged in them. Jai shooed her away, and she growled irritably as he bent to retrieve the leather file. Remy held out her hand, and he gave it to her, still prodding various parts of the Seer.

"I'm not going to lie, I expected him to melt. Or at least—"

Remy was no longer listening as she went through the papers in the file.

"He has everybody in the city in this." She recognized the names, descriptions of the people in West she had grown up with. Details about them she knew, details only she knew, and details she would like to have gone her entire life without knowing. Some of the pages had portraits affixed to them. Her father's face gazed back at her from beneath a collection of facts about him, and one fact in particular stood out.

She wrinkled her nose at the pile of beard and robes on the floor. Jai was studying the Seer's face. Aya was studying the Seer's shins.

"Is this the one?"

"I don't think so. The one that killed him was…much younger. Too much younger to have aged this way in ten years. But he is one of them."

"Where are the rest of them? The other three?"

"Close. They'll be close by. And the one…he'll be the most powerful." Jai scratched the back of his head. "The one coming for West. I think the others have used up a lot of their power already."

Remy looked back down at the portrait of her father. Jai laid his finger on it gently. "He drew blood on two of them before the one got him. I wouldn't have thought men like this should bleed so easily." He grimaced as Aya pulled the Seer off into a far corner of the bar. "Or fall, for that matter."

"You heard the part about the land?" He glanced up at her and back down at the file again. She ground her teeth. "You already knew about that."

"I didn't know for certain, but I guessed. It just stands to reason."

"None of this stands to reason, unless you are a madman."

"The land loves you," he said, to a spot just left of her shoulder. "Has to be a good reason for it."

"My mother's memories. How did they—" Remy did not know how to process a rage of this magnitude. "They could not have come for me…my eyes. They are not lavender."

A voice spoke from behind them. "An anomaly."

"For crying out loud," Jai muttered.

They turned, and Remy could see the three surviving Seers standing in The Row passages, just beyond the wide doorway in the back of the tavern. Seer Steve took a step forward.

"It was an embarrassing oversight," he remarked, inspecting the cleanliness of his fingernails in classic evil guy fashion. "The sorceress's eyes were lavender, and she had tampered with her own memories of the daughter's eyes. We took a gamble on the science of it. It would seem we are poor gamblers."

Jai spoke to Remy in a low voice, though he was sure it did not make a difference. "Are you burning your special incense in here again?"

"No. You're seeing what is really there."

The young Seer took another step, and then another. The other two remained in the passages, still unmoving. "Your way home is now blocked. You cannot get to the window leading out from all of this."

"In retrospect," Jai said, his tone amused, "we should have considered leaving through that window a long time ago."

If Remy could have elbowed him in his stomach without drawing undue attention to herself she would have. "There's nothing in that land but plants, and most of them hallucinogenic. It would not have been much of a life."

"Sounds like a great life considering the current alternative."

She made a face. "That's because you know nothing of plants. Too long in that world, and you would lose your mind."

Steve was only a few feet away from them now. He reached behind him and pulled out his staff; Jai recognized it from a decade earlier. The two older men followed suit from their spot rooted beyond the doorway.

"If only," he said carefully, "there were someone here with near limitless power to get us out of this."

"Mmm. That would be helpful."

Aya let out a low, mournful howl.

Remy sighed.

The passageways to The Row fell. Remy watched as the two Seers disappeared beneath the heavy beams, their staffs still in hand. Like the people of North, they died before the precariousness of their situation had a chance to set in.

"Those passages needed replacing anyway."

The force of the blast had knocked Steve to the ground. Jai had not seen Aya look so giddy in all the years they had known each other. He hauled the creature to his feet and kicked the staff away; it bounced off the far wall, and evaporated. He felt latent power within the Seer begin to bubble up through his fingertips, and he wrapped his arm around his neck more from force of habit than expectation of success.

"My dear..."

Remy had been processing the cacophony and the dust and the dog from a place that felt safe and far away. Jai's tone brought her back to the deeply unfortunate reality in which she now found herself.

"Stop," she stated.

The Seer stopped. It was clear to Jai it was against his will. In this regard, he felt for the guy.

"Speak."

The Seer made a vague face towards Jai's arm. Remy looked at her husband, who eased up just enough to allow him to find his voice.

"What would the lady wish me to say?"

"Explain yourself."

"It appears my associate—the one being consumed in the corner over there—" (Aya looked up briefly from her snack), "came before me and explained more than enough."

Jai started to smile, and Remy widened her eyes at him. As silent marital communication went, it was a smile that said: "Remember that neck I snapped earlier? I'm a man of many talents." Her answering stare might have been interpreted to mean either: "We can celebrate your many talents later this evening," or, possibly: "Now is not the time to be thinking about any of your talents, you infuriating man." Jai chose optimistically to believe it meant the former. The Seer began for the first time in many centuries to look uncomfortable.

"Why," Remy finally stated. "Why did you need this land?"

"You have been told why. Did you never wonder how the bloodlines strengthened people's natural gifts with each generation? That was not by chance; it was by design. Your mother's design. You were bred here, born here—exactly as she desired and planned—she left you on these hills so you would be more powerful than she was. Your mother wanted you to belong to the land, and you do."

"So why is this of value to you?"

The Seer's face transformed, his nondescript features twisting themselves into a grotesque smile. "Our number has diminished in recent ages. A new line of Seers was needed, and a line of Seers born on these hills, mingled with the bloodline of a sorceress's daughter? This world has not seen such a thing."

Jai came to some distasteful realizations around this time.

"You knew where I was from the beginning," Remy said. "You knew I was here. Why didn't you come straight to West?"

"We did not know your identity; your mother would not give you up. We thought with enough fear you might reveal yourself."

Her eyes darted to Jai and back to the Seer.

"You could have told...could have told the cities you were seeking my mother's daughter. My father knew who I was...Jai knew..."

Steve shrugged, or did his best imitation of a shrug around Jai's brawny arm. "We suspected you were unaware of the extent of your powers, and we wanted to find you before you discovered them. Your father allowed three cities to burn and said nothing of his daughter. As for this man behind me: he would not have given you to us. He suspected you were the one we sought all these years, and yet contented himself to share your bed and drink your spirits."

Jai tightened his grip on Steve's windpipe just slightly. Still, he waited.

"The people of The Row would have handed me over. Their loyalties were not so strong."

Steve tried to laugh but lacked the necessary amount of air. "In less-ah...progressive parts of the countryside, those suspected of sorcery are burned alive or drowned. We were trying to avoid mass panic."

"You incinerated three cities."

"We were trying to avoid mass witch-burning panic."

Remy's hands began to tremble. Jai maintained his unflinching grip on the Seer's neck, and his eyes never left hers.

Steve coughed. "We could not risk you. Not for any-one."

"Would I not have saved myself?"

The Seer regarded her steadily. "Would you have known how?"

Remy's hands stilled themselves.

Jai had not intended to begin his day by getting melted Seer all over his good boots, but at this juncture that is precisely what occurred. Remy had not moved, not a twitch, not a flinch. He thought perhaps he had seen her eyes flash a brilliant purple the moment Steve became a gelatinous stain on the tavern floor, but he was not certain. Neither of them could have anticipated it at the time, but it would be years before Remy would be able to get Steve out of the woodwork.

Aya was displeased at this culmination of events. She began to whine, but one exasperated look from Remy cut her off. "Are there not enough bodies here to fill you up?" The question was punctuated by a feeble, waving Seer arm from beneath the rubble beyond the doorway. Aya pounced upon the arm in an indelicate, un-wolflike manner, and put it out of the last of its misery.

Remy had not moved from where she stood when the Seers first revealed themselves. Jai continued to watch her, then turned to look at the ruined passageways adjoining the tavern. Something about their destruction was out of keeping with the woman who flatly refused to crush small spiders. "Was anybody—"

"No one was hurt, besides the monsters," she responded. "No one else was inside them." He turned back to her with a question, and she looked up. Above them, in The Row houses, they could hear the anger and confusion of those opening their doors to find they led to nothing but open air. "I don't know why the passageways were empty, but I knew that they were," she said.

She contemplated the act of moving her feet, perhaps stepping behind her bar to find a potent combination of colors to soften the situation, but it all seemed like too much effort.

Jai walked over to her, touched her hand, and said something that made her laugh.

They left Aya to enjoy her brunch.

She filtered down and through the boy's dreams like smoke falling from the end of his father's cigar. Tonight they were sitting on a rotting log in the woods at the edge of a large black pond. Blue Lotus floated across the pond's surface and black-green moss created a canopy that concealed them. In his mind, there was nothing beyond the pond but fog. The boy used his slingshot to skip small rocks the woman would hand him across the pond's glassy surface as they continued a conversation they had been having for many years.

"Remember boy. Keep her close."

"She's just a little baby. I don't see what the big deal is."

The woman with the lavender eyes smiled and handed him a smooth grey stone in the shape of a raindrop.

"You will."

THUNDERMOON
BRIDE

Sarah Bale

The door groans as I open it. I slip through, scraping my skin on the rough wood. I'm not supposed to be here. No, I should be locked away in the tallest tower of this castle, where dragons keep watch over every move I make. If caught, I face death. Or worse, and believe me, I know what that means. But, I can't help myself. I have to see him.

No one is about as I follow dark hallways designed to confuse. This palace is a den of secrets, and the King will do whatever it takes to keep them behind the palace doors. And I might be the biggest secret of all.

My breath comes out in short puffs; my heartbeat is equally erratic. I'm so close to the main door. The Thunder Moon bathes everything an eerie pink glow. I must act tonight. This is what the prophecy speaks of, and I've ignored the signs for too long. Reaching the door, I open it and step into the empty courtyard. It's too quiet. My skin prickles as the moon beckons me onward. My people have always looked to the sky for guidance, and I pray for protection on this night.

I pass not a single soul, making it to the trail that leads to the woods. We've always been warned not to go down this path after the sun has set. There are beings who live here that thrive on innocent souls. But, I am not innocent. Not since I gave my heart to the Night Prince. The creatures in the woods should fear me. Men should fear me.

The gravel cackles beneath my slippered feet as I walk further into the darkness. But I'm not worried now that I've escaped the palace.

And then I hear him—my love—far in the distance, calling for me. Yearning for me. Dying for me.

I rush forward, right into a trap. Guards grab me, and I can't escape their iron hold. *No!*

The King steps from the shadows, a gleam in his eyes. "You thought you could leave me? That I would allow this?"

My skin crawls as he tries to use his filthy magic to regain control of me. It snakes around my ankles, burning my skin. I've given in before—to stop the pain—but the moonlight gives me strength.

I square my shoulders. "Where is he?"

"You dare ask where that monster is in the presence of your King?"

I ask, "What have you done to him?"

The King laughs, but there is no joy in it. "The Night Prince is no more, slain by my own hand."

No! I would know if he was gone. I would feel it!

The King motions a guard forward. In his hand, he holds the severed head of my beloved. A cry works its way up my throat, but I refuse to let these beasts see my sorrow. "I will look past this incident, Diana, and let you back into my bed. Consider it a gift before our wedding."

Something inside me cracks and breaks. This is not how my tale ends.

"I will never become your wife."

He leans forward, sour breath hitting my face. "I plucked you from the gutters and saved you from the dark death, you ungrateful wench. I am showing you mercy and will make you my queen. You have no choice in this matter."

But there is always a choice.

I summon the magic that lives deep inside my soul. My people have always been blessed by the Goddess Selene. Tonight, under her moon, I will finally become a Priestess of her court. He rages as I pull away, too powerful to be controlled. The air swirls purple and blue, cutting the dark chains that bound my soul to this earth.

As I rise, I see the spirit of my Night Prince. He lingers in the shadows, Hades at his side. This is where I must make a choice. Do I ask the God of the Underworld to spare him, or do I let him go, where he will finally be free?

Hades bows his head at me. "Little one, this is not a choice you have to make. Your Goddess has chosen for you."

My love fades away, drifting toward the west. This is the will of my Goddess, but I cannot deny the ache in my chest. I rise high into the sky until I see her. She is even more beautiful than I imagined.

"You have served me well, child," she says, "and you never lost faith in me. For that I give you this gift. No man will harm you again, and you will be loved my many."

It is not the love of others that I want.

My gaze drifts to the west. "But my beloved—"

She smiles. "Trust in me, Diana. All will be as it should."

She is gone in the blink of an eye. For a moment I am lost. And then I see him, my Night Prince now bathed in light. He rises in the east, the sun at his feet. I rise, too, the moon at my heels. In that moment, I know my destiny.

We will always be together, my beloved and I. If you care to find us, just look to the sky.

TAVERNFALL

Ryan Swindoll

D*ear Reverend Scholar Godfrey, Dean of Oxford,*

I shall come straight to the point, which is a challenge for me, as I am prone to endless elaboration through the conjunction of a great many thoughts that swirl about my head at all hours of the day and night, probably induced by the unfortunate choices of my youth, for which I live in a state of considerable regret and from which I hope also for salvation: I need a job.

Not just any job; I would apprentice myself to your speculative and fantastical histories department. For I hear that your deanery possesses a unique collection of Saxon myth that deserves, in our Norman day and age, the most strict and humble protection.

I am uniquely qualified, you will see, for I have made my life's study our lately repressed histories, and in fact, I have first-hand experience with those things most uncommon. Thus, I enclose here a treatise of mine, for your eyes alone, which shall enlighten you to the purpose of my request for work. I trust you will read it and reread it diligently, for—and I do not mean to alarm you— the fate of the entire world may rest in your judgment.

Mr. Thomas Raen
November Anno Domini 1120

M AGICK and its invisible creatures, once accepted in the land of Saxony, are now commonly thought a gross FICTION of our world. Once a power impervious to principled investigation, now Magick is subjected to BURDEN OF PROOF. Once a noble profession, Magi are now called APOSTATE in our Norman churches. Once an aspiration of the young folk, Magick is now SLANDERED by the same. One used to hear the little children pray, "When I grow up, let me live nine hundred years like the faerie folk." Today, the same children insult one another wielding "faeries" as a moniker of cruelty.

Such is the destitution of Magick in our age. That within a span of two decades, Magick fell from veneration to obscurity, is due to its sudden and untimely demise in the events of **TAVERNFALL.**

On pain of inquisition by our Norman lords, I find myself compelled to speak against this, to make straight the public record. For my soul decries my guilt for Tavernfall, and also because I fear its related **CURSE:** that nine hundred years from now the time of Magick's banishment will cease and **BLABERT GALLOWSMATCH** will once again rue the human race "with sword and breath most foul."

Let me not belabour the point, but permit me once more to beat the proverbial horse. You must understand the machinations against me, horses be damned. For mere discussion of orks and faeries these days is liable to put one in the stocks for heresy against God and his Norman Pope. Ask any uneducated cleric and the consensus is that our fantastical histories are but allusions for ordinary things.

Take, for example, the **ORK** of Saxon lore. Normans say the ork is but a caricature of the Germanic barbarian that sacked the Holy City; their horned helmets representations of the perverse mind; their sandal-shod swine's feet an image of the trampling of the pearls. I argue, however, that the ork is real; their swine's feet really do pigeon nicely into sandals; and their known aversion to pearls completely breaks the analogue. When the barbarians sacked the Holy City, you will recall, they left the pearls but instead staged the burning of the library to mask a more devious plot: the pilfering of our magical tomes. This was the work not of human flesh and bone, but of orkish strength and cunning.

Again I say, the Normans wage war against the Saxon superordinary. **FAERIES,** they claim, are not tiny creatures, but mere metaphors for the temperamental humours that afflict us by the stars and the seasons, humours better left to Norman physicians and bloodletters. Nonsense. What they fail to account for is just how tiny faeries are. A breath of dust could conceal a veritable kingdom of faeries. For such is their tiny mission, playing mischief with our bodies in a window draught, or slipping our cellar keys from the sitting table to the gap beneath the chair. Even after Tavernfall, this type of magical trickery persists, indefatigable proof to the existence of faeries.

You must concede, then: the conspiracy is total; the threat to our public knowledge of Magick is real. Within a generation, the children of Saxony will deny all existence of magical creature, ork and faerie alike, and those like me who defend the true histories will be burned with their quills at the stake.

Lest the curse of Tavernfall come to pass, lest in nine hundred years our children's children's children (etcetera, etcetera) raise their fists and curse the heavens for our complacency when Blabert Gallowsmatch parts his war-mongering teeth, we must prevent this conspiracy. We must quench the Norman fires that lap at our precious remaining books.

We must gird ourselves with the **Truth.**

What is the Truth? First, that Magick and its creatures are real. Of this I have already persuaded you, no doubt, and thus I will only interject more examples when I deem them relevant to context. You will find them at the base of my pages in a form I have called "foot" notes.

Second, that the name of "Blabert Gallowsmatch and His Death Council" is not just the title of a lewd and igno-minious work of theatre—which it is—but also the name of an apocalyptic orkish power hellbent on the destruction of the good earth. Of this I have firsthand knowledge. The **Death Council,** hiding in their sunken hovels, wishes the total annihilation of the human race and the restoration of a barbarous ork society. Blabert Gallowsmatch, bane of breath, is their chosen warrior, a beast bred of infinite hatred and malice to destroy the world.

But few know this truth. For the play also called "Blabert Gallowsmatch and His Death Council" is a masterwork of pernicious evil: a mixture of fact and fiction, history and hearsay. A roving theatre troupe, vainglorious for fame, mocked the Saxon myth by putting it to artless play. One cannot cite the title in the public arena without eliciting a dirty chuckle. The troupe's arrest and execution by the Normans, I'll admit, was poetical.

Third, and last, that Tavernfall truly happened and how it happened, I shall demonstrate. Such is my misfortune that I am an actor in that tragic event that snuffed out the lives of faerie kingdoms innumerable, as well as a few human inebriates, which led also to my torturous **CAPTIVITY** and Magick's **BANISHMENT** from the mortal realm. Such is my cross to bear. You shall know all and everything. And should my testimony lead to an appointment in your office, we may yet save our mortal progeny from Tavernfall's most foul curse.

Let us then begin. Much of what has been written about Blabert Gallowsmatch has kindled a good many heretics who still speak of his return. It is of little importance, for those writings badly erred in factuality.

I shall begin with Blabert's birth, and its consequence, which was dramatized in the infamous play earlier mentioned. The troupe who twisted the truth of the orkish legend at least had the dignity to stop absurdly short of realism.[1]

---

1 Let the reader understand: I shall untangle the knot of truth within the play. Falsehoods abound. I suspect this is due to how the troupe always

Snerv reclines in the bed with child. Enter Throk.

THROK: Snerv, my proud wife, dost thou hold the orkish pupa of mine loins?

SNERV: Throk, you foul piglet. Who said you could enter my birthing chamber?

THROK: That pupa is mine by paternal right, according to Gallows Clan custom and law. Thou shalt render him unto me.

SNERV: You insult my intelligence with that drivel. The right granted me by the Smatch matriarchs overrules yours. And besides, I am his mother.

THROK: If thou meanst to imply that I am not his father, I shalt call thee a whore!

SNERV: Try it, and I shall beat you for the arrogant whelp that you are!

The scene continues thusly for many pages: **THROK** and **SNERV** holding the babe's swaddled birth sack, trading barbs. That Throk and Snerv hated each other is beyond dispute. They were son and daughter of dueling ork clans, a marriage conceived and arranged by the shadowy Death Council, meant to conceive the biological product of **GALLOWS CLAN** strength with **SMATCH CLAN** cunning. And, with the aid of some orkish mead on their wedding night, it did.

That Throk and Snerv gave birth to a **PUPA** is obvious equivocation on the part of the players, an ignorant jab at our racial incongruities. Few have studied the biologics of ork younglings, and their knowledge remains trapped inside their shrunken heads, serving as decoration for the youngling's cradle.

That Throk and Snerv spoke in the bawdy **ENGLISH**

improvised their scenes. And also how the only surviving scripts we have of their scenes were committed to quill by a hostile audience looking to report their heresy to the Normans.

of our day strains all credulity. Such are the more gross and unconscionable failings of the playwright's art. Yet, no doubt the improvised scene performed admirably with its Saxon audience: a crowd favorite for sure, exploiting the innate tension of the sexes.

I digress. The lesson comes when Death Councilor Hiccup enters the scene to record the naming of the child. You must understand that this child was the culmination of centuries of nefarious pedigree. Much depended on a good name. The Death Council, toiling unseen, had arranged countless ork marriages to produce keener stock. Every year the orks became more brutish, their marriages more hateful. This child was the pinnacle of strength and cunning meant to rule the world; a good name would solidify the child's ascension to power. A strong leader with a good name would mean marriages could go back to the lackadaisical fashion of coupling the orks had known before, in a simpler time. A good name like Roruk the Brawny, or Gadtheu the Glob Spitter.

> **HICCUP:** Hast the child raised his mighty fist? Hast he spoke his first words?
> **THROK:** Snerv clings the pupa too tightly. Mine son hast yet to breathe!
> **SNERV:** Shut your yap! He's wriggling right now.
> *The child emerges from the pupa.*
> **CHILD:** Bla—bert.
> *Hiccup gasps. Throk recoils.*
> **THROK:** What curse hast thou wrought, Snerv, that our child's name should be Blabert?

Indeed, the naming of orks is subject to much speculation, and this scene did little to dispel the baseless rumours. It does offer a rude approximation. The ork clans enforce a policy whereby the child's first words (upon transmogrifying from a birth sack) are taken for its name.

I can speak to this with accuracy, for reasons I will later disclose. While these conventions may seem to us absurd, in ork society self-naming represents the highest dignity of personage. A child self-named is guardian of his own destiny and will grow to surpass his parents in strength and in cunning.

> **Hiccup:** This will not do! The Council will be furious.
> **Snerv:** Damn your council of crooks and schemers! Blabert is uncommon, yes, but it has spunk. We can shorten it to Bert.
> **Throk:** That's worse! He wilt become the subject of much ridicule, called by his clanmates a sniveling human, no less!
> **Snerv:** Well, I'll not shorten it to Blab. Never met a Blab I liked.
> **Throk:** Councilman Hiccup, couldst we not simply name the child Throk and be done with it?
> **Hiccup:** I'm afraid… nothing can be done.

The play here is not strictly correct. I participated in some scholarly debate years ago on the subject of orkish names with a colleague who has since passed into the fire. We agreed that your average **Grok** and **Blog,** run-of-the-mill as ork names go, are almost certainly sounds an ork child would make upon ceasing the pupa. The child, you see, must cough up the fluid, which produces that guttural inflection so commonplace amongst the names. But we disagreed on the authenticity of other popular names: **Throk,** for instance, is not uncommon in the ork world, but the pronunciation of "thraww" with its oral nuance is not possible for an ork newborn, as the cleft has not yet hardened. Orks named Throk, I argued to the last, had their names embellished upon by their parents, perhaps to make the younglings seem more advanced. Careful inspection of an ork's name can usually determine its veracity. **SNERV,** for example, likely a sneeze. **HICCUP,** a twitch of the diaphragm. The legendary ork strategist, **GODSLAVER**, clearly an invention. The bane of Old Stratford, **GOOGOO-GOOGOO THE DESTROYER,** very likely authentic.

nd so Blabert Gallowsmatch received his unholy christening. Hiccup returned with tidings to the Death Council, who, fresh off the challenge of coupling the two warring tribes, now faced the obstacle of making said tribes obey their unfortunately-named offspring. But the Death Council was nothing if not patient.

Still, they resumed their regime of arranged marriages in case Blabert didn't work out.

As one can imagine, Blabert failed to excel socially amongst his peers. Neither the Gallows Clan nor the Smatch Clan embraced him, and Blabert endured a lonely childhood. He passed the time with books scoured from the human world; the Death Council used his isolation as a means to train him in the literacy of Magicks. What Blabert's name lacked in ambition, he compensated for as he overcame constant mockery and scorn. Blabert's name, curious as it may seem, made him what he would become: a brooding monster with a wicked pit of gastronomical anxiety. By the time Blabert's halitosis reared its ugly head at the cusp of maturation, he was universally feared amongst the orks. All that remained was Blabert's ascension to power.

Permit me here one calculated digression. You will recall the **SIEGE OF MADRID** in 1082 and the fall of that magnificent city to unknown barbarian marauders. As those who survived the siege attest today, the barbarians wore horned helmets and had the look "of one who had been at sea too long." Arguably this refers to the mauve pigment in their skin. The marauders poisoned the water supply and thus gained control of the city; Madrid was sacked and burned. The siege bears the infamy of bankrupting the Spanish government, which had relocated the treasury to Madrid in 1078. Those hapless Spaniards lost every last golden ducat to the marauders.

But what if I told you the raid of the treasury was a ruse, meant to distract the living from the real purpose of the siege? You will recall that the Spanish monks, slaughtered senselessly in their subterranean catacombs, never lived to tell their side of the story. For their monastery housed a secret vault: inside the vault, a secret collection of books and relics rescued from the Holy City before its inevitable fall; the most secret relic, the last of the seven **FAERIE BOOKS OF POWER.** Long had the Death Council pursued these tomes. With the acquisition in Madrid, their collection was complete. For those who held the Faerie Books of Power wielded the unspeakable fulcrums of Magick.[2]

Now the Death Council, seeing Blabert's potential to become the orkish conqueror they had always hoped for, gave him the seven Books on his fourteenth birthday. Because what better than the strongest, most cunning ork

---

2 Permit me one further digression, for the skeptical reader shall not abide such a claim without proof. Let me furnish your mind. As you know, all things animate and inanimate move in accordance with their inward spirit. The heavier the spirit, the more they cling to the earth from which they came. And Magick is the circumvention of that spirit. Magick may make an earthy spirit fly or a windy spirit plummet, turn a fiery spirit to ice or burst a watery spirit in flame. For years the Magi have used subtle incantations to manipulate the spirits of things, but the mechanism of this power eluded even the very wisest amongst them. One theory likened Magick to sunlight: a rarefied fluid aether imbuing the world with an invisible force. But this theory was roundly disproved by the discovery of the seven Faerie Books of Power. For when the Magi looked closely at the books, that is, peering through a lens of glass that made large the sight of its onlooker, they observed living in the pulp of every page innumerable creatures: tiny, black, leaping with sudden ferocity, and flitting with power unknown. All seven Books housed these fantastical creatures. Faeries, the Magi called them. And thus the nature of Magick revealed itself: it was tiny faeries all along.

in history becoming also the most imbued with Magick? When Blabert opened the dread Books, he became keenly awakened to a change wrought upon his body, **THE ITCH,** a harbinger of his burgeoning immortality, and he would routinely scratch as a testament to this fact. From that day forward, every ork he touched felt in his body a transfer of this power, as they too experienced the spreading tingle of **FAERIE ENERGY.**

Within a week, Blabert had mobilized a foul army. Within a month, he had unified the orklands. Within a year, he had conquered greater Europe. No human or ork dared stand before the young warlord; the heartiest man amongst us would faint before his gassy bellow.

Then came the day the orkish army advanced upon our good land of Saxony. I was a younger lad then, blissfully unaware of events on the continent. That fateful morning, the celestial bodies aligned and the sky darkened unnaturally; so dark, I slept through the entire day. But my friends tell me it was a day long remembered. Townsfolk flocked to the Norman cathedral to pray—to ask for God's deliverance—for though no one had yet seen the advancing army as it pushed out across the channel, they could tell in the air the **APOCALYPSE** was nigh. An awful growl in the breeze. The waft of death itself.

I must pause and reaffirm my purpose here. Blabert did not bring about the Apocalypse in the year of our Lord 1100, even though so many doomongers predicted the world's end with the century's turn. As a man of faith, I must think God a being of great mercy; he, having heard our prayers in that Norman sacrilege of a church, yet forestalled Saxony from its eminent demise. Forestalled, not saved. For though the wind that day blew ever stronger and more cunning, the smell lingers to this day.

I learned later that the waters of the channel had swelled upon Blabert's boat. The warrior-poet dropped his Faerie Book, and when he bent to retrieve it, slipped headlong into the sea. The Death Council panicked. The orkish armies clung to their rafts, halfway to Saxony, and when Blabert did not surface, they bickered over who was to don the mantle of his autocracy. The squabble ignited the **ORKISH TRIBAL WAR.** Their population on the continent plummeted. In the span of but a month, they numbered fewer than one thousand orkish souls.

The Death Council called a state of emergency and reconvened in their clandestine nooks.

HICCUP: What are we to make of this? Blabert is dead; our race nearly wiped off the earth!

FFFFPT: A travesssty. It isss thossse infernal Booksss.

LOLOL: They art certainly cursed. They brought only doom and pain and suffering on their own. Now we pay their heavy tax ourselves.

GODSLAVER: Gather 'round and hear my plot. We must return the Books to the humans, planting them where they least expect them. This will sabotage their fortunes, then we can stage a second and more successful invasion of Saxony.

HICCUP: It is decided. Surely some good may come of this yet.[3]

This brings me to Tavernfall. From here, dear reader, the events become fantastical, for Magick would soon enter its millennial sleep. Steel your soul for the unenviable

---

3 The excerpt of this meeting here is, I estimate, a fairly accurate representation. Few copies of the scene remain, however, as most of their audience by this time had fled the theatre square, or else fallen asleep.

Truth, for I shall give it to you in all its indigestible breadth and depth.

It begins like this: I was drunk. I fully admit it. I could say it was a consequence of my parentage; that my father never frequented church as he ought; that he poured himself into merchant toil; that he left his endowed coin purse loose for the occasional pilfer. He never noticed me anyway. I could say it was a consequence of the tavern's overly generous policy. The Hoof & Snout, they called it; I called it the **LITTLE PIGGY.** They served the most delicious moonshine to their most persistent patrons. O it tempted me more than I could bear. Fate is cruel. How could I have known what would come of my stupor? How could I have seen the Death Council crouching at the door?

At midnight, the regulars clung to the bar while I kept near the backdoor. My own little spot. I remember flicking beads of melting wax off the candlestick at my table. Then entered an imposing figure, black-cloaked, with a stocky gait that made me wonder if his pants were riding up. I sobered and squinted till he came into focus. He held under his arm a tome which he gently set upon the bar before turning to leave. I suppose I wanted to help. I snatched up the book and slurred, "Excushe me, lordships"—something shameful like that. I remember the fellow had a crooked jaw. He pressed his lips when I held the book out to him. They parted when I accidentally dropped it on the floor.

As a personal policy, when I am drunk, I do everything in my power not to call attention to myself. Especially at the Piggy, lest I fall out of favor with the night watch again. So at this moment, book on the floor, pages creased, I felt more than a bit foolish: akin to the feeling of suddenly falling off a trotting horse. I slunk to my seat and left the fellow to collect his book and be on his way.

Then, and I'm not pulling your hairshirt, he came and stood at my table, growling like he was tuning the

Doxology. He pressed the book on my lap. I remember the burgeoning itch. My crotch tingled like the devil; the pain was so intense, I knocked my elbow into my moonshine. It drenched the table bespeckled with candlewax. It doused the book, which, I would come to learn, was one of the seven Faerie Books of Power.

God. My shame never feels hotter but that I think of those tiny faeries bathing in a river of pure moonshine, losing their little minds.

Then the Piggy combusted spontaneously. I mean, the whole tavern was one minute serving drinks, and the next had dropped into the refuse fires of Hinnom's Vale. This was Tavernfall. Those little faeries: I think all the latent energies stored in their little faerie spires burst upon the room like a dragon's hot sneeze. Manic faeries. We were lit, all of us, and especially me. All the Magick in the world converged on me like lightning and threw up one final toast before the nine hundred year hangover. That was Tavernfall.

If only I'd died, the story could end.

When I woke, I was in a dark place. My head throbbed. My body felt numb and stiff. I was naked, swaddled in a black cloak. I reeked like pig slop. Something then probed my scalp. A knuckle, perhaps. What was it looking for? My eyes twitched. Nothing made sense.

When I woke the second time, it was still dark, but I had the distinct feeling time had passed. I laid on cold straw. The walls, stony and dark, featured only a barred window opening to the stars. I tried to move, but my body screamed with pain like it was Tavernfall all over again. I managed to bring my hand to my face, and that's when I learned how badly my skin had burned. The flesh felt hot, squeaked like black leather, and congealed like slick ooze.

When I woke the third time, morning light greeted my eyelids. A matronly figure sat in a rocking chair at my bedside, crocheting pigeon-toed socks. The musty scent of a charfire filled the simple cottage.

"Mother?" I may have said in my delirium.

"Call me Babu," I heard her reply, though her voice sounded manish, as if she'd been cursed from birth with a whooping cough. I tilted my head and waited until my eyes could assemble the scene. The matron smiled at me with two chiseled teeth that were certainly not human.

I started to sob.

"There, there, my son," she cooed like a foghorn. "You're home now. Safe now. I won't let them harm you."

I do admit to feeling strangely safe until that moment. Yet now a creeping unsettlement washed over me; and again when the matron bathed my pickled skin with a coat of herbal slime; and again when she sat me up to a breakfast of dried pill bugs drowned in sour goat's milk.

"Eat your breakfast. You need your strength."

I spoke to ease my nausea, "It's good to be home, Babu."

She broke into the most radiant gap-tooth grin. Seeing her happiness almost made it possible for me to stomach the horror of Tavernfall. The little blasted faeries. All those pill bugs bobbing in my bowl. I had yet to take a bite before the door burst open and a towering ork locked eyes with me.

"Is it true you've returned to us?" the ork barked over the raking coals of his voice. "Is it really you?"

The matron rose, slipped her hand around the other's waist. "It's true, Throk. He's home."

"I'm home," I rehearsed.

"That's Blabert's smile, just as it looked on the pupa," Throk (who was now my father) bellowed through his tears. "Would that I could embrace you, son, and slap your back with the fullness of my passion!"

"Would that you could."

"He's burned almost beyond recognition," said Snerv (who was now my Babu). "Not much is left of him in some places. Recovery will take months. He'll be fortunate to walk again."

"Then we'll count our blessings," said Throk huffing deeply. "Now to get the damn Council off our hides."

I go to great lengths here painting the scene because my CAPTIVITY WITH THE ORKS, which lasted a full Gregorian year to the day, has never before been dramatized by a theatre troupe, nor written down, nor ever breathed to another living mortal. You are the first to know it. Though the year proved most torturous for me, it also provided the ANSWERS we seek if the human race is to survive the curse of Tavernfall.

But first: I cannot abide falsehood, and that includes ignorance about orks. For you see, many unfounded rumours persist about orks and the way they endure a mortal life under the spheres. How are we to "love thine enemies" as commanded when we also assume the worst about them? On the matter of the PILL BUGS, many believe that orks maintain a slovenly home and eat grubs and insects because they know nothing of cleanliness. This is false. Should an ork roast a burger of meat and leave it upon the table until the maggots hatch, that is an improvement according to them—for there is more to eat. The ork digestion is considerably more advanced than that of their human counterparts, capable of such feats as devouring bones and shells and even the dirt itself in the most destitute of times. Rather than accost our mauve-skinned neighbors for their hardships, ought we not to praise them for their industry? Indeed, I did, and it's the only reason I'm still alive.

But the more damaging are public perceptions on the nature of ORK PARENTING, which suffers all manner of slander from the ill-educated amongst us. It is thought that because orks deliver babies via the birth sack, they take after the insects in disregard for the welfare of their young. This could not be further from the truth, as my captivity made plain to me. For I, too, held such unreflective beliefs until I became an adopted child of the Gallowsmatch Clan. I saw firsthand with what nurture and passion the orks feed their young. Never a minute went by but that I was offered a snack of sizzled spider legs or a gum grub chew. Unable to move and constantly eating, I got quite rotund in those early months.

Throk and Snerv, once proud and haughty personages of their respective tribes—forced into marriage and then thrust into parenthood—had been tempered by time and trial. The loss of their beloved genocidal Blabert shattered them. As all of ork society crumbled under the animosity of the Tribal War, they feared their marriage would succumb as well. Throk gazed at his grieving wife, the shrunken heads of her victims dangling from her temples like so many phylacteries; he realized how valuable her name had become to him. "Smatch," the sound a hatchet makes when it cleaves through the skull: truly Throk could swallow his pride and take her name with his own. And thusly their marriage remained resolute in the end. They became **Gallowsmatch.** When their kinsmen fought in the streets, they stepped upon the threshold with arms raised and hands enfolded, and together bellowed for the tribes to unite under their married name.

Thus the Tribal War ended. The wounds, however, never healed. Which is probably why, if I am to speculate, I was so easily mistook for the late warlord Blabert Gallowsmatch after my horrific burning at Tavernfall. Throk and Snerv were looking for a miracle. The day Hiccup returned to camp bearing me to judgment, the idiot who had destroyed a precious Faerie Book of Power, matriarch Snerv was quick to see resemblance in the charred features of my face. She looked past the missing horns, the pearly teeth, the mottled scabs and emaciated figure, and saw only the opportunity to love again.

Which brings me back to the Death Council and the final piece of this knotted yarn. When Hiccup returned to his colleagues of the cloak, singed by Tavernfall's flame, their immediate thought and earnest conviction was only to execute me.[4]

Thus, for the first six months of my captivity, as I grew fat on pocket worms and recovered my cheery gait, I evaded more murders than I have fingers and toes. I certainly don't withhold credit to God for the bliss that protected me in those anxious days, though I especially thank my surrogate mother for cleaving down the assassins that lunged for my throat. Nothing prefigured the wrath of God as pointedly as the crescent end of Babu's hatchet.

Eventually, to my relief, a new narrative supplanted the Death Council's edict of execution: that Tavernfall was not a misfortuned accident, but was instead a **SECOND COMING:** the Second Coming of Blabert Gallowsmatch.

It pained me dearly to continue under false pretenses, especially as I observed what great lengths the Death Council bent their theology to accommodate a Second Coming event. Truly, Metaphysics is not an ork's art. Hiccup, who tutored me the latter half of the year in the subjects of Magick and Death Theory, would explain their elaborate and lingering questions.

Was reincarnation made possible by the combustion of a Book of Power?

In a reincarnation event, did the spirit of the deceased

---

4 To comprehend: though the Death Council continued to debate where and how to dispense the remaining six Faerie Books, they considered the burning at Tavernfall a barbarous insult to their sovereign plans, an offense against centuries of collective plotting and scheming, undone by a human—and a drunk no less.

transfer wholly to the new body, or only in part? What happened to the spirit displaced by the reincarnated one?

Why did Blabert himself become reincarnate? Why not the soul of some other hapless ork?

Vexing questions, indeed. I, too, struggled to reason a meaning out of tragedy. I grew to accept my failed reincarnation as one of Magick's cruel and inscrutable mysteries.

Time skipped without incident until the first day of winter when orks take to **HIBERNATION.** I had stocked a few diversions to occupy myself through this lonely season, as I would be the only one awake. In my last tutorial with Hiccup, he appeared to me unusually withdrawn. I probed for answers until at last he confided a dark secret from the Death Council.

"There's talk of a Third Coming."

That's all he would tell me, but it started my thinking. The trajectory of the Death Council always tended toward **WORLD DOMINATION.** The first incarnation of Blabert had excelled so well at this. The purported reincarnation— that is, I myself—had his ambitions significantly lowered, such that the only thing on his mind right then was achieving a long run in solitary cards while his family slept through winter. The disparity between incarnations divided the Death Council into two theological parties: those that believed a **THIRD COMING** would correct the deficiency of ambition, and those that knew it would only make it worse. Both Hiccup and I were members of the latter party: staging a third coming would certainly make things worse. For I couldn't get my head around how they planned to engineer a Third Coming without knocking off the head of the Second Coming first.

As Snerv curled into her hibernation sack and Throk held her from behind, together they looked upon their son, eyes beaming with pride. I noticed how old Babu looked, how world-weary. When I bid them my fare-thee-well, they fell fast asleep, their gentle snoring wriggling in the night air. Then I doused the candle.

I would never again see my parents, never apologize for deceiving them so. But I could not dwell on the heartache of this. My enemies were waiting. Snerv could no longer protect me. I had to **Escape** and return to Saxony.

Hiccup had done me a final service to aid in my flight. He had tucked the remaining six Faerie Books of Power into my knapsack. Trembling now in the moonlight, I unsheathed one of the Books. I felt the tingle of immortality upon my hand and forearm. I struggled in the dark to decipher the Latin text, bending so near the page that the black faeries leapt onto my face. I whispered my confession, "It was me who killed your faerie brothers and sisters in the other Book. How can I ever make peace with your tiny kingdoms?"

I heard a quiet chorus, thin-pitched and singing from the Book. The faeries seemed most angry with me, biting my face and my hands. Faerie rage, tiny and true. I wept.

Then came the **Revelation of the Curse.** The faeries, seeing my abiding contrition, deemed me a vessel worthy to appraise the diminutive scales of their most poetic justice. Magick, they pronounced, was hereby banished for a faerie generation. Nine hundred years. No more would faeries serve the wielder of the Books. No more would faeries reincarnate the spirits of the dead. Until every last sprite who sings of Tavernfall perishes, Magick would hibernate.

Suddenly the tragic mysteries of my world made sense: why the Second Coming of Blabert Gallowsmatch had ultimately failed; why Throk and Snerv had lost a son not once, but twice; why the Death Council could not yet engineer Blabert's apocalyptic return; why, as I tried to incant the indecipherable Latin, nothing of magical happenstance occurred.

No dancing rock. No shooting star. We were **Post-Tavernfall.** I slipped the Faerie Book into my knapsack and made my fearful escape.

Thus I arrive at the culmination of my Truth. From that moment forward, my life's work became singular: Never again, I vowed, would the Faerie Books of Power fall into the grasping hands of the Death Council. For they surely know as I do that when Magick revives in nine hundred years, then they may revive their drowned champion. Should the Council steal back the Books, they would **Doom** us all.

The Council at my heels, I fled into the howling snowfall, wearing naught but the black linen they had wrapped upon me when I was first abducted. The bitter frost raked my flesh so that it bled again like it had after Tavernfall. But my only thought was to the keeping of my vow.

My body failed in a cornfield near Oxford, whereupon a farmer delivered my near-frozen corpse unto the local surgery. Saved, my relief proved short-lived, for the latch on my knapsack had broke in my flight. The Faerie Books of Power had tumbled out—God knows where.

Never have I touched a drop of liquor since Tavernfall. My daily penance is the constant anguish of knowing I may fail my vow. For all my years of searching, I have reaped not one sign of the Books. And Magick continues its daily forgottenment, with I as its last living advocate.

I pray the faeries made it, somehow, safely to your deanery of fantastical books. If they did, I should like the fortune to finish my sacred watch.

–Mr. Thomas Raen Gallowsmatch

To Mr. Thomas Raen, self-described as Gallowsmatch,

Your inquiry and treatise reached me at the most peculiar time. For when I opened your correspondence it had not been three days thence that our Master Tutor of Saxon Fantasies died of a sudden and heretofore yet unknown illness.

I had a generous mind when I began your treatise, ready to hire you on the spot if it proved even halfway sensible. But as I progressed through the literature, I became increasingly uncomfortable by its disturbed and perverse nature. While I share your enthusiasm for Saxon history and look favorably upon the mythologies of magick, ork and faerie, I cannot say I share your unbridled acceptance of their reality. You are fortunate I do not submit your superstitions to the authorities. The inquisitors are not as forgiving as I am.

I know not if you mock the venerated academy of Oxford with chicanery, or whether you are, as they say, "touched in the head;" however, I will not now, nor will I ever, allow you near our hallowed halls.

In short, do not ask for a position here again.

In case this reply does not dissuade you, I will also inform you that, as of this morning, the Saxon Fantasies department is closed. Given the loss of our only tutor and declining interest in the field, I auctioned our collection of books and antiquities to the highest bidder. Mercifully the collection sold quickly to a group of foreign tradesmen who purchased it for a princely sum of Spanish ducats. I know not what interest they have in the literature, but their generous payment assured me that the collection will remain in good keeping for a great many years to come.

The Reverend Godfrey, Dean of Oxford
December Anno Domini 1120

THE DOOR

Michael Hustead

"**N**obody ever mentioned the afterlife was so much work."

"My King?" Ini asked.

"Nothing," Tarik said, shrugging his shoulders. "I was thinking aloud."

"Of course, my King," Ini replied, bowing his head. "And the matter of last night's theft?"

Tarik scowled at the empty room, which had been full last night. All of the gold and jewels a king would need to secure his comfort in the afterlife had been stored here. In life, Tarik had been fabulously wealthy, and his treasure room had bulged with rare and wonderful things. Now it stood completely empty. Even the gilded tables and display pedestals had disappeared.

"The guards saw nothing?"

"No, my King," Ini replied. "But in their defense, the soldiers are here to help you protect the Door. No one thought to guard the treasure room. This is Paradise after all. There are no thieves."

"Paradise," Tarik grunted. "This is not Paradise. Paradise is supposed to be a place of rest and peace." He cast a final glance around the barren chamber and shook his head. "Very well, Ini. I want a second unit to patrol the corridors of the Palace in addition to the unit guarding the Door."

"Of course, my King," Ini bowed again. "But where will you be?"

"I am going to have a drink and lie down."

Tarik turned and strode from the room, rubbing his forehead. Nobody had warned him about thieves in the afterlife. As king, everything he could want, need, or desire was provided for him. Tarik had the best food, fine wine, and servants aplenty to see to his needs. His only task was to guard the Door with his warriors, and prevent evil spirits from crossing over.

He stopped at the base of the stairs to the second

floor, casting a nervous glance over his shoulder. Behind him, the stairs descended to the lower halls. Two guards stood at attention at the bottom steps, their spears held at the ready. Even from here, Tarik could feel the icy wind emanating from the Door in the chamber beyond. He massaged his chest at the memory of the cold ache that warned him when something was attempting to pass through.

Almost against his will, Tarik descended the steps to the lower hall. His warriors saluted as he passed, and Tarik gave a curt nod in acknowledgement. Evenly spaced torches filled the corridor with light, but were unable to overcome the icy chill that permeated everything. The walls were simple stone, but smoothed and polished to a sheen.

Tarik slowed and allowed his gaze to roam over the walls, every inch of which had been carved with runes and pictures depicting the exploits of the gods. He passed the creation of the world, the binding of the seas, the birth of living things from the dreams of the Great One. He lingered for a moment over the waking of the first man followed by the terrible war between the gods and the evil spirits. Tarik stooped and passed through the low doorway into the chamber at the end of the corridor and looked around.

The chamber was large and perfectly round, with a slightly curving floor reminiscent of a shallow bowl. The walls formed a single mural that depicted the gods defeating the evil spirits, with the help of the Great One, and bound them forever in the Abyss. Six of Tarik's warriors stood at attention around the perimeter of the chamber, their eyes moving constantly, taking in everything.

Tarik traced his hand over the image of the Fallen God who had attempted to release the spirits in order to overthrow the other gods. He had failed, but in the process had created the Doors, portals from the Abyss which could not be sealed, only guarded forever.

The Door itself loomed over him, an enormous, arched portal hewn from the living stone. Thick grey mist filled the space beneath the arch, swirling and twisting in upon itself as though alive. A pair of stone lions crouched on either side of the Door. Tarik knelt, paying homage to the Guardian Sphinxes, warrior spirits bound in stone to be called upon as the last line of defense in case the Door was ever breached.

Tarik approached the Door, his footsteps muffled by the soft sand, and reached out to trace the ancient runes that covered the stone. The runes were an old language, which he could never quite make out, but which never ceased to fascinate him. *Tarik,* a voice whispered from deep in the mists within the Door. Tarik backed away as his guards closed in around him, their eyes searching the mists for any sign of movement that might herald an attack. After several minutes, the guards relaxed and returned to their posts, spears still held at the ready. Only then did Tarik finally let out the breath he hadn't realized he'd been holding. Such incidents were not uncommon, but they unnerved him nonetheless.

He shook his head and swept out of the chamber, hurrying up the stairs, eager to put space between himself and the lower halls.

Entering his chambers, Tarik hooked a flagon of wine with his fingers in passing. He collapsed on his bed and took a long drink. His eyes closed, he massaged his temples with his free hand, pondering the mystery of the missing treasure. He was no closer to finding an answer when he drifted off to sleep.

Tarik dreamed of his family, the wives and children he had left behind. Ruling his kingdom was exhausting and stressful; what Tarik cherished most was relaxing with his family in the cool of the evening on the banks of the river. In his dreams, he watched the children squealing as they splashed in the shallows, his wives around him singing a soft hymn to the gods as the sun set around them.

He woke with a startled yelp as his body hit the floor. Tarik's head bounced off the stone and he swore, struggling to right himself. His flailing arms struck something in the darkness, and there was a crash of breaking pottery. He heard a shout, followed by the sound of running feet in the hall. Ini burst into the room carrying a torch; two soldiers followed him in, their spears held at the ready. The men skidded to a stop, staring at him, mouths agape. Tarik blinked in the light and stared blearily around. It took him a moment to realize he was sitting on the floor, and another moment to grasp what that meant.

"Where is my bed?" he asked.

Ini's mouth moved silently for nearly a full minute before he was able to squeeze words out. "Did you...move it?"

"Move it?" Tarik repeated. "I was sleeping in it. How could I possibly have moved it?"

"Someone must have taken it," Ini replied.

"Taken it while I was sleeping in it," Tarik said, raising an eyebrow. "How?"

"I don't know, my King," Ini replied, spreading his hands.

"Someone must have seen *something*," Tarik insisted, climbing to his feet. "They could hardly have missed a band of thieves carting a bed down the middle of the Palace halls. "Have Captain Asim make a complete search of the Palace. Every corridor, every room. I want all of the men interrogated as well. Whoever this thief is, I want him apprehended."

"Your will, my King," Ini replied, bowing low as he retreated from the room.

"And bring me more wine," Tarik shouted after him.

He paced the room, casting repeated glances over his shoulder where his bed had been. Out in the corridor he could hear shouts and the sounds of tramping feet as the search was organized. The noises were oddly soothing. Captain Asim was a thorough man, one of Tarik's most competent warriors in life. Tarik was confident he would get to the bottom of this mess. Ini returned shortly, wine in hand, which he handed over with a bow before slipping from the room again.

Tarik took a long drink and sighed. He started to sit on a stool, but the sight of the blank space his bed had occupied stopped him short. Not wishing to suffer the indignity of having his stool disappear from beneath him, he sat on the floor instead, staring into the corner, lost in thought. He couldn't say how much time passed, but it had certainly been no more than an hour before Ini ducked into the room. Tarik knew immediately from the drawn look on Ini's face it was bad news.

"My King," he said, bowing low to the ground. "Forgive me, but you must come quickly."

"What has happened?" Tarik leapt to his feet.

"Six of the guards have gone missing."

"What? When?"

"We don't know, my King. Captain Asim ordered the sweep of the Palace as you commanded. Everything was clear in the upper halls so they continued the search in the lower levels. When they reached the chamber of the Door, the men were gone."

"Was there any sign of an attack?"

"No, my King. They've simply...vanished. Like the treasure, and..." He gestured at the empty space in the bedroom. Tarik glanced at the place and looked away, noting Ini's uncomfortable expression. Somehow the disappearance of something as mundane as a bed was more unsettling than a room full of vanishing gold. You expected people to try and steal gold, but how often do they make off with the furniture while someone was sleeping in it?

"What happened next?" Tarik asked.

"Captain Asim ordered a full muster of the soldiers and doubled the guard in the Chamber. He awaits your presence."

"Very well," Tarik replied. "I will go at once." He made for the corridor but stopped and turned back at the door. "Ini, fetch my armor and spear."

Ini met his gaze, face pale and frightened. Tarik returned the look, hoping to project more confidence than he felt, and hurried from the room. He sped through the empty corridors of the Palace, trying in vain to ignore the feeling that he was being watched. The hair on the back of his neck rose, and the space between his shoulder blades itched. Twice he spun around to check behind him, but he was alone.

"No king should be afraid to walk the halls of his own Palace," Tarik muttered. His voice echoing off the walls did nothing to reassure him, and it was with a sigh of relief that he reached the guardroom on the lower level. He stopped for a moment outside the door to compose himself. Tarik took several deep breaths and gathered what dignity he could before stepping into the room.

Inside, four members of his guard stood huddled together, holding their spears close and whispering. Captain Asim stood a little apart, hands clasped behind his back lost in thought. The captain looked up and bowed as Tarik entered the room.

"Rise," Tarik said. "This is no time for ceremony. What have you found?"

"There is no sign of the men," Asim said rising smoothly to his feet. "I ordered the guard mustered to be sure they were missing. No one has seen them since they reported for duty. There is also no sign of the stolen treasure."

"It seems likely that the two events are connected then," Tarik scratched at his chin. "Perhaps the missing guards *are* our thieves."

"Perhaps, my King," Asim replied. "But where could they have gone? The Palace has no exits."

"There is the Door," Tarik said.

The men shifted uneasily and began to mutter until, at a glance from Asim, they fell silent.

"My King," Asim said, sweat on his forehead belying the calm tone of his voice. "They would not have gone through the Door. No one would be so foolish."

"Yet they are not here," Tarik replied. "Did the men guarding the stairs to the upper halls see anything?"

"No, my King," Asim replied. "No one passed them except for you since they went on duty."

Tarik shook his head. "Then the missing guards cannot be our thieves. Either they went through the Door on their own, or something must have taken them."

Asim opened his mouth to reply, but whatever he was going to say was cut off by a great crash in the corridor outside. Tarik spun around and sprinted into the corridor, Asim and the guards hard on his heels. The hallway was empty but for a set of gilded armor, a shield, and a great war spear strewn haphazardly across the floor.

Tarik bent down and picked up the spear, hefting it in his hands. "This is my spear," he said. "I...ordered Ini to bring it to me."

"But where has he gone?" Asim asked. The captain stepped forward, his own spear gripped tightly in his hands. He glanced each way down the corridor, his gaze focused and sharp. His men moved up to flank him, spears at the ready. "My King, please return to the guard room and wait for us. We will search for Ini."

Tarik turned to go and stopped, staring down at the discarded armor on the floor. "No," he said, clutching his spear for courage. "I will not cower in a room to be taken like a rabbit in a hole. We will all go."

The captain met his gaze and bowed his head in assent. "Of course, my King. Stay close to me."

The group set off together, the six men huddled in a tight mass as they searched the ground floor of the Palace. All was silent and empty; there was no sign of Ini. They passed four men guarding the stairs to the lower halls. Captain Asim broke away from the group and spoke with the guards for several moments before hurrying back.

"They say that Ini passed them carrying your equipment some minutes ago, but they have not seen anyone since then."

Tarik ground the butt of his spear into the stone floor, twisting it in frustration. "How could this be the work of the spirits?"

"Who knows what terrible powers the spirits possess?" Asim replied. "They have had ages to hone their powers in the Abyss."

"Yes," Tarik said. "But powers or no, I would feel it if something crossed over. I would swear that nothing has."

"Then let us continue the search, my King," Asim suggested. "Perhaps we will find the answer to this riddle."

The ground floor secure, Asim left two men at the base of the stairs and climbed with the others to the upper hall to continue the search.

"Asim," Tarik said as they made their way up the stairs. "Did you gather the servants together somewhere for their protection?"

"No, my King," the captain replied, his voice grim. "There wasn't time."

"Then where are they?"

The captain shook his head and didn't answer. They reached Tarik's chambers without incident and stopped. The room was now completely empty, all of the furniture gone, even Tarik's stool. The wine flask alone remained, sitting in the middle of the floor where Tarik had left it.

"What is happening here, my King?" Asim asked.

Tarik stepped into the room and picked up the flask. "I don't know, but I don't think this has anything to do with the Door. Something else is going on here."

"But, what could do all of this except something from the Other Side?"

"Nothing that comes through the Door would care about stealing furniture, Asim," Tarik replied shaking his head. "The creatures care nothing for gold or the possessions of men. Their only desire is to reach the lands of the living so they can feast."

"So, if our thief is not from the Other Side, how do we stop him?" Asim asked.

A scream came from outside the room. The men stared wildly at each other and then sprinted into the corridor and back to the stairs. One of the guards met them at the top of the stairs, his face ashen.

"What happened?" Tarik asked. The guard swooned and would have fallen had the captain not caught him.

"Quickly, my King, give him something to drink."

Tarik rushed to their side, the flagon of wine still in his hand. Asim took the wine and raised it to the guard's lips, pouring some of it down his throat. The man coughed and sputtered, but his eyes opened and he sat up.

"What happened?" Tarik asked again, squatting down beside the guard.

"He disappeared," the man replied. "Kefel and I were talking, and then he was gone. Vanished into thin air."

Asim caught Tarik's eye, his expression grim. "My King, how do we catch an invisible thief who can snatch men out of thin air? More importantly, how will we defend the Door if the soldiers keep being taken?"

Tarik swallowed and stared hard at the floor, his mind racing. "Captain," he said, without raising his eyes. "Gather any men you can find and send them to reinforce the guard on the Door, then meet me in the library."

Asim saluted then lead the still shaking soldier from the room. Tarik grabbed the torch from the sconce, cast a last look at the empty room, and then hurried down the corridor to the library. The room was dark and gloomy, and Tarik's skin crawled at the thought of being alone but he forced himself to go in, his torch held high. Many of the furnishings were gone, but the shelves that lined the walls seemed to be untouched for the moment, their spaces crammed with scrolls.

Tarik hurried from shelf to shelf, pulling the scrolls out and dumping them on the floor in his haste to find what he needed. With a shout of triumph, he clutched the scroll he was looking for and held his torch near it so he could read the markings. He knelt down and unrolled the scroll with his free hand, using a sandal to hold it open as he read. He was so engrossed in the reading, that he didn't hear Asim come in until the captain touched him on the shoulder. Tarik yelled and almost bounded clear off the floor in his fright.

"Forgive me, my King," Asim said.

Tarik waved him off. "Forget it, Captain. We are all rather tense at the moment."

"Everything has been done as you commanded, my King. The remaining men have been assembled in the chamber of the Door."

"It may not be enough," Tarik said, shaking his head. He was silent for a long moment. "We may need to awaken the Guardian Sphinxes."

"My King," Asim said his voice slow and measured. "The Sphinxes will guard the Door, but they will do so by destroying anything in the Palace. Including us. It is a desperate act."

"We *are* desperate, Asim," Tarik replied, pointing out the scroll. "I know what has been happening here."

"What is it?" Asim asked.

"Robbers," he said, his voice barely above a whisper.

"But we have found no one," Asim replied.

"Not here, Captain. *Tomb* robbers."

"But the tombs are hidden. They are sealed away from

the world and the entrance to the Sacred Valley is guarded ceaselessly," Asim replied, his voice shaking. "No one would dare…"

"They have dared," Tarik replied. He closed his eyes, leaning his head back against the cool stone wall. "I know not how, but someone has penetrated the Sacred Valley and is robbing my tomb. *That's* the reason for the disappearances. Someone is removing everything from the tomb, and once outside of the protective spells…" He waved his hand in the air.

At that moment, Tarik's chest constricted, and the familiar icy chill settled into his bones. He cried out and fell to his knees, clutching his chest.

"Captain," he said through gritted teeth, "Something is coming through the Door. Something big. I've never felt anything like this before."

The captain leapt to his feet and grasped Tarik's hand, hauling him up. He turned to leave the room, but Tarik grabbed his shoulder, halting him.

"Captain," Tarik said. "I don't know if we can stop this creature. Even if we can, who will protect the Door when the thieves have removed the last of us from the tomb? We must awaken the Sphinxes."

Whatever response Asim would have made was interrupted by a choking cry from beneath them, quickly cut off.

"Come, my King," Asim shouted, leaping down the stairs.

Tarik followed him, holding his spear before him like a talisman. They reached the stairs to the lower halls, and Asim hurried down without slowing. At the top of the stairs, Tarik stopped. The stairway was cloaked in shadows. He stared at his hands, which were clammy and shaking. From the lower halls, a second piercing scream rose. Tarik jumped and retreated from the stairs, staring around him wildly, but there was nowhere to go. He may have a Palace in the Afterlife, but it was also a prison.

"You are a king, Tarik," he said to himself. "*Act* like it."

He cast a final look back at the empty corridors of his Palace, and then, with his spear clutched tightly before him, he descended to the lower halls. He moved cautiously. Most of the torches had gone out, creating tiny islands of light besieged by seas of shadow. It was bitterly cold. Frost had formed on the walls, and little puffs of mist appeared each time he exhaled.

Tarik crept down the hall as quietly as he could, spear probing the darkness before him. The corridor seemed never ending. For a moment, he wondered if he had wandered into a dream, but at last the chamber of the Door was before him. He peered through the arch into the chamber, but could see no sign of the others. A cold wind blew from the room, brushing across his face like ghostly fingers. Luminous grey mist poured from the Door and filled the chamber with a pale, sickly light. Tarik's breath caught in his throat. In the light from the Door, he could see pieces of stone broken and scattered about the room. The Sphinxes were smashed, their spells destroyed.

Crouching low, Tarik moved into the room, but stumbled over something in the doorway. He knelt down. It was the body of one of the guards, twisted and ruined almost beyond recognition.

He let out a choked cry, and strong arms grabbed him from behind, cutting off his yell and dragging him from the doorway.

"Hush," Asim whispered in his ear. Tarik glanced back over his shoulder. The captain was crouched in the shadows behind him with one of the guards at his side. "This way, my King."

Together the men retreated toward the stairs to the upper halls.

"Where are we going?" Tarik asked in a hoarse whisper. "We have to protect the Door."

"We are too late," Asim replied. "Something has come through. The others are dead."

"What will we do now?"

"We make our stand on the stairs. It will not be able to ambush us that way, and we will have better ground for fighting." He shrugged his shoulders. "It's not much, but it's the best we can do."

Their feet had just touched the bottommost stair when there came a flash of movement from the darkness, something sensed more than seen. Tarik had a brief glimpse of a clawed, many-fingered hand, and then the last guard was yanked backwards off his feet, his body disappearing into the shadows behind them.

"Run!" Asim cried, sprinting up the stairs with Tarik hard on his heels. Behind them the guard let out a blood-curdling shriek that carried on and on before dwindling away into a final gasp.

The silence was deafening.

Tarik backed away from the stairs, shaking his head. "No," he said. "No, it isn't supposed to be this way."

Asim shot him a sideways glance, but held his position at the top of the stairs, spear pointing down into the lower halls. "My King, you must have courage. It is your duty!"

"No," Tarik said. "I can't." He turned and fled down the corridor, with no thought but to get as far away from those dreadful stairs as he possibly could. Behind him Asim called out, but Tarik ignored him and ran on.

He found an empty side room and hid inside, crouching against the wall. It took him a moment to realize he was in the guardroom where he had met with his warriors earlier that day. Only a few hours ago, but it felt like an eternity. The room was empty now, all its furnishings vanished. A single, guttering torch burned in a wall sconce.

In the corridor beyond, Asim yelled a challenge, and Tarik jumped. He heard scuffling from the direction of the stairs. Asim screamed once, and then silence fell. Tarik closed his eyes, resting his head against the cold stone, and prayed to the gods, but no help came.

He was alone.

Tarik stared around the empty chamber, picturing the furnishings that had been there. He could almost see his guards standing around talking and joking with each other. His warriors. They were his servants, yet his friends nonetheless. And he had abandoned them. His mind wandered from the empty halls of his Palace to his former life. He pictured his wives and children. What would become of them if this monster came through to the living world? What paradise would await them when they died if the Door were breached?

"You. Are. A. King." he said to himself through gritted teeth. If the Door were breached, it would not be because he ran away. He could not fail his family or his people.

He rose to his feet, wiping his sweat-soaked hands on his clothes and gripped the spear with new determination. Outside, he could hear movement, like a great weight being scraped along the floor. He uttered a final prayer then leapt out into the hall, stabbing with his spear and screaming his defiance into the face of damnation.

The room spun around him, and he faltered, his spear falling away as the ground tilted around him. He closed his eyes, his teeth clenched against a wave of nausea.

Tarik opened his eyes, but could see nothing. The Palace had vanished around him. He tried to move, but his body was bound with cloth. A cold fear settled in the pit of his stomach. The thieves must have removed his sarcophagus from the tomb, and now he was trapped.

"Help," he cried, but his voice was thin and pale, the voice of a shade. Removed from the spells of the burial chamber, he was powerless to act. Outside the sarcophagus, he could hear voices, but their words were faint and garbled. He did not recognize the language.

Put me back, he pleaded silently to the nameless robbers,

trying by sheer will-power to reach them. *Return me to the tomb before it's too late.*

The sarcophagus shifted around him, and he felt himself carried along. Hope flared in his heart, and then he felt warmth bathing the sarcophagus, heat seeping in to warm his ice cold limbs. His heart sank. He was outside. They weren't taking him back to the burial chamber at all. He was carried a while longer, and then his sarcophagus was set down with a jarring thud. Once again, he could hear men talking, their words unintelligible and harsh to his ears.

Who are these people? He wondered, his mind racing frantically. *Have we been conquered by an invading army?*

Sudden movement jostled him as his sarcophagus was shoved several feet forward, scraping against some sort of metal with a terrible screeching sound. Something clanged, and then the voices faded away. A terrible roaring arose from beneath Tarik like the ceaseless growl of a ravenous beast, and they began to move at a tremendous speed.

Within the sarcophagus, Tarik cried and raged and screamed, praying to the gods to deliver him. No answer came. He felt himself carried along faster than any chariot he had ever ridden, and for the first time, Tarik wondered how long he'd been buried.

His chest tightened with a cold grip. *You fools! The Door! The Door!*

The sun sank, casting the empty tomb in shadow. In the darkness within, something moved.

THE
CANDLEMAKER

Adam D. Jones

Dorian hefted the pitcher and poured beeswax into the narrow, clay vase, keeping his hands steady so the wax fell past the upheld wick without disturbing it. Each layer smothered the next until beeswax filled the vase nearly to its rounded brim. Dorian unwound the wick from the stick that had kept it in place, cut it to a fingerwidth's height, and nodded in satisfaction as it stayed upright, tilting only a little as it towered over the hardening wax.

This candle would be completely ordinary, giving light and slowly burning down to a nub like any other. And as far as anyone in Ostwik knew, all of Dorian's candles were ordinary.

The bell that hung over the door rang from the next room. Dorian checked one last time to make sure the wick was still standing before turning toward the main room. He had spent almost his whole life in these two small rooms where his parents had taught him to make his own candles before he could write his own name.

The front room was lit by a single tall candle that stood on the counter where Dorian talked to his customers. Dorian stepped over his mattress (sleeping in the same room as the smelly tallow was impossible), leaned over the counter, and saw a familiar face stumping through the front door. Burt, one of the oldest townsfolk, and certainly the heaviest, was dragging himself through the doorway as if he didn't have a broken leg.

"Sit down!" Dorian shuffled his only chair around the counter and brought it near the door. "Burt, I would have come to your place."

"Nonsense. There's nothing wrong with me," he said, but he still sat down in Dorian's chair; he'd only made it one full step inside. Burt held up a narrow clay pot, empty except for bits of wax stuck to the inside. "This one's all used up, Dor."

Dorian took the pot from his old hands. "Got any

more at home, Burt, or will you be in the dark without another one?"

"All out," said Burt, who was trying to pretend he wasn't catching his breath. "Gets dark sooner this time of year. I use my candles faster. Reckon everyone does."

Dorian returned to the back room. He kept certain candles on a rickety shelf in the corner farthest from the door, candles that had been made with *different* recipes. They looked and smelled the same to most people, but each of these candles, set aside on the corner shelf, had a special use and a special design carved into the bottom that helped Dorian tell them apart.

"How's your leg, Burt?" he called out. Dorian stood in front of rows of candles, some bare and some hiding within ceramic vessels like the one Burt had just handed him. Dorian's eyes settled on a series of candles near the middle. He had been giving Burt candles from that section since that wagon had knocked him down a few weeks ago. "Resting Candles," they were called.

The Resting Candle was the first recipe he'd learned after finding his mother's candle-making book hidden under a floorboard. Dorian had wondered why a collection of simple candle mixtures should be kept secret, but after studying the recipes, Dorian realized it was a book that needed to be kept away from curious eyes.

The Resting Candle
—*A twice-wound wick soaked in snake's venom.*
—*Grind rose hips into beeswax and pour with eyes closed.*
—*Keep lit for hours; especially uplifting while afflicted and needing rest.*

The recipe, like all the others in her book, had seemed normal, albeit whimsical, but Dorian couldn't shake the idea that he was looking at more than mere mixtures.

The next time someone in Ostwik fell ill, Dorian followed his instincts and whipped up his first Resting Candle. The patient had been Dorian's neighbor, a fisherman named Yuri who had eaten a spoiled fish and couldn't keep anything down. That evening, Dorian placed the Resting Candle on the sill outside Yuri's window where its golden glow spilled over the fisherman like a blanket. When the sun rose, Yuri rose along with it and hauled his nets to the sea with a spring in his step.

As he watched Yuri head to the docks, Dorian knew he had discovered something powerful. Powerful and dangerous. And, with this discovery, Dorian finally understood why his parents had put aside their mystical talent and made their home in a sleepy coastal town: they had been hiding.

The people of Ostwik were simple and unassuming, mostly honest merchants, but even they knew that the word "candlemaker" meant "spy" in every corner of the empire. No matter which side they served, a candlemaker always meant trouble. Dorian was smart enough to keep his experiments secret so his work wouldn't attract the marshals who patrolled the empire's outskirts. The empire maintained that these patrols kept the frontier safe, but the marshals were mostly known for antagonizing anyone on the frontier suspected of practicing mysticism.

Not every candle was as easy to make as the Resting Candle. When Dorian got an experiment wrong, it usually filled his shop with colored smoke—he'd learned to keep a bucket of water handy. It was a dangerous hobby, and he knew being found out would land him in an imperial prison, but the allure of working magic was irresistible.

"Leg's much better!" Burt called. "I couldn't walk 'tall two weeks ago. Seemed to get better faster than the travlin' doc thought possible."

You don't say. Dorian turned away from the shelf and grabbed an ordinary candle from a pile on a dresser. *His leg will have to heal the rest of the way on its own.* Too much miraculous healing would bring questions, and questions would bring the marshals. Dorian smiled at his secret. The people of Ostwik didn't know he was helping them, and that was just fine with him.

Even so, the worst part of unlocking magical secrets was not being able to tell anyone about it. Ten years ago, a sickness had taken a third of the town, leaving Dorian without parents and without anyone who could understand his work. More than once he'd walked past the shop where Claire sold books and considered confiding his secret to her. Claire was young, like Dorian, and her parents had also been taken by the sickness. And she was smarter than just about anyone who passed through their town. But one glance at her bright blue eyes and the raven-black hair that tumbled over her shoulders, and Dorian always found his words slipping away.

Since his tongue invariably failed him whenever Claire was around, Dorian settled for making sure her candles included a hint of jasmine so that her home, Ostwik's bookhouse, would smell of more than dusty books. But she never mentioned it. Maybe she never noticed; maybe she didn't care.

"No…" Burt moaned from the other room. "No!"

Dorian spun around, hearing the distress in his voice. "Something wrong, Burt?"

In the main room, Burt was struggling to move in a hurry. Limping and staggering, he reached a wrinkled hand for the candle on Dorian's counter. "Get down, child!" He pressed two fingers together against the flame.

"Burt, you'll fall—"

Burt's fingers snuffed out the candle with a quick *hiss*. Faint, mid-day light streamed through the narrow windows and the front doorway, but the room fell mostly dark without a candle. The old man collapsed, making a horrible sound as he hit the floor.

"Stay…stay back…" whispered Burt from the other

side of the counter. "West...western brig..."

The pain from falling on his injured leg took over, and Burt's whispering turned into a whimper, but Dorian knew the rest. *The Western Brigands.*

Hailing from the Black Wastes where they hid between raids, the Western Brigands rode their caravans along the coastal roads and took what they wanted along the way, always disappearing before the marshals could catch up.

Dorian fell into a crouch and peeked out from behind the counter. He was covered in shadow, but he knew someone outside could make him out if they looked hard enough. He considered moving to a better hiding spot, but the sound of wagon wheels froze him in place.

The wagon crawled past, pulled by two scrawny horses. *They'll keep going.* Ostwik wasn't wealthy, and even bandits knew it wasn't worth stopping there. *Please, don't take anyone...*

The wagon was led by a man with only a few teeth and face full of wiry whiskers. He stared hard into the candle shop, looking through the doorway Burt had left open. The brigand raised his hand and pointed a crooked finger toward Dorian.

"No..." Burt pushed against the ground, trying to rise. "Not the boy."

Burt, you old coot, knock it off.

Dorian steeled himself to get up, prepared to stand and get to the door before Burt could do anything foolish. Dorian wasn't a child anymore, but Burt tried to look after everyone in Ostwik like they were his own. Even when he could barely walk. Dorian decided it was best to stand up and take his lumps before the Western Brigands hurt them both.

Here goes.

Dorian began to rise. But as the wagon rolled past, the bandit continued to gesture while he laughed at a joke Dorian couldn't hear.

He wasn't pointing to me at all—just motioning while he spoke. And I nearly ran out there like a fool!

Dorian stayed low and crept over to Burt on his hands and knees. The old man was wincing in pain, but at least he wasn't trying to rescue anyone.

He'll need the special candle after all.

"Help me up, lad." Burt held out a shaking hand.

"I'm sure they'll just keep going." Dorian held his arm while Burt got to his feet. "You can rest here if you want…"

Burt limped to the doorway and leaned against the frame. He stared out, watching the departing wagon with narrowed eyes, and, for a moment, Dorian saw Burt as the young soldier from his old war stories.

"Don't have to dote over me, lad. I'm fit as a fiddle."

Dorian knew Burt was about to fall apart, but he let the old man have his way. Dorian walked back to the counter and ducked behind it to look for a taper so he could relight his shop candle. At the sight of his own shaking fingers, he remembered a candle in the back that was supposed to calm nerves. Not that it would work for Dorian, but it might help Burt relax.

Suddenly, Burt let out another cry.

"Dorian! Something's wrong!"

Dorian jerked his head up, expecting to see Burt falling again, but instead Burt stood in the doorway pointing across the street.

"Those monsters are in the bookhouse!"

Dorian bolted into the back room. He grabbed a corner of the rug and threw it aside; then he knelt down and ran his fingers along the floorboards until one of them shifted under his touch. He pulled up the loose plank, revealing a dark hole just large enough to fit his secret recipe book and a few special candles he didn't dare keep with the others. He picked up a small, black candle with a short wick, completely covered in dust. Something he had made as an experiment but never found a reason to use. Dorian replaced the board and hurried to his feet, barely aware that the rug was still thrown aside. *No time.*

Hands trembling, he tilted the top of the bare candle toward the lit candle he kept at his workbench. He frowned at his nervous hands. He closed his eyes and forced himself to count to ten, letting his fingers and hands relax. He tried again.

This time the wick grabbed the flame from the other candle and began to burn. Dorian cupped the candle in both hands and ran past Burt through the open door. He winced at the bright sunlight and moved as quickly as he could while making sure the candle remained lit. The wagon had stopped just at the start of the woods, and what Dorian saw there froze him in his tracks.

A rope had been thrown over a tall tree branch. The leader of the brigands held one end in his tattooed hands while another man shoved Claire toward a dangling noose.

"Gather 'round!" the leader yelled. "And bring what ya' got!"

Laughter came from the other two bandits. Dorian realized there were only three of them. A proper town wouldn't be afraid of three men, but Ostwik wasn't much of a town. Just a bump in the road for most travelers. Some folks stopped to look out over the cliffs that rose above the green sea or to make conversation with the friendly merchants, but people tended to forget Ostwik after a few bends in the road.

Dorian could already hear his neighbors scrambling for their goods. It was well known that the Western Brigands would hang someone unless the victim's neighbors turned over their valuables, and Claire would certainly hang if these thieves thought the good people of Ostwik were holding back.

But it was a devil's bargain; Ostwik already hung by a thread. The town depended on road-weary travelers who stopped for food and supplies; it would be a rough winter if the merchants lost their stock today. Dorian shuddered at the thought of Ostwik becoming a camp of hermits, like so many along the empire's roads, where people only left their homes to beg for handouts from passing caravans. Dorian knew everyone in town was thinking along the same lines, but they were marching out their doors carrying their best goods anyway.

He glanced over his shoulder and saw Henk, the ferrier, trudging toward the scene. Henk was leading his horse, saddle and all, shaking his head and looking down. It was the town's only horse. Behind Henk, Annette, the seamstress, struggled to carry her fine rocking chair, the one her father had built before his hands started to shake. She held it high as she walked, and Dorian could see the intricate horses her father had etched deeply onto the backboard.

Dorian felt his own hands tremor, and the candle nearly tumbled through his fingers.

Focus, Dorian!

He looked down, blocking out everything but the candle and concentrating all his efforts on holding it steady. And making sure no one could see its light. Not yet. The small flame burning at the top of the wick was only meant for the brigands. This candle created darkness...but not the kind of darkness you can see. Dorian was *pretty* sure he knew what that meant.

A Candle to Make Darkness
—A wick wound 'round the stem of a corpse flower.
—Bones of birds and blood of vermin, mixed with mildewed tallow.
—Useful for creating darkness, where moments are minutes and memories are light.

The recipe hadn't made sense at first, but the meaning

slowly became clear as Dorian reread the odd instructions and remembered that candlemakers were known for their clever tricks and lies.

He kept the candle close, covering it in the shell of his hand to keep its fire out of sight. He wasn't worried for himself; these candles couldn't affect a candlemaker. In more peaceful times, children were tested for the gift by placing them in front of a special candle to see if they were resilient to it. Now that candle making had been thoroughly outlawed, these tests were only used on suspected spies.

We'll all starve if we give this much of our stuff away, thought Dorian, as more of his neighbors emerged from their homes, burdened by their own goods.

Dorian took careful but purposeful steps directly toward the scoundrels standing in the town square. Stunned by the clear heading of his path, the rest of the townsfolk stopped moving. Before anyone could lay down their valuables, Dorian had arrived in front of them all. The man holding the rope locked eyes with him, and Dorian felt his belly clench at the man's hard gaze. Next to him, Claire staggered in place, the noose resting on her shoulders. A few red cuts marred her face, and a bruise was emerging on her left cheek.

The leader of the three brigands stepped forward. Dorian knew it was time to see if his candle was going to work, and, more importantly, if he had interpreted its recipe correctly. Just as the bandit opened his mouth to speak, Dorian moved his hand and exposed the candle's flame. Claire's view was obscured by the man's burly body, but all three brigands had a clear line of sight.

One.

They took a step closer. One of them drew a blade from his belt.

Two.

The leader blinked and frowned, but remained distracted by the flame.

Three. That should do it.

Dorian blew out the candle. "The marshals are coming?" he asked loudly, as if he was repeating something that had just been said.

"What?" The man in front of him glanced around. The rope fell from his fingers. "The..."

"...Marshals," Dorian supplied. "That's what you said."

He stared back, his mouth trying to form the word. "M....ma-marshals..."

It's working.

He wasn't *completely* certain he understood what this candle did. He'd never tested it. But if his assumptions were correct, a few seconds of looking at the flame was enough to clear out a man's memories of the last few minutes. *Moments are minutes*, the recipe said.

"The marshals are coming?" he asked Dorian. The two other men began to squirm.

"That's what you told me." Dorian said. He knew confused people tended to be highly suggestible. In their stupor, they might believe anything.

Realizing no one was paying attention to her, Claire flung the noose off of her shoulders and stepped away. The men saw but made no move to stop her. *They don't even remember capturing her. How much of their memory did I steal?*

The man in front of Dorian began nodding his head. "Marshals...coming..." He backed away. "Marshals..."

The other brigands watched their leader and then turned back toward the wagon.

Good...they all saw it.

The bandits picked up their pace, nodding to one another as they retreated away from Dorian.

And don't come back!

Dorian felt Claire standing next to him.

"What did you do?" she whispered.

"Me? Nothing."

"Don't lie!" she hissed. "You stood there and locked eyes with him, and now they're running away! You were... holding something—"

"No!" Dorian gripped the black candle tightly, hiding it in his hand.

The brigands, confused, began loading themselves onto their wagon.

"What happened?" Helene, the alchemist, asked as she approached them from behind with her arms full of stoppered bottles. "They're just...leaving?"

Dorian realized he hadn't prepared an explanation. "Maybe...something scared them off."

"It was marshals!" shouted a man carrying a few blankets over his shoulder. "Marshals are comin'!"

Dorian shook his head. "They said something about marshals, but there aren't any—"

The man merely pointed past him. "Marshals!"

Dorian was about to speak again when Claire tapped his shoulder. "Dorian, you dummy, *look!*" He turned around and peered toward the woods.

Tall, narrow flags flew just above the treeline, carrying the sigil of the empire above the path that led to Ostwik.

Oh, perfect.

A carriage roared around the path. At the sight of the Western Brigands, a tall woman in the driver's seat cracked an ugly whip and screamed a warning at the top of her lungs. A door opened on the side of the wagon, and a soldier looked out with a grim frown. While the brigands stood in place, three soldiers leapt down from the wagon and began running alongside, weapons drawn. It was even numbers, three against three, but the brigands didn't make a move to defend themselves.

What...exactly did I do to them?

With all eyes on the approaching carriage, Dorian tossed the candle away. It landed under a bush at the edge of the clearing. No one saw him. Of course, with the scene unfolding before them, Dorian figured the people of Ostwik wouldn't notice if he lit himself on fire.

As the soldiers neared, one of the brigands fell to the ground in a fit. The other two raised trembling hands in a hurried surrender.

Not good. Not good at all. You've really stepped in it now, Dorian.

All three brigands were cowering on the ground as the marshals closed in on them. The marshals stood around them in a circle, but made no other move except to glance back at the carriage.

The tall woman jumped down from the driver's seat. Dorian saw that her leather uniform bore more insignia than the others. "A commander," someone whispered. Her boots kicked up a cloud of dust with each step, and her long fingers rolled the whip into tight coils as she strode over to the brigands.

I should have stayed in my shop. The marshals were only a minute away! Idiot!

The commander towered over the brigand leader, the one who had nearly hanged Claire. "We meet again, Griff. Thought you lost us in Nakal, didn't you?"

He looked up into her face. "Na...Nakal?" His jowls quivered. "Nakal?"

Blast it!

He stammered a few more words, then half-heartedly pointed a trembling finger toward Dorian. At his side, he felt Claire grip his hand.

The commander marched their way. "Start tying them up!" she barked to her soldiers. In an instant, she stood before Dorian and Claire, one hand on the coiled whip that now rested on a hook of her belt. "Tell me what happened here."

As she stared Dorian down, he realized that he would make an awful candlemaker if there was a war on. Sure, he could mix ingredients from a recipe book, but Dorian had no idea how to come up with a quick lie to save his life.

"I just asked them to leave," he said, trying not to squirm under her glare.

"My name is Commander Rela, and you are lying." She planted her fists on her hips and looked around. "Or someone in this town is."

Claire moved closer to Dorian and squeezed his hand. "Did...did that awful man say something about my husband?"

Dorian had heard of courageous men, the sort who could be confident and calm in dangerous situations. In this moment, Dorian learned he was not one of those men. Hearing Claire utter the words "my husband," even though it was a ruse, set his heart beating faster than he would have thought possible.

Commander Rela pointed toward the brigands. "Those men have been...*affected* by something." She narrowed her eyes at Dorian. "And he seems to remember talking to you."

"Stupid." Claire punched him. "You should have brought our things out! Every other person in town was trying to save me and you were protecting your useless books."

Dorian felt his mouth dry. "My...books. I...didn't want them to—"

"Stop talking!" Commander Rela ordered.

She turned away with a sneer and cast her eyes around the scene. Behind her, the soldiers had tied up each of the bandits and made them sit in a circle with their backs to one another. Rela scanned every inch of the ground, looking, to Dorian, like someone who knew exactly what she expected to find. Her eyes stopped at a bush at the edge of the clearing.

No.

Rela hurried to the bushes and knelt. The onlookers stood tall and silent, watching her reach beneath the bush's branches and retrieve the black candle. She turned it over as she stood, then put it to her nose and sniffed. Her jawline tightened as she slowly stowed the candle into a pouch on her belt.

"...Candlemaker..." She whispered. Her gaze rose until her eyes settled on Dorian's shop. The swinging, wooden sign said nothing, only bore the image of a burning candle so travelers would know what he sold.

Rela unslung her whip and let it fall, coiling at her boots. She pointed to one of her men, then marched toward the candle shop; the soldier clumsily fell in line behind her.

Dorian felt his hands curling into fists. He shoved them deep into the pockets of his apron while he watched Commander Rela march across town, the soldier at her heels. They seemed to reach his shop in a single step. As they disappeared inside, Dorian's mind raced to the false panel on his floor and how he'd failed to re-cover it with the rug.

Dorian saw movement just inside the door frame. *They're leaving already? She couldn't have found anything that fast.*

A shape appeared in the doorway, but it didn't look like a soldier.

Burt stumbled out, his arms flailing to keep him balanced. He was prodded and pushed into the middle of town, where he would have fallen to the ground had Commander Rela not grabbed his shoulders and held him up.

"Are you the candlemaker?" Rela yelled at him.

Burt's face wrinkled in confusion, but only for a moment. Quickly, his old eyes turned to steel. "Of course I'm the candlemaker, ya lout! That's been my shop for years! Built it when the emperor's *da* was less 'an knee high to a—"

Rela released him, and Burt collapsed with a howl of pain.

Dorian looked around. The citizens of Ostwik silently watched Burt. A few glanced toward Dorian, but none of them spoke up. *Why are they all going along with him?*

Dorian took a step forward, but Claire's hand gripped his tighter and she pulled him back.

"He's lying for me!" Dorian hissed.

From the center of the clearing, Commander Rela pointed at Dorian, and he felt his feet stumble. Even Claire tensed, but after a moment they both saw that Rela's pointed glare had settled on something behind them.

"You!" She shouted. "With the horse!"

Dorian turned around. Behind him, frozen in the tableau, stood Henk and his old horse. Henk looked over at the reins in his hand like he'd forgotten he'd been holding them.

"Ride that thing to Nagran's Fork. You'll find a magister's patrol heading south; we left them before we came here."

A defeated sigh ran through the people of Ostwik. Nagran's Fork was just outside of their town; a rider could find the magister's patrol and be back in well under an hour.

Henk shot a worried look at Burt. Seeing his hesitation, Rela turned to the nearest soldier and shouted, "Find that man's house and set it to the torch. Then find his family—"

"Wait!" cried Henk, but he still didn't move. "Just…" He looked back at Burt with desperation in his eyes.

Burt gave Henk a slow, understanding nod, and Henk scrambled up into his saddle. "I'll go! I'll go!"

The small crowd parted for Henk, who was still settling into the stirrups as he rode. Rela brandished her whip, and Henk kicked his paint horse into a gallop. Dirt and grass kicked up from the ground as Henk rounded the path into the woods and disappeared. In the center of town, Burt wheezed and tried to sit up.

"Nothing you can do about it now," whispered Claire. "Come on."

The crowd began backing away. Rela ordered her men to tie Burt up while she turned her attention to the brigands. Dorian couldn't stop feeling guilty, but Claire tugged on his hand until he was following her into the bookhouse.

Dorian felt slightly embarrassed at the smell of jasmine in Claire's bookshop. It was faint, but his senses easily picked it out over the scent of old books.

He'd never been inside of Claire's home. Most of it was taken up by a large room filled with tall, solemn shelves, all bursting with books. A small kitchen just inside the door with a table big enough for one was the only evidence anyone lived here.

They both froze and wrinkled their noses at the arrival of a new, unwelcome smell. In a huff, Claire dashed into the kitchen where a pot sat atop her metal stove. "Was about to make stew." She stood tall and glared down into the ruined mess, scowling while a pungent odor overtook the scent of Jasmine. "Stupid men. Made me ruin the whole meal!"

Dorian stood next to her at the kitchen window. Outside, a pair of soldiers tied Burt's hands in front of him. One of them stayed with Burt while the other began a patrol around town, looking into windows and barns as he walked. The third stood by Commander Rela, who was trying to interrogate the bandits.

"They'll turn over everything in Ostwik looking for evidence." Claire lifted her head and stared out the window. "I suppose you hide your things well."

He looked at her. "I didn't do anything, Claire."

She scowled, and he felt all the warmth leave the room. "You're not the only person who knows things around here," she said.

"I know that. But don't think—"

"Don't think? Is that what you want? For me to stop thinking?"

He tried to apologize, but she wasn't finished.

"You want me to believe that three men just turned into pudding at the same time while you were standing there holding a candle? I'm not an idiot."

"I'm sorry." He looked back out the window where Burt was putting on a brave face.

"I'm worried about Burt too," said Claire, "but this is his decision to make."

"I know. But it won't only be him. They'll arrest anyone they think is helping. Sometimes entire towns get carted off if marshals suspect they've been hiding someone..."

Someone like me, he almost finished.

"All right, then let's think about this. Can you use... another candle? Something to trick the marshals into leaving?"

Dorian wanted to keep lying, but it was obvious there was no point trying to hide who he was from her. "...Maybe."

She added, "Have you got another one of those candles that makes people stupid? Or whatever just happened out there?"

"I think that would leave a pretty large hole in their memories. It would raise questions. Besides, I haven't got another one." He glanced down into the pockets of his apron. "If only I had a..." He remembered one of his experiments. "...Decision Candle. That's what the book calls it. It's grey."

Her eyes widened. "Is that...a candle that can change people's minds?"

"Yes." He had promised himself that he would never use it. Taking away someone's choices felt like villainy. "But it's all the way in my shop."

He felt her hands reaching into his apron. "Can any of these help?" She produced a handful of his candles.

"Doubt it." He took a blue candle from her hands and looked at the bottom mark. "With this one...it's hard for people to notice you. I've tried it once, and I...I'm pretty sure it doesn't work if they're already looking at you." Dorian used it when he wasn't in the mood to talk to customers. As long as he kept quiet, and held that candle in his hands, people tended to look right past him.

"What about this one?" She held a white candle.

"Calms people down. Makes them want to agree with you and go along with what you say."

"Let's use it!" She jutted her chin outside. "We'll just ask them to go on their way."

"No good. It's very temporary, and they always change their minds once they're looking away. I don't think I've mastered that recipe yet. And if someone's angry, or *real* determined, well, I don't think it'll work at all."

She looked at the candle with a frown.

"I'm going to check on Burt," Dorian said, pointing to a waterskin hanging on the wall near the kitchen table. "Is that fresh?"

"Filled it at the well this morning."

"Good." He took the waterskin from its peg. It was heavy, nearly full. "I need to see what Burt knows, and what he thinks he's up to."

Claire turned the candle over in her hands. "You do that."

Dorian carried the waterskin toward the center of town. The soldier standing near Burt held up a restraining hand as he approached.

"You can't deny him water," Dorian said.

The soldier motioned for him to pass. Dorian thought he looked relieved to see someone helping the old man.

Dorian knelt next to Burt. "Drink up, you old fool." The soldier stood a few steps away, looking out across the square.

"You're welcome, boy." Burt sat up with some effort and took the waterskin. "Shouldn't you be running away, or doing something clever?"

"Not as long as they think you're a candlemaker," Dorian whispered.

Burt's face grew more stern. "Lad, you and I both know there hasn't been a candlemaker stupid enough to operate in the empire in ages. But I also know how these military commander types are. They'll take someone away on that cart, guilty or not, just so they aren't empty-handed. We all know that person is never coming back. Don't argue with me, now. I'm old. I get to play the part of the town hero if I want."

Dorian could see Burt wasn't going to budge, but it wasn't clear whether the old man was only pretending to be ignorant. "Burt...what do you know about what's *really* going on here?" Dorian urged with a penetrating stare.

"I know that commander woman has something to prove." He pointed to Commander Rela, threatening a brigand with her whip. "Look at her soldiers. All ruddy-faced lads who don't look old enough to be out of the crib. That's a rotten assignment if I ever saw one. Take my word, that woman'll turn this into a career opportunity if she has to wipe us off the map."

Dorian sighed. "Burt, they'll test you once the magister's here. You can't just lie about being a candlemaker. They light a candle, and, oh, I don't know how it works, but Burt, they'll know right away if it affects you or not."

"A test, you say!" Burt managed to laugh. "Ol' Burt's

bluffed his way through worse, lad. Don't you worry about me. I'll have 'em all singing along with my tune 'fore the day's over, and Ostwik will be fine an' dandy. Just you keep an eye on Claire. They're leavin' you alone for now, but I'll wager they still don't trust you two."

"You're right. But she should be safe in the…" Dorian turned around and looked toward the bookhouse. "Oh, no."

Claire was walking across town in plain sight, holding one of Dorian's candles.

"She must be inside still," said Burt with a nod of his head. "Smart girl."

"Burt…she's right there." Dorian pointed.

"Eh?" Burt squinted. "Well, so she is, lad! Didn't even see her right in front of me. Isn't it strange how that happens?"

Claire continued her stroll. The guard standing near Dorian didn't notice her go by, and neither did the next soldier she passed when she was almost to the candle shop. She casually held the candle high enough for everyone to see as she walked inside Dorian's shop and closed the door.

The soldier's ears pricked at the latch's *click.*

Claire! They can still hear you!

The soldier turned his full attention to the door. He waited in place for a moment, listening, then approached the door and walked inside.

"I need to get in there," Dorian whispered. The nearby marshal was watching the candle shop intently.

"Say no more." Burt motioned for the guard. "Hello! Hey there! Is this an *official* arrest?"

The marshal tore his gaze from Dorian's shop and looked at Burt, puzzled. "I suppose. We are the emperor's marshals, after all."

"Good, good, lad. In that case, I've got a list of demands."

"I'd…I'd better get Commander Rela," the soldier stammered.

"Are you daft? Interrupt a commanding officer's interrogation? If that's not against regulation, then I'm a crow's canary! Now, I'm entitled, by the emperor's own decree, mind you, to tell you my demands for fair treatment as a prisoner. Or do you want to tell the emperor yourself you didn't listen to the pleas of a legal citizen? A war veteran at that!"

"No, sir—of course, not! Go ahead."

Dorian slipped away. Rela was yelling at the brigands, trying to get information out of them, while one of her soldiers stood nearby looking like he wanted to be anywhere else. *One soldier's with Rela, one's listening to Burt, and the other's in my shop.* Dorian picked up his pace. Rela and her soldiers were all too busy to notice him slip through the door as Burt droned on.

"Now, lad, you might write this down," Burt wagged his finger at the marshal. "My right foot's got a strange shape to it, and that means you can't march me in the same way as the others. If you force me to walk anywhere you'll have to slow down every other step. One...two—one... two—one...like that, boy. Try it. No, no, slower. Slower..."

Dorian stepped inside. He saw no one in the front area, but as soon as he shut the door he heard the unsheathing of a sword coming from the workroom.

"Who's there!" came a man's voice. "You're under arrest!"

"No he's not," came Claire's voice.

"He isn't?"

Dorian inched forward and stopped in the doorway that separated the two rooms. Claire stood in front of the hearth where Dorian's fire still roared high and hot, and in front of her, stood the soldier, his sword in hand.

At the sound of Dorian's footsteps, the soldier spun his head around like a great horned owl and locked eyes with Dorian.

"Don't move!" the soldier barked.

"Shh." Claire put her hand gently to his cheek and turned his face back toward her blue eyes. The white candle rested on her flat, outstretched palm, its flame dancing between their gazes. "It's fine. Remember? He's with me," she said slowly.

"Oh, I understand." He smiled and nodded. "But… you're not supposed to be in here. Are you?"

"Yes," she said sweetly.

"Yes?"

"Did you find anything?" interrupted Dorian.

Putting a finger to her lips, Claire moved so he could see the book-shaped bundle under her arm. She'd found the loose floorboard before the soldier followed her in. She'd even had time to spread the rug back over it.

Dorian stepped quickly to the corner shelf where he kept his unusual candles. "We'll need a few things."

The soldier raised his hand. "I'm pretty sure you're not supposed to take anything."

"It's fine," said Claire. "Put your sword away, Lewin."

Lewin?

"That's a good idea." Lewin slid his sword back into its sheath, never taking his eyes off of Claire's.

I don't even think she needs the candle to hypnotize that one.

Dorian's gaze settled on the candle he would need. Simple, short, grey. If Rela so much as glanced at it, he could make her believe anything. *Not here. Back at the bookhouse.* He wanted soldiers and magisters to spend as little time in the candle shop as possible. Dorian grabbed the grey candle and dropped it into his apron.

"You know what's funny, Claire? That candle affects you, too. It's lucky your friend Lewin hasn't given you any orders."

"I don't think that's how it works," she said, her eyes fixed on the soldier.

Dorian shrugged and held out his hand. "Give me the candle."

"Sure." Without thinking, she placed it in his palm. "Hey!"

Dorian smirked and then turned to Lewin, ignoring the glower that darkened Claire's face. "Stay here 'till we're gone, then go and tell your commander we're in the bookhouse."

His eyes were transfixed by the orange flame. "Should I just go now?"

"No!" Claire took the candle back, giving Dorian a quick, pointed glare that said, *I do this better than you.* "Wait until we're gone. Promise?"

He smiled. "Promise."

Lewin's content gaze convinced Dorian they were safe. If Claire asked him to bring her a piece of the moon, this man would have found a way. Dorian grabbed Claire's arm and guided her toward the back door. "C'mon. If we go out this way it'll be easier to—"

Dorian threw open the back door and saw the stern face of Commander Rela.

"No!" He slammed it shut and threw the locking bolt. The doorknob rattled, then the entire door shuddered as Rela threw her shoulder into it from the outside.

"Will that...*calming* candle work on someone that upset?" asked Claire.

"Not a chance."

"Hey!" Rela's pounding seemed to stir Lewin. He slowly wrapped his fingers around his sword handle. "You two...are under arrest—"

Claire held up her candle again. "No we're not!" She looked at him with wide eyes. "Don't be silly! We're just a few friends talking." She nodded while she spoke. "We're friends, right?"

He relaxed his grip. "Friends…"

Dorian saw the soldier getting lost in her blue eyes. *Poor guy's melting faster than that candle.*

The entire wall shook as Rela continued to barge her way in.

"Dorian!" shouted Claire.

"I'm thinking!"

Dorian could hear footsteps approaching the front door. *That'll be the third soldier in her company. Glad my shop could bring everyone together.* He considered the shelf that held his experiments; many of them were untested. He didn't always get the recipes right…some were bound to be failures.

He frowned as an idea formed in his mind. *I'm about to do something stupid.* He shook his head. *Here goes.*

Dorian grabbed the flimsy wooden shelf and hurled it toward the hearth, candles and all. It fell into the fireplace. Every one of his special candles rolled off the shelves and tumbled into the flames.

Behind them, the front door banged open in the main room, and the third soldier ran inside, sword drawn. "Lewin, what are you doing?" he bellowed. "Arrest them!"

Lewin blinked a few times then looked at Claire accusingly. He swatted the candle from her palm, and she backed away with a gasp. In a blur, Lewin's sword was in his hand. He was about to shout at Claire when the back door to the shop finally gave in.

The old door shattered into pieces. Rela's manic eyes bore into Dorian as she stomped inside.

But neither Rela nor her soldiers reached Dorian before red smoke filled the shop.

"Close your eyes!" he whispered, and Claire gripped his arm with both hands.

A velvet cloud puffed out of the fireplace like smoke from a giant pipe, and all three of Rela's men fell to the ground before the billows even reached them. They grabbed their heads and convulsed into balls of pain, but not all of them were affected in the same way. Lewin thrust his arms and legs in every direction; the soldier nearest the door began to scream accusations at the others; the third ran from wall to wall, eluding Rela's grasp.

The smoke stung Dorian's eyes, but he could make his way out of his old shop and home blindfolded. He took the long step over his mattress and slipped around the counter while the howling soldiers continued their pandemonium. All but Rela. Dorian didn't hear her voice at all.

She must not have seen the flame. She's good at this.

Dorian led Claire outside. They emerged surrounded by a red cloud that billowed out from the open door. Everyone who lived in Ostwik, all except Burt who was still tied up, stood on their porches to watch.

"They aren't following us!" said Claire. "What did you do to them?"

"I wish I knew." Dorian didn't slow down as they hurried across town. "But it's buying us time."

They ran into the bookhouse and slammed the door shut. Through the window, they could see Dorian's shop pouring smoke from every window and doorway.

The people of Ostwik gathered in a tentative, murmuring crowd. A shape appeared in the candle shop doorway, and then Rela and one of her soldiers emerged carrying a second soldier between them. They laid him down beyond the reach of the smoke. Rela looked back at the billowing door and took a deep breath before rushing back inside.

"She's going back!" said Dorian.

"One of her men is still in there."

The crowd had grown so large that everyone who lived in Ostwik had to be standing in the clearing, quietly watching the shop burn. They gasped when Rela returned, her face sullied by smoke. She dragged Lewin out of the fumes and laid him on the ground, then knelt to catch her breath.

Claire patted at his apron. "Did you get the candle we need?"

Dorian reached into his deep pockets, pushing past broken tapers and loose wicks, and grasped the candle he had pulled from the shelf. "She'll be at your door in a minute. I don't think she'll rest for more than a few seconds. All I need to do is light this thing and wait for her to come storming in…"

Dorian turned the candle over and looked at the bottom.

No.

This wasn't a Decision Candle. He'd been in a hurry, and in the dim light of his shop, he'd grabbed a candle that only looked like the one he needed. They were even a similar recipe, but the only thing the candle in Dorian's hand was good for was helping people fall asleep.

"It's the wrong one!" He gripped the candle in a fist, feeling it crush under his fingers. "All that work!"

"Are you sure?"

"Of course I'm sure!" He showed her the symbol on the bottom, a simple flower. "It looks the same, but, oh—burn me, it even has the same wick! The recipe's only one ingredient different. I should have—"

Claire pressed her hands against his chest. "Dorian, think. What's the other ingredient?"

Dorian closed his eyes.

A Candle for Having Your Way
—A Beeswax core and a wick made of rat's tail.
—A dollop of royal jam.
—Ground mint.
—Mix in a melted spoonful of…

"Jasmine!" He looked around.

The bookhouse had many candles, all purchased from

his shop. They sat inside their simple ceramic pots where they had been placed around the kitchen and atop book-shelves, all glowing with the same orange light...and all emanating the same aroma. "Is your stove hot?"

"I'll throw another log in!" Claire ran into the kitchen and opened the side door to the stove. "What else do you need?" She took a log from a nearby pile and tossed it inside, then shut the metal door and wiped her hands as she stood.

"Time." Dorian took a candle from her table. Inside the clay vase, the wax had more than half melted away, but what remained contained enough jasmine to complete the recipe. "This might actually work."

Dorian placed Claire's candle onto the stove, then dropped the smaller grey candle on top of it. It only took a moment for them to start melting together inside the clay vessel.

"Can you just...*mix* them like that?" asked Claire.

"I think so." Dorian nodded. "Yes...yes. It's the same as mixing it any other way."

They both looked up at the sound of shuffling feet. Through the kitchen window, Dorian saw the crowd part to make room for Rela. Her soldiers remained in the clear-ing by the well, apparently too dazed to understand what was going on, but the commander marched on, unfazed. Rela unfurled her whip and cracked it over her head for good measure.

Claire rolled up her sleeves. "She'll have to go through me."

He wanted to tell her to be careful, but his tongue stammered while she darted out the door.

Dorian carefully lifted the candle's wick so it wouldn't drown in the melting wax. He could see Claire outside the window, walking on a collision course straight toward Rela.

"Wait!" shouted Claire. She stood in front of Rela with

her arms held up in surrender. "Just wait!"

Commander Rela advanced closer, and Dorian knew Claire's attempt at diplomacy would be no good.

But instead of talking, Claire lowered her head and charged. She landed square in Rela's belly, but the taller woman merely stepped back to absorb the attack and then moved to the side, letting Claire fall to the ground.

I need more time! Just one more minute!

Claire snatched out at Rela's feet; her fingers grappled with the boot leather. She crawled and lunged with her hands outstretched, but was stopped by Rela's strong grip. Rela lifted Claire by the hair and then dropped her back to the ground. Claire looked up as the whip unfurled.

"No you don't!" came a voice.

Ysold, the silver-haired beekeeper who was old enough to have *great* grandchildren, was running across the courtyard in a flurry. She fell on Claire and threw her arms around her and then looked up with a glare as sharp as Rela's whip. Rela turned on her heel as more of Ostwik's citizens stepped closer. They weren't as brave as Ysold, though most of them were nearly as old, but they gathered in a half circle around Rela and stood their ground, tremoring hands and all. Rela, her hard face still smudged with soot, brandished her whip; its barbed end danced along the rocky ground.

This won't end well.

The mixture needed more time for the two candles to merge, but Dorian had already given up. He was out of ideas and out of time, and the crazed woman with the whip had murder in her eyes. Dorian had no trouble imagining Rela cutting right through his neighbors as she marched to the bookhouse, laughing with each step. He took a deep breath and prepared to meet her, to beg her to leave Ostwik and just take him away. That time had come.

Rela raised her weapon overhead and then froze. Every eye in the courtyard turned toward the forest path.

Around the bend came Henk, galloping on his old mare and looking twice as desperate as when he'd ridden away. He made it to the courtyard just as the biggest carriage anyone in Ostwik had ever seen rolled in, led by six horses and covered by soldiers who rode on top and clung to the sides. The people of Ostwik took a step back; only a magister rode with that many soldiers. The coach came to a slow stop, and the soldiers peeled off the sides, none of them in a hurry. Magisters were too important to be seen in a hurry.

Dorian looked down. The blended candle was ready. While the magister took his time walking into town, Dorian placed the newly mixed candle on Claire's kitchen table and lit the wick. By the time Rela threw open the bookhouse door, Dorian was sitting on the far side of the table watching her walk in. He smiled, looking over the glow of the candle, knowing she couldn't approach him without seeing that tiny, dancing light.

Beyond the open doorway, Dorian could see the magister's soldiers moving toward the bookhouse.

I've only got a few seconds to convince her.

"There's no candlemaker here," he said, as soon as she stepped into the kitchen.

Rela shook her head and lifted the whip.

"There's no candlemaker. Not here!" Dorian insisted. Couldn't she see it?

She shook her head as she walked. Each of her boot steps rattled the dishes in Claire's cupboards.

"You were wrong!" He slammed his hands on the table. "You didn't find a candlemak—"

The whip lashed out. For a moment, Dorian saw it suspended in the air like a ravenous snake, and then it struck out at the candle. The hard clay split open and sent shards flying across the room as the whip slammed onto the table like a fist.

Dorian jumped at the sound. Rela laughed and lashed

the table again. The whip shuddered the wood with a *crack* that shivered Dorian's spine. Rela threw the table aside and lifted her weapon again as Dorian fell against the wall and threw his hands over his face.

"Commander Rela," came a dry voice.

Dorian peeked out between fingers.

The whip stopped its motion and fell to the ground. "Magister." Rela bowed.

A thin, wrinkled man stood in the doorway, his hands together at his waist, fingertips touching. Dorian lowered his own hands and watched the magister enter the book-house. The magister turned to take in Claire's collection of books for a moment and then looked away, unimpressed.

That candle was perfect.

The magister was followed by a large soldier who wore the same insignia as Rela. Another commander. More soldiers came after and filled the room, blocking light from the door and windows.

The mixture was right. I know it.

"Thanks to this detour, we've lost our timetable," said the Magister. "So, Rela, that hysterical man you sent riding after me said you found something important here."

Dorian looked at the scattered pieces of wax around the floor. Even now, he could see how the candles had mixed properly. It made no sense.

It should have worked.

He slowly lifted his gaze and, for the first time, looked steadily into the eyes of Commander Rela, the eyes of a woman who had run into his burning shop and faced his candles unaffected, the eyes of a woman who knew every one of Dorian's tricks and had faced the flame and flicker of his magic without a trace of fear.

His mouth fell open as he realized the truth: there was nothing wrong with the candle.

Rela turned to the Magister. "What did he tell you?"

"Believe it, or not," the magister sighed, "that frantic

man said you had a candlemaker in this town."

"We do," Dorian heard himself say. All eyes turned to him while he slowly stood and raised his arm to point a finger at Rela. "It's...her."

Her eyes flared.

I knew it.

"You?" The magister's voice raised.

"She's got one of those candles in her pouch," Dorian added.

"Is that so?" The magister gestured, and his soldiers moved to surround Rela.

"He's lying!" Rela spun around, turning the pouch away from them.

Two of the magister's men grabbed her by the arms. Another fumbled for the pouch, and in his attempt to reach it, he managed to pull apart the opening. The pouch turned over, spilling its contents. Dorian smiled as his black memory candle fell out and rolled onto the floor.

The magister's commander picked up the candle and turned it over. He showed the bottom of it to the magister, and they shared a nod.

"I guess it's hers?" asked the commander.

The magister sneered and waved a thin hand. "Never guess. We have a test for these things. But...the ones who resist always turn out to be guilty. Always. Come along, Rela. You've hidden your secret long enough."

Finding the last of her dignity, Rela lifted her chin and marched out with the magister and his soldiers. The bookhouse fell quiet.

Dorian realized he was breathing hard. He tried to calm himself while he pushed away from the wall and made his way, shakily, to the door. Outside, he could see that his candle shop still stood, despite the blackened walls and windows.

By the time he staggered to the door, the magister and his soldiers were gathered near the wagons. A few soldiers were dealing with the brigands. Rela was shoved into the largest carriage.

In the center of town, Claire knelt, untying Burt while the others gathered in a quiet circle, each keeping an eye on the wagons. The three marshals who had arrived with Rela stood nearby, shrugging and asking each other questions. Dorian could tell they were still dazed by the red smoke.

As he approached, the townsfolk turned his way one by one, the same question etched on each of their faces. Even the marshals watched him, desperate for something to make sense.

Claire spoke up. "Why are they taking Rela?"

"Because…she's a candlemaker," said Dorian. His neighbors shared a look of confusion, and so did the soldiers, but none argued.

Understanding dawned on Claire's face. "That… actually explains a lot." She turned toward the marshals. "Doesn't it?"

The marshals looked blankly at each other. One of them scratched at the back of his head and said, "The last thing I remember is…chasing the brigands this way." He looked up. "Wasn't it raining?"

Dorian grimaced. *At least none of them are hurt.*

They watched the brigands get loaded into their own wagon. One of the soldiers climbed into the driver's seat and took up the reins, sighing at the sight of the old horses in front of him. The magister's commander walked away from the rest of the men and approached the center of town where Dorian and the others were gathered. He stood before them with his hands clasped behind his back.

"You have the empire's apologies. It appears a candle-maker is to blame for…some of what's happened here. The empire thanks you for your assistance in capturing the Western Brigands, as well as that spy." He looked at the three confused soldiers. "Come along, marshals. We'll add you to our company for now." He took them in, shaking his head. "Gods only know what that woman did to you."

"What about my shop?" hollered Burt. "Seems we deserve something for our trouble!"

The commander raised an eyebrow. "Surely...serving the emperor is reward enough?"

"Oh, aye, and what a reward it is." Burt frowned and gave a mocking salute. "Off with you, now."

The commander turned around in a huff.

Shaking their heads, the marshals followed him back and then climbed into their own wagon. When the commander boarded the larger carriage, he closed the door behind him just as the driver snapped the reins. All three wagons shambled up the road, their wheels creaking as they disappeared up the path and into the trees.

The sound of wagon wheels faded quickly, replaced by the crashing of ocean waves and the music of waving branches. The people of Ostwik remained still and quiet; no one wanted to be the first to break their newfound peace.

Dorian knelt next to Burt, who was rubbing his old wrists. "Why'd you do that, Burt? I bet you broke your leg again." Dorian looked around at the other townsfolk, the brave neighbors who had stood between him and Rela's whip. "Why did *any* of you do that?"

"We don't need your permission, lad!" laughed Burt. "'Sides, we like Ostwik the way it is."

There was a general nod of agreement from the others. Dorian looked up and saw Claire smiling down at him. "I'd sure hate it if my bookhouse stopped smelling like jasmine."

Dorian flushed. A few people laughed at him while sharing a look of understanding, and Dorian realized he had been doing a lousy job of keeping his secret.

Burt reached over and tousled his hair. "And don't worry about my leg, boy." He winked. "I have a feelin' it'll heal up quick."

Copyright Information

Made in the USA
San Bernardino, CA
31 August 2019